THE AIRSHIPMEN TRILOGY

VOLUME THREE

TO ASHES

Two girls study the airship on which their daddies will fly away—perhaps forever. *Cardington R101* at the tower 1929.

THE AIRSHIPMEN TRILOGY

VOLUME THREE

TO ASHES

BASED ON A TRUE STORY

THE GRIPPING, HIGH-STAKES CONCLUSION

DAVID DENNINGTON

THE FULL CAST OF CHARACTERS FOR THE TRILOGY
MAY BE FOUND AT THE BACK OF THE BOOK.

Printed by Amazon.

Available from Amazon.com and other retail outlets.

Also available on Kindle and other retail outlets through Amazon.

DESCRIPTION: This special edition of *The Airshipmen* is now published as a trilogy, (originally published as one volume).

TRILOGY IDENTIFIER: Paperback.

THE AIRSHIPMEN TRILOGY VOLUME THREE
TO ASHES ISBN - 9798687363068

BY DAVID DENNINGTON

THE AIRSHIPMEN
(Now also available as a three-part series below)

The Airshipmen Trilogy	Volume One	*From Ashes*
The Airshipmen Trilogy	Volume Two	*Lords of the Air*
The Airshipmen Trilogy	Volume Three	*To Ashes*

THE GHOST OF CAPTAIN HINCHLIFFE
Based on a true story

For Christian and Ava with great love.

TO ASHES

The events so far:

Lou Remington has returned safely from Canada aboard the private enterprise-built airship, *Howden R100*. Whilst in North America, Lou made a personal trip down to Washington, D.C. and Virginia to see his family. It is the height of the Depression and Lou was shocked to see the state of affairs in America. He was also saddened to see what has become of his family during his ten-year absence.

Whilst in the States, Lou had a brush with the Ku Klux Klan, reconciled with his father who is dying, and also with his brother who had become hostile and jealous. He also met his old flame, Julia, who revealed she is still in love with him and whom the family believe he has jilted.

The stakes were high with *Howden R100's* trip to North America. The Vickers team had been approached before leaving in a bid to postpone the trip, as the government airship was not in shape to make its own transcontinental flight to India. An extra bay must be inserted in order to provide more lift – she is perilously overweight.

The private team has triumphantly achieved its goal – a round trip to Canada – although not without some terrifying moments. Now, with the gauntlet thrown down, can the government-built *Cardington R101* match *Howden R100's* splendid accomplishment?

TABLE OF CONTENTS

VOLUME 3

PART THREE—AFTERMATH

PART FOUR—EPILOGUE

BACK OF THE BOOK MATERIAL

"Airships are the devil's 'andiwork in defiance of God's laws and we should avoid them like the plague!"

Lord Scunthorpe, House of Lords. July 4th, 1929.

PART ONE

Bringing in the hay while *Howden R100* is moored at the Cardington tower

THE DAYS BEFORE
THE
INDIA VOYAGE

1

WELCOME HOME!

Wednesday August 12 - Saturday August 16, 1930.

L ou talked with Ezekiah and thanked him as the train approached Montreal. Ezekiah wished him luck and told him to 'stay strong.' For Lou, this whole trip to North America had been like a fantasy—another world. Norway was waiting on the platform.

"How was your trip?" he asked.

"Oh, pretty quiet," Lou grunted.

The return voyage had been uneventful, except for one night on Lou's watch. After everyone had retired, Cameron fell asleep. Lou suddenly realized the ship was descending rapidly toward the water and grabbed the elevator wheel, slapping Cameron around the head. Lou didn't report the incident, realizing Cameron had lost a lot of sleep over Rosie lately. Apart from this incident, the journey turned out to be boring, and the Canadian journalists who'd been invited to travel with them, said as much. Scott kept a low profile the entire voyage.

On the way home, Lou lay in his bunk hoping the feelings of euphoria would return, but all he could think about was his father. His mission became clear: as soon he returned from India in October, he and Charlotte would take a steamer to Montreal and travel down to Washington by train.

Wouldn't it be great if Ezekiah was our steward!

Aside from the worry about his dad, he was glad he'd gotten things straight in his mind. He'd had plenty of time to think. Things were going to be different from now on. They'd pay their visit to America. On their return they'd start a family—adopt if necessary. Everything was going to turn out swell!

They got back to the Cardington mast around 11:00 a.m. on Saturday, August 16th. The journey home had taken less than fifty-eight hours. Two hundred cars were parked on the field when they arrived and a crowd had gathered—tiny compared to the reception in Montreal. Lou was in the control car for the docking with Booth and Meager. He scoured the fence, hoping to catch a glimpse of Charlotte, but couldn't see her anywhere. Mooring the ship took an agonizing forty-five minutes. Lou was scheduled to be on duty at noon the following day. He hurried off the ship behind Booth and Steff, leaving Meager on watch with a skeleton crew. Thomson waited with Brancker at the foot of the gangplank where they shook hands with each man, uttering words of praise and welcome.

From the top of the tower, Lou could see a BBC crew waiting with their broadcasting equipment in front of Shed No.1. A small brass band was playing a march. Thomson was obviously planning to make a speech and Lou didn't intend to stick around, anxious to get home to Charlotte. He glanced over the tower rail. No Binks. No motorbike.

Dammit! He's late as usual.

But then Lou looked across the field and saw Binks roaring toward the tower. Lou went down. Binks raced up to him.

"Here she is, sir, good as new," he said, chirpy as ever. "Voyage okay?"

"Yeah, not bad."

"Someone put sugar in your tank. I 'ad her in the shop and me and Mr. Leech stripped her down. She's all right now, sir."

"Damn! Who would do such a thing?" Lou asked, knowing *exactly* who.

"And I mailed the envelope a week after you left, just like you asked me to."

"Thanks. I owe you a pint, Joe."

While Thomson and the crowd moved toward Shed No.1, Lou strapped on his kit bag, and after dropping Binks off in Shortstown, drove to the florist's at the parade of shops near Kelsey Street. He bought a big bunch of violets and tied them on the gas tank. Then he nipped into the corner store and bought a box of Cadbury's chocolates —her favorite. He slipped them in his side pocket and rode slowly home.

Thomson went from the tower to the front of Shed No.1. The doors had been opened to reveal the bow of *Cardington R101*. The public turnout for *Howden R100's* return had been disappointing, but the broadcast would give things a boost and the usual battery of journalists and photographers had been summoned. The publicity derived from this little homecoming event would pressure the R.A.W. to keep up with the schedule he'd imposed on them for the *Cardington R101*.

Thomson stood at the microphone with Capt. Booth and Second Officer Steff, a small group of R.A.W. personnel on either side. The crowd that had been at the fence was allowed in and people gathered around to listen.

"It is with pleasure that I welcome you home from your voyage to Canada," Thomson said, smiling at Colmore and Scott and then at Burney and Norway who were standing off to one side. "I want to congratulate the Howden team and Vickers for their magnificent achievement. This will be recorded as a landmark flight in the history books. In undertaking this journey across the Atlantic Ocean to North America, you have succeeded in taking a giant step in the development of a new generation of British airships."

Thomson looked directly at Capt. Irwin standing beside Lt. Cmdr. Atherstone. Irwin appeared thin and drawn. "We shall now move forward with complete confidence toward a successful conclusion of this grand experiment."

Thomson turned his gaze on Colmore, Richmond and Rope. "All that remains is for this great airship behind us to make its *own* landmark voyage. This will demonstrate to the Dominion Prime Ministers the advantages of this mode of travel—a demonstration of *incalculable importance!* Thank you."

Thomson signaled to the BBC announcer it was time to end the broadcast. The brass band struck up again with the rousing "Royal Air Force March Past," heard by thousands all over Britain.

On reaching home, Lou looked up at the front door step, remembering the image of Charlotte when he'd last seen her there. He'd had it imprinted on his mind for the last fifteen days. He bounded up the steps and knocked on the door. While he waited, he removed the present, the wine and the card from his kitbag, ready to hand them to her. He'd hastily bought Charlotte a small, white marble replica of Abraham Lincoln from a gift shop at Penn Station when the train stopped en route to Montreal. At the station, he'd also bought a bottle of Cabernet from Napa Valley and a gift card. They'd celebrate. She'd like that. He stood at the door and studied the brass knocker. He'd never seen it polished so brightly.

Must be looking forward to seeing me. She's been busy. Bless her heart!

He knocked again and waited.

No answer.

She must be in the garden.

He put down his kit bag and, holding the flowers in one hand, the gift box and the wine under his arm, and the card between his teeth, he searched for his key. He finally fished it out, dropping the wine as he did so. The bottle smashed and the wine ran down the concrete steps. Lou cursed under his breath as he unlocked the door, pushing it into a pile of mail scattered about the floor. His heart sank. He put the flowers on the hall table with the present, chocolates and card and gathered up the mail. His birthday card in the brown envelope was the first thing he spotted with the two telegrams he'd sent from North America. Something must have happened to her.

Oh my God, I hope she's all right!

His mind began racing He thought of the sugar in his gas tank.

What if Jessup's been round ...Damn that son of a bitch!

He called out, although he realized it was futile. The place felt like a morgue.

"Charlotte!"

She obviously wasn't home.

Maybe she went up north.

Everything in the house was pristine and in its place—*too pristine.* He went down to the kitchen. Again, all was clean and perfect. Even the rubbish bin was spotless. The sink shone white with nothing on the draining board or table. He peered inside the metal bread bin. Empty, not even a crumb. He heard Fluffy at the door mewing and let her in. She wanted fussing over, but he didn't have time for her. He bounded up the stairs, two at a time, Fluffy on his heels.

Their bedroom door was ajar. He pushed it open and gazed around the room. *Immaculate.* The bed was made, not a crease anywhere. His guitar hung on the wall on his side of the bed where it always was. Shined to perfection. A dead bluebottle on the windowsill seemed out of place. The candle holder, usually on her bedside table, had disappeared.

He opened the wardrobe. All her things were gone. His clothes, newly washed and ironed, hung on his side. His heart began to pound.

"Oh, no, oh no," he gasped.

He went to the chest of drawers, without noticing the envelope, and opened 'the baby' drawer. Empty. He yanked open the rest of Charlotte's drawers. All empty. The house looked as if Charlotte had never set foot in it, except for a few photos—that said it all.

Reminders she doesn't want.

"Oh, Charlotte. What's happened to you?" he whispered.

Suddenly, he noticed the white envelope propped against the photo on the chest of drawers. It came like a hammer blow. He knew instinctively what it was and froze, staring at it with dread. The way it was placed in front of *that* particular photo in its special gold frame had to be a statement. His name was in her hand. He snatched it up, tore it open with shaking hands and pulled out the letter. He sank down onto the bed, his hand against his head in despair.

Dear Louis,

By the time you read this, you will have been to Canada and returned safely—I hope. I am sorry to tell you I have left you. I am not cut out for this life. All I ever wanted was for us to be an ordinary family with children and a dog—and we both know how that turned out.

We have had good times and bad—mostly bad for me, though. I have given it all much thought, and I must face the fact that I no longer love you. Please do not come after me, or contact me. That would be futile. I wish you all the luck and happiness in the world doing what I know you love most.

Goodbye – Charlotte

He had a vision of her standing on the doorstep the night he left—like a goddess.

"Goodbye, Lou," she'd whispered.

How had he missed that?

Fluffy jumped on the bed beside him, mewing and purring, wildly happy he was home.

"She's left us, Fluffy," Lou said quietly, his eyes fixed on Binks' three pencil portraits on the wall: he, the intrepid airman, she, the stunning flapper. Binks had portrayed her beautiful, full lips perfectly. Her smile so captivating. So chic … Then it hit him.

Robert!

"Son of a bitch," he whispered.

He must have materialized from somewhere.

"No, surely not ..."

She's obsessed with getting pregnant.

Suddenly, his incredulous eyes blazed and his anger erupted.

"God damn it!"

He leapt to his feet and smashed his fist through the wardrobe door, splintering it.

"Bitch! Bitch! Bitch!"

Fluffy flew out the bedroom door in terror. Lou stumbled after her down to the kitchen in a daze, holding his bleeding fist. He held it under the cold tap. It hurt like hell. He opened a cabinet and pulled out the Scotch Norway had brought before Christmas. He ripped the top off, poured some in a glass and swilled it down. He tried to think. This wouldn't help, but he needed something to numb the shock and the pain in his hand. His wild thoughts went to Charlotte, his father and back to Charlotte again. *Agony*. He sat at the table with his head in his hands. A monotonous wood pigeon cooed from a tree in the garden. He wished he could kill the damned thing! He poured out another shot and put the bottle on the counter. No point in drinking any more. He finished his glass and went back up to the bedroom and laid down, his face in her pillow, her familiar scent now replaced by soap powder.

At Shed No.1, with the broadcast over, the journalists were ready with questions. They raised their hands. Thomson pointed to one. "It's Tom Brewer—the *Daily Telegraph*, if I remember correctly?"

"Quite right, sir. When do you propose setting off for India—I presume you *are* still going, are you?"

"Yes, of course. As to the date, I leave that to my team."

"If you go, don't you have a deadline to be back to attend the Prime Minister's Conference?"

Thomson smiled at Colmore. "I have every confidence we'll be back by 20th October."

Thomson singled out another journalist.

"Bill Hagan, *Daily Mail*. When do you anticipate completion of the modifications?"

"I'm told by R.A.W. the extra bay will be completed this month." Thomson glanced at Colmore who nodded.

"And ready to fly when?"

"In September."

"So you'll definitely leave for India in September, then?"

"I expect it'll be *late* September, yes," Thomson said, eyeing Colmore again. He pointed at another reporter. "Mr. Haines with the *Times*, over there, yes, sir."

"Will that leave adequate time for testing?"

"I shall be guided by my Cardington team."

"It doesn't seem to me like you're allowing enough time. Is it wise to go flying off to India without the airship being properly tested?" Haines asked.

"As I said, I'll be guided by the experts." Thomson glared at Irwin, sure he was in agreement with the premise of that question. "Look, I want to make myself perfectly clear. While I'm in charge, unnecessary risks will not be run and lives will not be sacrificed."

Bill Hagan came back with another question. "Sir, you said yourself in your speech 'this is all experimental.' Does it make sense for you to be flying around in an *experimental* aircraft?"

"I'll just say this: I will not ask of others what I won't do myself."

Thomson pointed at another reporter, remembering him as the troublemaker with the five o'clock shadow.

"George Hunter, *Daily Express*, sir. Has the fact that *Howden R100* has flown to Canada affected the R.A.W.'s judgment? Are they now obligated to fly to India when, perhaps, their ship isn't ready? Do you *really* think this ship's up to the task?"

Thomson frowned.

Damn this man!

"I'm completely confident in this airship and in the Royal Airship Works staff and its officers. That's why I'll be on board when she casts off. One last question—you're Jacobs with *Aeroplane Magazine*, I remember."

"*Sixty tons* of disposable lift. That was the stipulated requirement if you remember, sir. I remember distinctly you telling us—"

"Yes, well, er—"

"They've managed to achieve only thirty-five tons—that's *twenty-five tons* short."

Thomson gave a dismissive wave of his hand. "The team is working hard to rectify that—"

"Wouldn't it be wiser to stop the clock and the schedule until the ship is proven—just to be on the safe side?"

Thomson saw Irwin exchange glances with Brancker. He wondered if these questions had been planted. Irwin actually nodded his head as he glanced at Atherstone.

The nerve of the man!

"I've already stated my feelings on all this."

Another journalist raised his hand.

"All right, one more."

"Sir, stories are filtering out to the press about morale: that it's at an all-time low and there's a breakdown of discipline at Cardington. Would you care to comment?"

"Who are you, sir?" Thomson asked. He'd been caught wrong-footed and cast around helplessly toward his R.A.W. team. They gazed at him blankly, while Irwin stared at the ground.

"Edmund Jones, *Daily Mirror*, sir," the reporter replied.

The Daily Mirror! I thought these people were supposed to be on our side.

"Edmund Jones," Thomson said, filing that name away. "I haven't the slightest idea what you're talking about, sir. Good day, gentlemen." Thomson marched off.

From the car, he watched the reporters gathering around Burney and Norway. They appeared eager to talk.

They would be!

2

OLIVIA

Tuesday July 29, 1930.

After Lou had climbed on his motorbike and left for the Cardington tower in the middle of the night, Charlotte returned to the bedroom. She removed a blanket from the bed, went down to the kitchen and opened the French doors. After turning off the lights, she sank into one of the deckchairs. She remained in a semi-catatonic state until she heard the sound of Lou's airship passing over. It was as if it were trying to seek her out. She glared at the massive, black shape, droning like a prehistoric insect.

Damn you! You can't see me here in the dark.

The airship passed over, its red navigation light clearly visible. She watched it vanish into the darkness. She felt relieved—never wanting to set eyes on the thing again. That chapter was over.

Charlotte sat in the deckchair through the rest of the night, wrapped in the blanket, staring at the stars. At dawn, she went back to bed and slept until noon. Three times she'd been woken by someone knocking on the front door, which she ignored. When she finally got up, she washed and dressed and walked to the Irwin's house on Putroe Lane. She rang the doorbell and stood on the front step like a waif. Olivia opened the door.

"Come in, you poor dear. I came round to visit you earlier, but you weren't home."

Charlotte's face was grim. "I'll not stay long. There are things I need to tell you, Olivia."

Olivia put the kettle on and then sat down with Charlotte.

"I'm leaving Lou," Charlotte said.

Olivia's eyes widened and her mouth dropped open. "What do you mean? You can't be serious. Have you told Lou?"

"No. I thought it better he didn't know. I'm leaving Bedford this week."

"Charlotte, are you *sure* about this? You're such a lovely couple. Come and stay here with us while he's away and think about it."

"Olivia, you can't imagine what I've been through. It's made me so ill." She broke down and began to cry. "I can't go on. I tried to warn him. I wanted to persuade him. I'd made up my mind last year to tell him how I felt. I had it planned when he came home that day when Thomson came up after he'd got back in office. I'd worked it all out; what I was going to say. We would quit all this and go back to the cottage like he promised. Mr. Bull would take him back. But when he came home he was so happy—he got two promotions that day. I *just* couldn't do it."

"Oh, dear, Charlotte. But I think you should wait until Lou returns."

"No, my mind's made up. Truth is Olivia, I don't love him anymore. I can't be the wife of an airshipman—*not for one more day.*"

Charlotte wiped her eyes and blew her nose. They sat in silence for a few minutes. Charlotte became mesmerized, dulled by her thoughts.

"I was *there*, you know. I saw everything," she said finally, her voice flat.

"Where, love? What did you see?"

"When his ship went down in the Humber."

Olivia put her hand to her mouth in disbelief. "You were there?"

"I was standing right there on Victoria dock."

"You *saw* it?" Olivier closed her eyes.

Charlotte gazed at the wall, experiencing the horror again.

"*Everything*—that thing on fire and breaking in half, the control car breaking away, spinning in the air like a top, men on fire, men falling, bits of bodies flying everywhere—"

"Dear God! I didn't realize you'd actually witnessed it."

"We never talked about it."

They ignored the whistling kettle in the kitchen.

"They laid out the bodies in the garden next to the hospital—too many for the morgue—dozens of them—or what was left of them. We had to chase the kids off. They were peeking through gaps in the fence. They must've had nightmares for years after that. They had to post policemen outside to keep them away. Later, from the ward, we watched a massive funeral pass along the waterfront. It was a dreadful sight."

"Oh, Charlotte. You poor dear."

"When he left last night, I thought to myself, 'I have no idea whether you'll come back.' I will not live my life this way anymore, Olivia. It's over. I don't want to witness another funeral like that."

The kettle continued its howling.

"I'm sorry," Olivia said, getting up. She went and made tea and returned to let it brew.

"Olivia, You're the first person I've told."

Olivia sighed and sat and thought for a while. Charlotte sensed Olivia was deciding whether to confide in *her*.

"I spoke with Captain Booth's wife about Bird. We're pretty close. All this with the Cardington ship is making *him* ill. I asked her what would happen if Bird decided to give up flying—maybe we'd go and live in Ireland."

"What did she say?"

"She asked Captain Booth and he said they'd make *him* fly it to India."

"I suppose they would. That's obvious, isn't it?"

"Bird knows that and he wouldn't shirk his responsibility and put it on another man like that."

"So, you're worried?"

"Yes, I am. It's become a nightmare. The other day, before he went to work, he sat down on the edge of the bed, in his uniform, staring at the floor. I sat down beside him and put my arm around him and put my face against his. I begged him to give it up and he said 'I must go on with it, Olivia, it's my duty.'"

"He really *should* give it up," Charlotte said.

Olivia went to the window, glaring at the overcast sky. When she turned, Charlotte saw, she too, had tears in her eyes.

"Duty! Duty! I'm bloody *sick* of it!" Olivia said, as she shuffled wearily into the kitchen. She returned with a tray of cups and a pot of tea. Olivia obviously had more on her mind.

"He told me Emilie Hinchliffe came and spoke to him. You've heard of her?"

"Yes, she's always in the papers. What did she say?"

"She'd asked to meet him. He didn't tell me at the time. Nothing in it, of course. He didn't want to worry me. Bird and Captain Hinchliffe had been friends. She gave him messages from her husband telling him airships were a lost cause. Gradually, it told on him. It's dragged him down ever since."

They sat and commiserated for another hour until Charlotte got up to leave. They hugged and Charlotte went home, leaving Olivia in a similar state of misery, but feeling her own now had resolution.

Charlotte took a bus to Bedford Station after leaving Olivia's house, to check on train times to Wakefield. While at the station, she ordered a taxi for Friday morning. On her way home, she went into the chemist's shop and bought a large pair of scissors.

She got home around 6 o'clock and sat in front of her dressing table mirror with the scissors. After swinging wildly at a bluebottle intent on annoying her, she began snipping. With Fluffy watching closely from the bed, she started at the top by her left ear and cut her hair off in great swaths. Charlotte turned and glared at the cat.

"What are you looking at Fluff?" she said.

The cat remained silent.

"You really miss him, don't you? I guess you're his cat. I wonder if you'll miss *me*."

Her thick, shiny locks fell to the floor around her feet and after half an hour they looked like the remains of a dead animal lying there. An hour later, she had a bob-cut, finally—short as a boy's. She took a hand mirror from the drawer and inspected the back. It was pretty uneven, but it would have to do. She picked up the hair and threw it in a brown bag and placed it in the bottom of a suitcase on the bed. What would Lou say? It didn't matter.

She spent the evening sorting out drawers and clothes and items to wash, including some of Lou's things. She went to bed early and slept soundly for the first time in months. She got up at six and cleaned the house from top to bottom until late into the night, stopping occasionally to chase the irritating bluebottle that was always just out of reach. It became a battle of wits.

"Damn you!" she shouted.

The following morning she stripped the bed, washed the sheets and pillowcases and hung them on the line in the garden. By midday, they were dry, before the rain came. She ironed them and put them back on the bed and then spent the rest of the day packing.

That evening, Charlotte laid a small, black suitcase on the bed. She opened the 'baby's drawer' and pulled out the clothes she'd made over the years. While rummaging around and pulling out a collection of old Christmas and birthday cards, she found Bobby's message from *R38*. It was still in its cardboard tube buried at the back of the drawer. She pulled out the note, wincing as she read it.

Marry me and come away. I promise to love you forever. Bobby.

"Pathetic! Wasted lives!" she said aloud.

She replaced it in the tube and put it on the bed, making up her mind to find Elsie and give it to her. Though pointless, she owed it to that foolish girl.

Her child must be almost ten now. God!

She held up a woolen shawl, examining it through tears, her face deathly white in the mirror. The shawl smelled of mothballs. She roughly folded it and flung it into the suitcase. She did the same with the rest of the clothes, unwrapping them and throwing them in the case. After screwing up the tissue, she took it down to the dustbin and threw it out with the cards and a heap of half-used cosmetics. Dumping the cards was bit of a wrench, but there was no point in keeping them, and that was not half as bad as what she had to do next.

Around midnight, she put on a headscarf, left the house with the suitcase and walked to the ancient bridge, and although the roads were deserted, she sensed she was being watched. She walked to the middle and looked down into the river, swollen by rain. She listened to the swirling, babbling water. After looking around and seeing no one, she dropped the suitcase over the stone balustrade. She leaned over and watched it splash into the water in the moonlight. It floated for a moment and then moved from side to side in the current before disappearing into the depths. She stood staring at the spot for a few minutes feeling drained—as after an exorcism, or more accurately, a water burial. She wept.

There, it's done. It's over at last.

She felt a weight, or not so much a weight as an expectation, had been lifted and torn away—one that couldn't be fulfilled, but which had finally been confronted and eradicated. Charlotte trudged home and slept fitfully on the couch, grieving for her phantom child and for a husband who was as good as dead.

The next morning was overcast and chilly. She spent time going around making sure everything was in its place with no sign of her existence. The exception was the collection of framed photos, which she had dusted and left where they were. She didn't want them. She took down his guitar from the wall in the bedroom and dusted and polished it until it shone. She stared at it before carefully replacing it. That thing had made him so happy and she'd worked so hard to get it for him. She could hear it now. Oh, how he could play! He made it sing. He made it cry. The sound of it had often made her weep. But not now. Not anymore.

The last thing she did was to dust and polish her precious piano. She made that shine, too. When she'd finished, she stood back to look at it. She thought about taking it somehow, but couldn't cope with it. Maybe when she was settled he'd have it sent to her. The thought of leaving John Bull's present behind made her feel bad about John—like a spit in the eye.

The taxi arrived ten minutes early. She put on her cloche hat and went down and asked the driver to take her cases. She was standing at the bottom step when she heard a familiar voice behind her.

"You're leavin 'im then, ain'tcha?"

Charlotte spun around and stared into the face of Jessup. For the first time in years, she studied that face, noticing the scar. It was on the opposite side to Lou's. She found him attractive in a repulsive way, as many women did, even with his twisted jaw. Strange. His manner was humble. This was certainly new.

Maybe he's changed.

"He's no good, you know. He done me out of my rightful place on that ship. I was in the crew an' everythin'. He got me kicked off."

"I don't know anything about that."

"It wasn't right what he done to me."

"That has nothing to do with *me*."

"I want you to know, I still love you, Charlotte, despite all the beatings and suffering he put me through. I'd endure it all again for you. I love you and always will. I want to say how sorry I am for all the upset I've caused you. I'm a changed man. I walk with the Lord now. I have accepted Jesus Christ as my Savior."

The taxi driver approached them. "And *this* one, too, miss?"

"Yes, please."

The driver worked his way around Jessup, who stood in his way. He gave Jessup and irritated glance as he picked up the other case.

"Will you *both* be traveling, miss?"

"No, just me."

"Charlotte, give me a chance. I'm not really a bad person, you know. I never 'ad much of a chance really, what with me dad an' all," Jessup begged.

Charlotte showed him mild indifference—not the usual complete brush off.

"I've got the baby clothes. I rescued them from the river. They're all at 'ome with me landlady, dryin' out. I saw you throw 'em in the river last night. I dived in and saved them for you, Charlotte."

"You did *what!*" Charlotte screamed, her eyes wide in disbelief.

The taxi driver was getting impatient. He kept looking over at them. Jessup responded with a venomous glare. The driver looked away, scared stiff.

"You need to be with me, Charlotte. We could 'ave a family. There's nought wrong with *me,* you know."

Charlotte shut the front door with a bang and walked toward the taxi. Hearing Charlotte's front door, Mrs. Jones came out and stood on her top step. Jessup hung around, following Charlotte with pleading eyes. Then Church's girlfriend, Irene, showed up. She gave Jessup a funny look and rushed to Charlotte as she was climbing into the taxi.

"Charlotte—"

"I'm sorry, Irene. I can't stop," Charlotte said, not meeting her eye.

"Are you all right? I just—"

"I've got a train to catch. I'm really sorry," Charlotte said, slamming the door.

As the taxi pulled away, she glanced at Mrs. Jones and Irene, who both looked very concerned. Fluffy sat on Mrs. Jones's windowsill staring at her with accusing, green eyes.

3

ROSIE

Sunday August 17, 1930.

At 9 o'clock Sunday morning, Lou woke up with a groan as the alarm clock made its ugly sound. He'd slept uneasily and when he came round, the nightmare hit him again, sending him into a freefall.

She's gone.

Fluffy lay beside him. She stretched herself and nuzzled his face. He stared at the photo on the chest of drawers with both sadness and bitterness. He remembered exactly when the picture was taken. Charlotte had sat on the five bar gate opposite her parents' house on Station Road during his first visit to Ackworth, while he stood beside her. They both looked very happy—and they *were* happy. It was Lou's favorite photo, and he'd put it in a special gold frame. Charlotte's dad had snapped it with his Brownie.

He went down to the kitchen and let Fluffy out, then made coffee. A knock came at the front door. Mrs. Jones stood on the step with a shopping bag of groceries. By her expression, she must have been aware of events of the past couple of weeks.

"There was a lot of glass on the steps. I cleaned it up," Mrs. Jones said.

Lou had forgotten. "Oh yeah, I dropped a bottle of wine. I'm sorry."

"Lou, can I—" she began.

"Sure come in, Mrs. Jones. Come and have a cuppa Joe with me."

"All right. Your milk's here on the step. I'll bring it in," she said. She handed him the shopping bag. "I picked up a few things for you." They went down to the kitchen. "Charlotte told me the milkman would start delivering again this morning."

"That was *real* nice of her!" Lou said. He placed the groceries on the table, poured out the coffee and put the milk in a jug.

"I'm so sorry, Lou."

"Did she talk to you?"

"I knocked on the door the morning you left, but I got no answer."

"Probably asleep," Lou said.

"She came and talked to me the Friday before she left in a cab. Gave me money for cat food. Fluffy's been living with us while you were away. She's such a sweet cat."

Lou kept his face expressionless.

"Charlotte didn't say a lot, except she was leaving and wasn't coming back."

"Did she say where she was going?"

"No, I didn't like to pry—but I wish I had now."

"Don't worry. Did she say *why*?"

"She said she'd been unhappy for a long time—that was all. And I must say she looked very sad. But you know, she often seemed like that to me—like something was gnawing away at her inside."

"She was desperate for a kid."

"I don't know, Lou. It seemed more than *that,* to me."

Lou felt depressed hearing all this from a neighbor. Charlotte had been low, but he hadn't realized the extent of her unhappiness. Now *everybody* knew.

"I thought we could sort things out. I guess I was wrong."

"If you find out where she is, you can talk to her—you *must!*"

"She's probably at her mom's place. She said clearly in a letter her mind's made up. She's a stubborn Yorkshire girl."

"Oh, dear. Lou, please don't give up."

"You're very kind, Mrs. J."

"She gave me the key and asked me to get some shopping in for you. I didn't bring it in. I didn't like to."

"Thank you."

She finished her coffee and stood up. "The girl's mad, going off like that," she said.

"She's unhappy, and *I'm* to blame," Lou said.

"Takes *two* to tango, love—that's what I say."

When Mrs. Jones had gone, Lou stared out the window at the sunlight on the flowers. Charlotte must have planted them this spring. He hadn't noticed them before. He took out the pad from the writing case she'd given him and sat trying to put his thoughts together while the mind-numbing tap dripped in the sink. Finally, he began.

My Dearest Charlotte,

I found your note when I came home and I was devastated. I looked forward to coming home and seeing your lovely face at the door. You have no idea how much I have been longing for you. I had lots of time to think and wanted to surprise you with some definite plans when I got back. I suppose that's all out the window now—unless you don't mean the things you said. When you said in your letter you didn't love me anymore, it was unthinkable to me—I believed our love was forever. Please say it isn't true and please meet me and let's talk— I'm sure we can work things out, if we try ...

Lou glanced at the time: 11:30 a.m. already. He needed to get going. He'd finish it later. He put on his uniform and went down to the front door, gathering up the dying violets on the hall table. He took them out and threw them in the dustbin. When he reached Cardington, the gatekeeper glanced at him with what Lou took to be sympathy. He wasn't sure.

"Mornin', Lou," he said.

"Hi, Jim. What's up? Everything okay?"

"I'm not sure. I'd been expecting another officer this morning, but no one showed up. The watch crewmen are on the ship, though."

"I'm supposed to come on at noon."

"Something else is a bit funny."

"What's that?"

"That Mrs. Cameron came through here earlier dressed up to the nines. Said she had something for her husband. I'm certain he's not on the base—bit fishy if you ask me."

"I'll find out what's going on. Thanks, Jim."

Lou rode up the driveway passing Cardington House and coasted silently over to the fence. He left the motorbike and walked across the field to the tower, climbing noiselessly up the stairs and gangplank. He heard shouting and laughing as he moved along the ship's corridor.

The place was a disgusting mess. Empty bottles of Canadian Club, various bottles of spirits and beer lay on their sides on the dining room tables on a carpet of bread crumbs, crackers and scraps of cheese. The noise was coming from the promenade deck on the port side. He stood at the opening.

Disheveled, unshaven watch-crewmen sat slumped on the loungers, couches and easy chairs, their feet on tables. It was Jessup's crowd. A fat lout in his twenties spotted Lou. He downed the remnants of a beer and released a loud belch.

"Aye, look what the cat's dragged in, lads," he said, his mouth curling into a sneer.

"It's our old mate, *Lucky* Lou," a tall, skinny one said, waking from a stupor on a couch.

"What's 'appened to the other big shots? No one's been 'ere all day but us," said one with a Birmingham accent, his face sallow and spotted like a frog.

"But you don't need to worry, mate. Everything's under control. Come and have a drink," the fat one said.

"What the hell do you men think you're doing?" Lou shouted.

"Easy, Lou, me old pal—or should I say, Lieutenant Commander, Third Officer, United States Navy, *sir!*" the skinny one said.

"You're supposed to be on watch," Lou said.

"Yeah, so we *are* on watch, ain't we? See us 'ere!" said another with rotten, goofy teeth.

"We're just having a little drink. It's Sunday—the day of rest. Relax. Come on, sit down and 'ave a drink, me boy."

"He's got nothin' to go 'ome for, 'as he?" the fat one said, roaring with laughter.

"You men are a disgrace," Lou said.

The fat one and the goofy one got up and moved toward him.

"Perhaps the fancy Navy man's going to get us all in trouble," the goofy one said.

"Trouble? You have no idea what trouble you're in," Lou muttered.

"We're not in your precious bleedin' Navy, Lou, me old cock," the goofy one said, putting one hand on his hip and shaking his backside around.

"Go on, Micky, give 'im one!" someone said.

Goofy moved in, but Lou stopped him with a blow under the chin which lifted him off his feet. He crumpled to the floor out cold, minus a few teeth, which fell on the floor like gravel. The other five rushed at Lou, but were surprised by a great shout from the dining saloon.

"*That's enough!*" It was Capt. Irwin. "Step back and get in here, all of you," he bellowed.

"*Very* merchant service!" Sky Hunt, shouted from behind Irwin.

"Very merchant service *indeed*, Mr. Hunt!" Atherstone echoed.

The five crewmen did as they were told, rapidly sobering up, fear registering in their faces. Hunt tilted his head back, sniffing the air.

"Apart from whisky and beer, there's *something else* I smell," he said.

The five sorry crewmen glanced at one another, their worries compounded. Sky Hunt left the dining saloon and marched off to the officers' cabins. In a few moments, he was back, dragging Rosie Cameron by the wrist. She wore only her brassiere and a pair of pink knickers. In her other hand she clung to the rest of her clothes and a pair of high heels. Jessup slunk behind, putting his braces over his shoulders. He glanced across at Lou and smirked.

"Out, you little whore!" Sky Hunt roared.

Rosie bolted.

"You might have let her put some clothes on, Mr. Hunt," Irwin said.

"*I did*," Hunt replied.

"There's gonna be an inquiry and charges," Irwin thundered.

"They've broken into the ship's bar and all the officers' lockers— add that to the charges. They've stolen all Steff's Canadian Club," Hunt said.

"And drunk it, by the looks of it," Atherstone said, surveying the empty brown bottles lying everywhere.

"He struck one of our crewmen," the skinny one whined, pointing at Lou.

"And you men are all *drunk!*" Irwin said.

"All right you lot, on yer bikes!" Hunt snapped.

Later, Lou went home to finish his letter. Irwin had asked him to come by Putroe Lane later for something to eat, but he declined. He sat at the table with a mug of coffee, brooding. His dark thoughts were interrupted by Mrs. Jones knocking at the door again. She came in carrying a plate of sandwiches covered with a clean tea towel.

"Lou, there's something else I must tell you," she said, following Lou into the kitchen. "The morning she left, a young man showed up and was talking with her. I couldn't hear what they were saying—but it seemed odd to me."

"What was he like?"

"Blimey, if I didn't know better, from a distance, I'd swear it was *you*—must be your ugly twin. I didn't like the looks of him. About your build ... scar down his face ... 'orrible greasy hair. And his eyes ... satanic—like one of them hyenas. His chin was crooked to one side, like this ... Oh, and he had a limp."

Lou got the picture.

"He came around here once or twice while you were away. Once, walking past and another time on a motorbike. Does he sound familiar?" Mrs. Jones asked.

"Nothing to worry about, Mrs. J. We're old friends."

"Oh good," she said, relieved. "Oh, yes, and a girl showed up. She's been here with one of your crewmen. Don't remember her name —nice looking girl."

"Long blond hair?"

"Yes, that's it, and a lovely face."

"Probably Irene," Lou said with a frown.

Everybody knows.

"Lou, there's something else."

"What?"

"Charlotte has cut her hair."

Lou shrugged.

"No, I mean *all* of it. All that beautiful hair! I couldn't believe it. I saw her from the window when she was pegging the sheets on the line."

His heart sank. "You're kidding me!"

When Mrs. Jones left, Lou made more coffee and ate the sandwiches. He hadn't eaten all day. He was deeply saddened about Charlotte's hair. She knew how much he loved her shining locks. He sat down to finish his letter, but couldn't think of anything to say. He was lost for words.

Lou got up at 4:00 a.m. the following morning. It was Monday. He went to Cardington field where he assisted in the removal of *Howden R100* from the mast and 'sticking her back in her box.' He returned home at 9 o'clock and put on his best suit, a clean shirt and a tie.

He went to the post office and sent a wire to his family in Virginia letting them know he was still in one piece. Next, he paid a visit to the bank to check their joint statement, not from a mercenary standpoint— he wanted to understand Charlotte's frame of mind. He saw where she'd taken out fifty pounds on July 31st—about a quarter of the total. He pondered this.

She didn't even take half of it—some women would have taken everything!

He left the bank and drove to Bedford Hospital, feeling like a cuckold and a sleuth on the trail of an unfaithful spouse. But maybe she wasn't unfaithful, just devious and deceitful in planning her escape, which she'd carried out with precision.

Did I deserve this? Was I so bad? Perhaps I was ...

He asked for the matron on Charlotte's ward. After about ten minutes, a pretty nurse showed him to Matron's office. She sat at a table in the corner of the room, her uniform stiff and white, like her personality. She gave him an accusing glare.

"This is—" the nurse said, giving Lou a furtive glance.

"I *know* who he is, nurse. Go out and shut the door. What can I do for you, young man?" she said unsmiling.

"I've come to speak to you about my wife, Charlotte."

"I've been expecting you."

"I got back from abroad on Saturday and Charlotte wasn't home."

"She gave me her notice three weeks ago, Mr. Remington."

Lou almost choked. "*Three weeks* ago!"

"Yes. Said she was leaving Bedford."

"Are you sure?"

"Of course I am. No, it was more than that." She consulted her log book. "She gave in her notice on the 15th of July. Her last day was July 25th and it's now the 18th of August. She'd been working nights."

She'd given in her notice two weeks before he left and served her last shift while he was still with her. He was stunned. How did he not see this coming? He'd missed this and the fact that his father was dying. He was usually so perceptive. Matron sensed his terrible disappointment and self blame. Her attitude softened.

"Don't be too hard on her, or yourself, son. She is a wonderful girl and she has really suffered—she had a *lot* of problems—believe me, *I know*. She was trying, in her own way, to be kind. Maybe one day, you'll understand that. Not all these girls are cut out to be the wives of airshipmen, you know."

But while the matron was speaking, all he could think about was how they'd made love the night he left. She'd even lit the candle for cryin' out loud!

How could she do that?

What he'd learned about Charlotte's actions over the past few weeks was the *coup de grace*. He got home feeling utterly betrayed. He sat down and read his unfinished letter and realized he had nothing more to say. If he put down what he thought at this moment, he'd certainly make matters worse. He signed the letter curtly, 'Fondest love,' addressed it to Charlotte's parents' home and stuffed it in an envelope. He walked to the pillar box on the corner and dropped it in the slot. At that moment, he realized how Julia must have felt.

Poor Julia!

4

SUNDAY PAPERS

Sunday August 17, 1930.

T homson had a restful Sunday. He rose at 8 o'clock, donned his silk dressing gown and went to the breakfast room, which was bathed in morning sunshine. He opened the *Sunday Sketch*. He enjoyed these Sunday mornings, leisurely going through the newspapers while Gwen served him tea and toast with his favorite thick-cut marmalade.

Every newspaper had a photograph of *Howden R100* arriving at the Cardington mast and some had pictures of him welcoming home the officers and crew. The articles were fair with the questions and his answers reported accurately, though he perceived the right-wing papers were a little snide in talking about the Cardington ship, whereas the rest appeared more objective, more even-handed.

He opened the *Sunday Express* to find a picture of himself shaking Burney's hand—like best friends; they stood together smiling happily. The interviews with Burney and Norway he found annoying—they were crowing. But then he had to admit, they'd done what they set out to do—he had to give them full credit. Now it remained for him to drive the R.A.W. to better this achievement. A voyage to India and a safe return would do just that.

The caption read:

HOWDEN R100 AIRSHIP WELCOMED HOME
SIR DENNIS SAYS HIS SHIP PERFORMED FLAWLESSLY
THE BAR HAS BEEN SET—NOW IT'S UP TO CARDINGTON

Thomson scoffed out loud. "Huh! We'll show you, *Sir* Dennis!" he said.

He turned to the *Sunday Telegraph*.

HOWDEN R100 AIRSHIP BACK FROM SPECTACULAR TRIP
WILL CARDINGTON AIRSHIP BE READY IN TIME?

The Times, business-like, alluded to the 'great competition.'

VICKERS FULFILLS CONTRACT WITH HOWDEN R100.
CAN ROYAL AIRSHIP WORKS COMPETE?

The Sunday Pictorial appeared more light-hearted:

HOWDEN AIRSHIP WOWS CANADIANS
WE DID IT. NOW IT'S YOUR TURN! SAYS SIR DENNIS

Overall, publicity was satisfactory. Thank God, no mention had been made of that damned fool's question concerning morale. He considered the issue again. What were Irwin and Brancker up to? Was there still some undermining going on? Was Irwin demoralizing the whole damned organization? He went to the bedroom and, with Buck's help, got dressed. Later, he sat in his new study overlooking the rear courtyard and worked on ministerial papers for the rest of the day. In the evening, he sat in his spacious living room at his credenza and wrote to Marthe, while listening to a sad violin on the gramophone. Marthe smiled down from her picture frame.

> *122, Ashley Gardens.*
> *17ᵗʰ August, 1930.*

My Dearest Marthe,

Thank you for asking, but I cannot get over to Paris this month. I could come in September if you're there, say during the first week.

I have moved from No.100 (as you can see by my new address) to a larger flat No. 122 with room for a comfortable study, a nicer aspect, a bigger kitchen—which pleases Gwen—and since I plan to keep it a long time—a longer lease. Now all that's necessary is for you to bestow your blessings upon it, along with me and Sammie, who misses you almost as much as I. So, dearest, I hope we can be together before I leave for India so that you can work your magic upon my spirit and fortify my soul for the journey. Please let me know soonest.

Ever my devotion,

Kit.

Thomson received Marthe's reply a week later. She wouldn't be available since she'd be in Romania attending a reception for a group of professors from America. After that, she'd be hosting a garden party for them at Posada. These arrangements had been made a long time ago. Marthe sent her love and best wishes, remarking that she'd been 'outwitted by Fate.' Thomson had a rash of unhappy thoughts about a herd of virile, good-looking American intellectuals in Marthe's house. He hated the thought and tried to push it aside. He wrote back immediately.

122, Ashley Gardens.
25th August, 1930.

My Own Dear Princess,

No, it is I whom Fate has outwitted. I hope these headwinds we are up against abate soon. Though you are not actually with me, please know that you shall be forever present in my heart throughout my journey. Let's hope we return from India in triumph, and that all our new days are glorious. If only we had a crystal ball to glimpse the future. Meanwhile I shall sit helplessly by, watching for hopeful signs.

Always and Forever,

Kit.

5

QUESTIONS

August & September 1930.

Lou carried on with his life as best he could. He constantly wondered what Charlotte was doing and what she was thinking, not to mention where she was. He got home each evening hoping for a letter. But none came. He asked Billy to move in with him. Work would be nearer for Billy and Lou could keep and eye on him, as he'd promised Fanny. The lad would be company, too; he was miserable being in the house alone. Lou decided to write John Bull. Perhaps he had news of Charlotte. He dashed off a note.

58 Kelsey Street,
Bedford.
22nd August, 1930.

Dear John and Mary,

I don't expect you have heard—or maybe you have? When I was inCanada, Charlotte left Bedford (and me) and did not say where she was going. I wonder if you have heard from her? As you can imagine, it came as a terrible shock. I guess it's my fault. We are preparing the other ship to fly to India in September. Please drop me a line as soon as possible.

My fond regards as always,

Lou.

Lou received a letter from John Bull three days later.

Croft Cottage, Brough, Near Hull,
Yorkshire.
24ᵗʰ August, 1930.

My Dear Lou, Mary and I are deeply shocked. We had not heard a
word about this until your letter arrived. We have heard nothing from
Charlotte. You are a wonderful couple and you know we love you both
very dearly. We hope you can resolve everything and get back together
soon. Please let us know if there is anything we can do. Anything at
all!

Much love, John and Mary.

Lou spent the rest of August and most of September in Shed No.1
monitoring the alterations, as he'd done during construction. As the
deadline loomed, a toll was exacted on everyone, nerves fraying,
tempers flaring. Furious activity continued around the clock in an
atmosphere of general panic. Morale and discipline sank to new lows.

A preliminary inquiry had started regarding the altercation between
Lou and the drunken watch crewmen, but nothing of consequence was
expected from it. The man Lou had knocked out was still off with a
broken jaw—a reminder for Jessup to stay out of Lou's way, which he
did conscientiously. One afternoon, Lou tracked him down in the
crewmen's locker room lavatories. Lou had been worrying about
Charlotte and brooding about Jessup's visits to Kelsey Street all
morning and was in foul mood. Lou worried that if Charlotte was in
Ackworth, Jessup might go up there and harass her. He was also sore
about the episode with Rosie. He'd not acted on any of this until now.
Jessup was standing at the urinal trough. Lou came up behind him,
grabbed his neck and slammed his face into the brick wall, causing
Jessup to spray himself.

"Mr. Jessup. Question: I understand you were hanging around my
house when I was away." Jessup made babbling noises. Lou leaned
against his ear and yelled. "What were you doing there, shithead?"

Jessup remained silent.

"Cat got ya tongue, boy?"

"I was passing by, that's all," Jessup whimpered.

"I warned you to stay away from my wife," Lou said, letting him
go.

"She's gone. She's fair game now."

"You stay away from her!"

"Don't come near me. I'll have you up for assault. I'm gonna lodge a complaint with my union. We'll go on strike and you'll be court-martialed."

Lou knew these things were possible, particularly the way the mood was in the shed just now. He didn't get too rough. He'd bide his time.

"Watch yourself, Jessup," Lou said, walking out of the locker room.

"Yes, an' you watch yourself an' all," Jessup muttered.

During the last week in August, Thomson summoned Colmore, Scott, Richmond, Rope, Irwin, Atherstone and Lou to Gwydyr House for a progress meeting. Knoxwood took minutes. Thomson was showing his most affable side.

It was the first time Lou had been to the Air Minister's office. The first thing that struck him was the Taj Mahal in its ornate gilt frame. He smiled when he saw Churchill's airship and wondered who the 'daubing fool' was. The painting looked pretty damned good. He noticed Richmond studying it, too. He looked mystified—as though he was seeing things.

"Good morning, gentlemen. I have a few questions about your progress and the schedule. First of all, update me on the modifications, Colmore," Thomson said.

"The work on the extra bay is almost complete, with the additional gas bags being installed and inflated. The bags with holes are being repaired.

"What about the padding issue?"

"Padding is almost complete—and monitored by the inspector."

"The fellow who caused the rumpus?"

"Yes, sir, Fred McWade."

"Good. When do you expect to schedule the re-launching?"

"Hopefully mid-September—leaving two weeks for tests."

"So, we'll start for India before the end of September?"

"Providing the tests are satisfactory."

Thomson glanced at Irwin, sitting behind the others. "What testing is required? I thought most of it was done last year?"

"Captain Irwin has drawn up a comprehensive schedule of tests. I'll let him brief you," Colmore said, turning to Irwin.

Irwin stood up. "First of all, I must stress this ship's only *ever* flown in near-perfect weather. Initially, a flight of twenty-four hours will be conducted in *moderately* adverse weather, followed by forty-eight hours in *adverse* conditions—six hours of this flight at full speed, the rest at cruising speed. After that, the ship must be put in the shed for a thorough inspection."

"This all seems rather extravagant, after all the flying this ship's already done." Thomson growled.

"After the insertion of the additional bay, she'll be a different ship with different characteristics—we'll need to start from scratch. These tests are required in order to be declared '*fit to fly*'," Irwin said.

"Seems to me we're asking an awful lot of the weather—we want conditions '*dead calm*' to bring her out—'*windy* and *rough*' for seventy two hours, then '*dead calm*' to put her back in the shed. What are the chances of *that* in your two-week window? *Zero*, I should think!" Thomson sniffed.

"We'll have to play it by ear, sir and adjust the schedule, based on experience," Colmore said, his eyes shifting to Scott.

Scott was glad to step in. "I'll keep an eye on the situation, Lord Thomson. We'll make these decisions as we go along. We can be flexible, I'm sure."

Thomson saw Irwin didn't appreciate Scott's accommodative tone.

Irwin is a spoiler!

"One request: I want you to lay a nice blue carpet from the bow to the passenger public area. The interior needs dolling up a bit," Thomson said.

Colmore winced.

"What's that for, Colmore? You don't like *blue?*"

"It's *weight* I'm worried about, sir."

"Come on, Colmore! It won't weigh that much. What's the story with the cover?"

Richmond wanted to answer this one. "Most of the cover's been replaced and waiting to be doped. The rest of the areas are under inspection," he said.

After the meeting, Thomson left Gwydyr House where George Hunter from the *Daily Express* and Edmund Jones from the *Daily Mirror* were lying in wait outside. The C*ardington R101* saga had become a drama closely followed by the public.

"Lord Thomson, do you mind if we ask a few questions?" Hunter asked.

Though caught off guard, Thomson smiled broadly. "By all means, gentlemen."

"We're getting reports *Cardington R101* may not be ready in time for the voyage in September."

"My staff from the Royal Airship Works informed me less than an hour ago, she *will* be ready to fly."

"Will that leave time for testing, Lord Thomson?" Hunter asked.

"We'll have to *make* time won't we!" Thomson snapped, but then caught himself and smiled pleasantly.

"What about morale and discipline? Apparently, an inquiry is being held to look into brawling and drunkenness. Can you tell us about that, sir?" Jones asked.

"I've no idea where you're getting all this. Morale, gentlemen, has never been higher," Thomson said. "Good day to you."

The next day the two newspapers carried headlines.

The *Daily Express* asked:

WILL R101 BE READY IN TIME FOR VOYAGE TO INDIA?

The *Daily Mirror* would not let go of the morale and discipline story:

AIR MINISTER DENIES RUMORS OF BREAKDOWN IN MORALE

6

RACE AGAINST TIME

September 1930.

They toiled through September at a feverish pace. Richmond arranged to make an inspection before bringing the ship out, with Lou, Rope, McWade, Irwin, Atherstone and the shop foreman, Ronnie, in attendance. The group trooped around the ship's interior, looking at the padding.

"They've done a *fine* job, Mr. McWade," Richmond said.

"They did what you asked. Not *my* idea of a fine job!"

"You've carried out your instructions. That's all that matters."

"What matters sir, are the lives of these young men. I maintain padding is *not* a satisfactory solution."

"Yes, yes, Mr. McWade, we're all aware of your feelings on the subject. Let's move on, shall we? I want to examine the cover."

They moved to the exterior of the ship and stood looking up at the canvas. The foreman pointed out that the cover had been replaced with the exception of the area between Frame 1 and Frame 3 at the front end. Richmond stood under the frames in question.

"What about the rest, then?"

"It's in fairly good condition. We would replace every piece, but we don't have time," replied the foreman.

McWade wasn't satisfied. He made them follow him up on the scaffold. "I want you people to focus your eyes on *this*," he said. "You think you've removed all the rotten fabric from this ship. Well, you haven't." He led them around poking his finger at the cover. Sometimes the cover held, other times his finger went clean through, like rotting paper.

McWade glared at Richmond. "So, *now* what?"

Richmond addressed Rope and Ronnie. "Get the *whole* crew on this. Put patches over the holes and weak areas and anywhere it looks doubtful," he told them.

"It's *all* very doubtful, if you ask me. I'll be surprised if you make it to Dover!"

Richmond stormed off.

"This ship's gonna have more pads, bandages and sticking plasters than the bloody Red Cross," McWade sneered. Lou worried about Irwin. He looked physically ill.

The Air Ministry decided *Howden R100* would also receive an extra bay. Norway came down to discuss these modifications, although he didn't believe it was necessary, and told Richmond as much. Naturally, his views were not well received. But he was glad of the work; Vickers was still paying his salary, for the moment anyway. Most of the staff at Howden had been laid off and he expected the axe to fall at any time.

New designs for bigger and better dirigibles were on the boards at the R.A.W. Many in government urged a freeze until the two existing airships proved themselves before committing more money. One successful return trip across the Atlantic could've been due to sheer luck.

While in Bedford, Norway stayed with Lou on Kelsey Street. Since their triumphant return from Canada, Norway had been treated with even more disdain by the R.A.W. (if that were possible). His only safe haven was in Booth's office in Shed No. 2, where *Howden R100* was presently housed. After Richmond's inspection of *Cardington R101*, Lou took a piece of the cover to show them. None of them seemed happy when Lou stepped inside.

"Come in, Lou. Nevil's complaining because no one loves him," Booth said.

"There's tea in the pot," Meager said.

Lou closed the door and poured himself a cup.

"They're treating me like a b-bloody leper," Norway complained.

"What do you *expect*, Nev? You've caused all this panic, all this worry and all this misery," Lou said.

"Many a true word spoken in jest!" Booth said.

"Everything's rubbed off on *us*. They won't include us in anything either," Meager grumbled. "We're sitting in here with nothing to do all day. It's all *his* fault."

"We upped the ante. Now you're the enemy, too," Norway said.

Lou laid the cover sample on the table in front of Norway, without a word. Norway put on his thick-framed reading glasses and carefully picked up the fabric in two hands. As he did so, it crumbled to pieces.

"Oh, my good Lord!" Norway gasped, while Booth and Meager gathered round. "W-w-what the hell is this? Where did this c-come from?"

"Don't panic, Nevil, it's not off your ship. This is part of the old cover from *R101* next door," Lou replied.

Norway turned the remaining piece over in his hands. "Look at this. They've stuck tapes on the inside as reinforcement and the adhesive is having a chemical reaction to the dope."

"You could be right," Booth said.

"I hope they d-don't leave any of this on that ship."

"Most of the cover's been replaced—they're patching the rest."

"They need to remove *all* this r-rubbish!"

"They're trying to, but they're running out of time," Lou said.

In late September, while the October fair was arriving in the village and setting up opposite Cardington field as usual, *Cardington R101* was going through her lift and trim tests, which came out as follows:

Fixed Weight	118 tons
Gross Lift	167 tons
Disposable Lift	49 tons

These results were as expected, although still shy of requirements originally laid down by Thomson in 1924. The good news was that the two forward engines, Nos.1 and 2, were both now reversible, so they would no longer be carrying one engine as dead weight and had the benefit of much needed forward power on all engines. This would increase dynamic lift and help them stay airborne.

7

TRAIN RIDE NORTH

September 25 - October 1, 1930.

T he ship was handed over to the flying staff a week behind schedule, but now the weather was taking the final bite out of allotted time for testing. It remained atrocious for the next five days. As the departure date loomed, Lou felt the need to make an effort to try and meet Charlotte. She hadn't responded to his letter and Charlotte was all he thought about.

Who knows? Maybe she didn't receive it. Perhaps she hasn't gone to her parents' home. Maybe they haven't heard from her either. Maybe she's with this Robert guy. At least I'll be able to talk to her mom and dad if I go up there.

Lou went to Capt. Irwin and asked for permission to be away for one, possibly two days. Irwin encouraged him to go. Lou also spoke to Colmore, who was kind and sympathetic and wished him well. On October 1st, the weather abated and Lou went with Norway to witness the handling party walk *Cardington R101* to the tower. Once moored, *Howden R100* was brought out of Shed No. 2 and put into the longer shed for work to commence on the insertion of her own additional bay. This would be the first time the two ships had actually been visible together and Norway wanted a photograph.

Afterwards, Norway ran Lou back to Kelsey Street, where he put on his best suit, clean white shirt and a smart red tie. Before leaving, he placed the writing case Charlotte had given him on the bed to take with him. Maybe he'd draft some letters home during the train journey. Then, as an afterthought, he removed the photo of them together from its gold frame and stuffed it in an envelope. He put it in the writing case. Lou wanted to travel by rail so he could dress decently. He decided against wearing his leather greatcoat.

On the way to the station, Norway aired his employment woes.

"I met with Richmond this morning," he said.

"How did *that* go?"

"I asked him if they'd put me on the payroll while they insert the extra bay and do the modifications to our ship. I offered to stay here as consulting engineer for half my salary."

"I'm sure that went over *real* big!"

"He flatly refused!"

"You're out of work then, basically?" Lou said.

"They're talking about more ships—but goodness knows when that'll be."

"I don't think they like you much, Nev."

"I know."

"This is the perfect opportunity to write another novel!"

"I'm out of ideas right now," Norway said.

"Hey, I got one for you. How about this: An American naval officer flies to Canada in a British airship. After escaping death twice on the way, he goes to visit his family in the U.S.A., ravaged by the Depression. He finds he's run into a shit-storm; his family have lost everything; he gets mixed up with moonshine, the Ku Klux Klan, his old Army buddies in Shanty Town, the government and the military— and then his *old girlfriend* shows up!"

They arrived outside the station.

"Lou, Lou, Lou!" Norway said, shaking his head. Lou got out and stuck his head in the window. Norway continued. "I don't know where you come up with these silly ideas. They're daft! That kind of ph-ph-phantas-m-mag-g-goria would never appeal to my readers. They're f-far too sophisticated for that kind of unrealistic silliness."

"You're probably right—whatever that means."

"Lou, I wish you the very best of luck today," Norway said. "I'd ask you to give her my love but it might q-queer your p-pitch."

"Make sure Billy's okay. Tell him to get his stuff ready for *India*."

Lou bought two dozen red roses at the florist next to the station before purchasing a ticket. He arrived in Wakefield two hours later and waited for the local train to Ackworth. Pretty soon, a steam train trundled in. The journey to Ackworth took twenty minutes.

A wave of nostalgia overcame him. He remembered arriving there the first time with Charlotte to meet her parents. It was this same time of year—leaves on the ground rustling underfoot—their colors as bright as daffodils and plums in the sunshine. All the thoughts he'd had at that time rushed into his head. Now here he was, back to ask what had become of his bride. *Humiliating!*

Under heavy cloud and spitting rain, Lou, clutching the roses, walked up the dirt road between the stone houses. As he got closer to Charlotte's house, he had feelings of both dread and excitement. Would she be there? Perhaps she'd be thrilled to see him on the doorstep. Maybe she wasn't there. Maybe she *had* found someone else. What sort of reception would her parents give him? Would they blame *him* for everything?

His whole life depended on this unrequested (and perhaps unwelcome) visit. But the more he thought about it, he believed he was right to come. He should've come before now. Staying away meant he didn't care. He felt confident and his spirits rose with every step.

This is what men do—pursue. It's what we're meant to do.

At last, he stood at the front gate. He glanced up at the rooftop. Smoke was coming from the chimney. The net curtains in the front window were drawn, preventing him from seeing in.

The room where she was born!

He hesitated for a moment, looking at where Charlotte's swing used to hang from the oak tree. It was long gone—but he could see marks on the bough where it'd once been tied. He pushed down on the gate latch. The gate squeaked as he opened it. They'd surely hear it. He figured the whole neighborhood must have. He went to the front door, sensing an aura of unfriendliness. He felt like a stranger, his confidence began to dwindle. He lifted the brass knocker and gingerly knocked once. He waited. Perhaps they couldn't hear it if they were in the kitchen. He waited patiently for a few more minutes, his heart racing. No one answered.

He knocked again, louder, twice. He waited, but no one came. He knocked three times, this time much louder. Hell, all the neighbors must have heard that! Still no one came. He carefully put the flowers down on the grass next to the stoop. They were beginning to droop and some of the petals had fallen off.

He bent down and peered through the letter box. A few coats were hanging on hooks in the hallway—he spotted Charlotte's—the blue one she wore in Switzerland. Beyond the foyer, the coal fire glowed in the grate in the living room—probably stoked less than half an hour ago. On the coffee table in front of the couch, he noticed a cup and saucer.

Someone's home.

There was nothing next to Father's easy chair on his shelf. No cup and saucer. No cigarettes.

He must be at work.

Lou left the flowers on the ground and went back to the front gate and into the street. He walked along the stone wall, past the house next door and into the alleyway leading to the back of the houses. He felt like an interloper. He'd ridden his motorbike round to the backyard many times. This place used to feel welcoming. Not anymore.

He got to the back of the house, passing the outhouses, and went to the kitchen door. Hearing Lou's footsteps on the gravel, the dog behind the fence next door started barking, while nearby chickens clucked and carried on. The curtains had been drawn across the window over the sink.

That means they're out—or they know I'm here.

He knocked with his knuckles and got the same response. He tried the door. Locked. He glanced up at the windows next door. The curtains were also drawn, but he could swear they moved. Probably someone had been asleep. Many of these people were miners on shift work who slept during the day. Now the neighbor would be irritated. He thought about knocking on their door and asking about Charlotte.

No, that would only make her mad as hell.

Lou retraced his steps along the alley and returned to the front stoop and peeped through the letter box again. He could swear the cup and saucer had been moved. He was sure someone was home and knew he was there.

Well, if they're home and they won't open the door that tells me all I need to know. No point in sticking around here.

He scanned the windows again on the second and third floors—nothing. It began to rain. He took out a sheet of paper from the writing case and wrote:

Dear Charlotte

I had hoped to talk to you before leaving for India. Please remember I always loved you, and always will. I guess old Mrs. Tilly got it wrong.

Lou signed the note, smudged by raindrops and put it in the envelope with the photograph of them together at the five-bar gate across the road. And then, on an impulse, he pulled off his wedding ring, slipped it in the envelope and sealed it. He pushed it through the letter box and, leaving the wilting flowers on the ground, left the front garden. He walked off toward the station, collar up, shoulders hunched against the cold rain. He wished he'd worn his leather greatcoat.

"Go after him!" Charlotte's mother implored.

Mrs. Hamilton had spotted Lou first from her bedroom on the second floor as he came in the front gate. She rushed down to Charlotte who was sitting in the living room on the couch, reading and drinking tea.

"Lou's coming to the front door," she whispered hoarsely. She didn't know why she was whispering, but had anticipated Charlotte's reaction.

They heard a light knock on the door.

"Don't you *dare* open that door," Charlotte hissed.

Charlotte got up and went to the kitchen and pulled the curtains across the back window over the sink and turned the key in the lock. It was stiff. She couldn't remember the last time it'd been locked. She returned to her mother in the living room and picked up her cup and saucer, and then put it back down. He must've seen it there.

"Come on, we must go upstairs," she murmured, her eyes determined. The two women sneaked up the staircase, to Charlotte's parents' bedroom, overlooking the front garden. They peeped down through the net curtains and saw Lou standing at the door. There were two more knocks.

"Charlotte, why don't you go down and talk to him."

"No, I won't!"

"Oh, Charlotte, he's come all this way. You can't leave him standing out there in the rain."

"Mother, I will *not* speak to him. I don't want any more to do with him."

"How can you be so cruel? He's such a lovely fella."

"I don't love him anymore. There can be no happiness with an airshipman."

"Perhaps you could talk him out of it."

"No, he's committed. You don't understand. I've tried a thousand times. He has his reasons. I've no control over that. Now leave it be."

They followed Lou's movements as he tried the back of the house. They saw him returning to the front door. A minute or two later, they heard the letter box snap shut. They watched him walk off up the road toward the station.

"Oh, Charlotte, go after him. He's so thin and gaunt. Look at him! He's your husband. You made a vow—for better or for worse." Tears were springing from her eyes. "Go after him! I can't bear it—it breaks my heart to see him like this."

"Let it be, Mother!"

It was raining hard now, with gusty winds. The leaves fell on the road, leaving a slippery, mustard and brown carpet. Surreal, ominous clouds shifted overhead, occasionally revealing vivid blue sky and shafts of sunshine, illuminating fields each side in patches.

Lou trudged up the deserted street toward the station. Rain soaked through his jacket, chilling him to the bone. A spectacular rainbow arched over his road ahead. The vicious irony of it infuriated him, and with every step he took, he became more angry. When he got to the station, the stationmaster told him the next train was due in twenty minutes. He slumped down on the bench in the empty waiting room, fuming. He was mad at himself for bothering to come. She'd made it plain she didn't want him to make contact.

Stubborn Yorkshire b...

He couldn't bring himself to say it again, even to himself.

Charlotte's mother came downstairs, wiping her tears with a handkerchief. She went to the vestibule and picked up the envelope from the mat, then opened the front door and warily peered outside. Petals were being beaten off the roses by water cascading from the roof. She gently scooped them up and took them to the kitchen table. She was cutting the stems and placing them in a vase when Charlotte entered the room.

"Where did these come from?" she snapped.

"He left them for you."

"I don't want them."

"I'll not leave them out there. They came with his love. I'll keep them, even if you don't want them," Mrs. Hamilton said.

"Do as you please."

"And there's a letter for you."

"I said leave it be!"

"You've *never* done right by him, you know. You kept him in the dark all this time. It wasn't right!"

"Don't go on about *that*, Mother ...anyway, it doesn't matter now."

Charlotte sat down at the kitchen table, scowling at the envelope.

Later, Mr. Hamilton returned from Ackworth Colliery. After getting them to unlock it, he came through the back door wearing his bicycle clips on his overalls, grimy with coal dust.

"What's that locked for?" He noticed the flowers, "Hello, hello. What's all this? Have you got a secret admirer, Mrs. Lena Hamilton?" he said, smiling at his wife and then Charlotte. But then he saw they were both upset.

"Lou's been here and left them for our Charlotte. She wouldn't open the door to him."

His face lit up for a second and then fell. "*What!* Has he gone?"

"He was on foot. He walked back up to the station. Poor Lou, he looked so sad." She started to cry again.

"How long ago was this?"

"He left about fifteen minutes ago. Oh, that *poor* boy ..."

"I'll go up and see if I can catch him. I'll bring him back."

"Don't you dare, Dad!" Charlotte said.

But Mr. Hamilton was resolute. He put his cap back on, rushed out the back door and jumped on his bicycle. He began peddling like mad.

Sick at heart, he returned twenty minutes later. The station had been empty. Mr. Hamilton got washed in the kitchen, changed, and went to sit in his armchair by the fire. Mrs. Hamilton brought him a cup of tea and sat down. He lit a cigarette. Charlotte came and sat on the couch with Lou's letter. It felt stiff and there was something else inside making it bulge. Mr. Hamilton turned on the radio beside him in time for the news. Charlotte tore the letter open and Lou's ring fell into her lap. It stunned her and she felt a knife in her heart. She clasped it into her palm and closed it, hoping her father hadn't seen it. But he had. She caught a glimpse of sadness in his eyes. After the sound of Big Ben striking the hour, there were six beeps on the radio and then the familiar BBC announcer's voice. Charlotte was surprised to find the photograph as she pulled it out with Lou's damp note. She read his brief words before raising her head to listen.

'This is the BBC Home Service. It was announced today by the Air Ministry in Whitehall that His Majesty's Airship Cardington R101 is expected to leave her mast in Bedfordshire on the 4th of October to begin her passage to India. The Secretary of State for Air, Brigadier General, the Right Honorable Lord Thomson of Cardington, will be on board for this, her historic maiden voyage…'

Charlotte left the room with Lou's letter, his ring still in her palm, and went to the attic bedroom where Lou had once slept. She sat on the bed and pulled out the photograph and studied it. Lou looked younger. He wore a sweater (she remembered it was light blue) and black trousers. She looked closely at his face. He was looking into her eyes and smiling with such love. She lay down, burying her head in the pillow. She thought about the things old Mrs.Tilly had said on her deathbed and remembered kissing the palm of her hand where his tears had been on that horrible, beautiful night in Hull. She opened her hand and looked at his ring.

Lou's anger simmered throughout his journey back to Bedford Station. He sat alone huddled in a carriage with his feet up on the seat opposite, trying not to shiver. On the journey up to Yorkshire earlier, he'd mulled over the idea of foregoing the voyage to India and quitting airship business altogether. He had a good excuse. He could've said he needed to rush back to see his dying father. He'd thought about taking Charlotte with him. They would've taken a steamer from Liverpool to Montreal (as he'd dreamed of doing) and then hopped on the train to Union. But that would've meant deserting his captain and his crew and leaving them to their fate with that damned airship. Would he have done it? For her, yes. For *her,* he would've done it! Then he thought about the guilt that would've been associated with that—especially if something happened to them all. But she wouldn't open the door, so it was all moot. And, in some ways, he was glad.

What the hell! It doesn't matter. I'll fly with them and take my chances. I could care less now anyway.

He couldn't help thinking of Charlotte's words when Freddie died.

That ship is cursed! And this city is cursed. And we're cursed, too.

He looked at the impression on his ring finger where his wedding ring had been. Perhaps she was right. He dwelt on what she'd said as the train approached Bedford. He thought about *Cardington R101*. It wasn't up to *Howden R100*—although that ship was Spartan and without frills—it didn't even have any damned fuel pumps for God's sake! *Cardington R101* was ornate and bloated, a testament to overspending and a desire to impress.

I'll talk to Colmore again. I'll give it another try. You never know, he might grow a set of balls—but I doubt it. Time's getting short.

Richmond had conscientiously done his best to design a strong airship that wouldn't break in two, and this and the extravagant touches, had caused her to come out heavy. And now they'd added an extra bay—what had that done to all their calculations and to the factor of safety? Lou still didn't know if the ship was really and truly airworthy. He hoped they'd find out more during the twenty-four hour test. But the lack of testing was crazy! And for what? To satisfy an old martinet, hell-bent on using it as his own personal plaything! It was maddening. *Colmore* was maddening! They were *all* maddening!

This just ain't no way to run an empire!

Had *Cardington R101* become the symbol of the Empire—too big, too heavy, too vainglorious to fly?

Lou got home late, after stopping at The Swan in Bedford near the old bridge, where he downed a pint of bitter and a couple of double whiskies. He didn't expect them to be up, but Norway and Billy were waiting to hear his news. Lou sat down with Norway while Billy made a pot of tea.

"We're dying to know. Did you see her?" Norway asked.

"They wouldn't answer the door."

"What!"

"I'm positive she was home. I saw her coat hanging in the hallway. The fire was burning. Place was locked up tighter than Dick's hatband."

"Who's Dick?" Billy asked.

"You tried the door?" Norway asked.

"I tried the *back* door."

"It was locked?"

"Yes."

"Nobody locks their doors up there. Especially the *back* door."

"I guess somebody must've seen me coming."

"Probably. Did you try the *front* door?"

"No. I didn't."

Lou was mad with himself. "You know something—if she'd let me in and said 'Give it all up,' I'd have done it right then and there. She obviously doesn't care for me anymore and that's that," Lou said.

"Damn!" said Billy.

"What happened with the flight test?" Lou asked.

"Irwin took his ship up today. They had the new AMSR on board —Air Vice-Marshall Dowding. He knows absolutely nothing about airships."

"Sounds a lot like you, Nev. Are they doing the twenty-four hour?"

"It got shortened to sixteen hours. Booth told me this afternoon."

"What about the forty-eight hour?"

Norway put on his most exasperated face. "No time for that."

"Irwin's gonna be mad as hell. It's flat calm out there. No use at all!"

8

A FEW LOOSE ENDS

October 2, 1930.

The following day, Lou sat at the kitchen table and wrote some letters. The first was to his mother. After delivering the bad news, he'd try to keep the rest positive.

58, Kelsey Street,
Bedford,
England.

2nd October, 1930

Dear Mom,

I am heartbroken and I have only myself to blame. Charlotte has left me and gone away. Please keep this to yourself, for now. I guess Dad was right. Perhaps it was all a mistake. I hope he is not feeling too bad. Tell him I think of him always and I will be with him soon. I am praying for a miracle. I hope he is taking an interest in Jeb's new house.

We are off to India this Saturday aboard Cardington R101. I hope, all being well, to see you on my return. I will come home for good after we get back from India. My job here will have been done and there is no reason for me to stay—although I will miss this place and these people more than I can say.

There's a chance of a place on the U.S. Akron or Macon and I will probably try for one of them, unless I become a farmer! Give Dad my love—and also Tom, Anna and Julia, and of course, Jeb and family.

Fondest Love, dearest Mother,

Your son, Lou.

He took a long deep breath before addressing his next letter.

President Herbert C. Hoover,
President of the United States of America,
The White House,
Pennsylvania Avenue,
Washington, D.C. U.S.A.

58, Kelsey Street,
Bedford, England.
2ⁿᵈ October, 1930.

Dear Mr. President,

Please forgive me for taking the liberty of writing to you, sir, but I believe it is important I do so. I served in France during the war with the Marine Corps and now I am serving as an airshipman with the U.S. Navy, seconded to the British Airship Program.

I recently flew in the British Airship Howden R100 from England to Montreal and came to Washington, D.C., where I was met by a delegation of Army veterans who asked me to intercede on their behalf. I promised I would do my best to help. As you know, they are camped out in Anacostia and are lobbying for their Army Service Bonds to be paid now instead of later, due to the hardship caused by the depressed state of the economy.

Therefore, I am respectfully appealing to you to help these men, who have done so much for our country, by urging the Congress to pass a bill which will give them financial relief and ease their suffering.

Yours faithfully,
Louis Remington Lt. Cmdr. United States Navy,
Chief Petty Officer U.S.N. Airship ZR-2,
Third Officer HMA Howden R100 and HMA Cardington R101,
Special Assistant to Director of Airship Development of Great Britain.

Lou wrote a similar letter to the senator in his grandmother's district. Lou sealed the letters and took them to the pillar box on the corner. He next went to two insurance agents on the High Street in Bedford. At the first one, The Prudential, he took out a life insurance policy on himself for the sum of one thousand pounds, the beneficiary being Charlotte Remington of 11, Station Road, Ackworth, Yorkshire. The second, with the Pearl Life Assurance Company for the same amount, but with Mrs. Louise Remington of Remington's Farm, Great Falls, Virginia, U.S.A. as beneficiary. The premiums were high, due to his occupation, but he paid the money willingly.

Lou stopped next at Midland Bank, also on the High Street, where he arranged for a draft of one hundred pounds to be sent to the new account he'd set up at Riggs Bank in Georgetown. This left him with ninety pounds in the joint account with Charlotte. No activity, apart from his own, had occurred in the account since she'd gone.

Lou went from the bank to Needham & Finley, Solicitors-at-Law, where he asked the receptionist if he could get a will drawn up immediately. She told him to come back in an hour—Mr. Needham would take care of the matter personally.

On his return, he was ushered into the white-haired solicitor's office, a dark room surrounded by leather-bound books. Lou explained the will would be simple—he had few assets. Lou told the solicitor he was an airshipman aboard *Cardington R101,* which intrigued the old gentleman. On leaving, Mr. Needham asked Lou if he wouldn't mind paying his bill before leaving the premises.

At 6:00 p.m., Thomson sat at his desk at Gwydyr House. Knoxwood looked in to tell him his visitors had arrived.

"Send them in and come in and take minutes, would you?" Thomson instructed.

Colmore and the new AMSR (Air Member for Supply and Research) entered. Dowding was a tall man in his late forties, with graying hair and strong features. Thomson, though tired, perked up as soon as they came in, taking their hands and greeting them with warm smiles.

"Come in, gentlemen, come in! Just a few loose ends to sort out this evening. How did the test go—well, I hope? That was her final—yes?"

"Major Scott reported the test went well. 'Wonderfully,' actually. No major problems, except for the oil cooler," Colmore replied.

"Anything serious?"

"Oh, not too serious, but it prevented them from doing the speed test."

"And what about the additional bay?"

"The extra lift has helped considerably. No question," said Colmore.

"You were on board, Dowding?"

"Yes. I must say, it was a *most pleasant* experience—surprised me!"

This pleased Thomson.

"I should point out that Air Vice-Marshall Dowding had to be back by 8 o'clock this morning, so it meant the ship only did sixteen of the twenty-four hour test. And of course, we've not done the forty-eight hour test—required in rough weather," Colmore said.

"Required by *whom?*"

"The schedule drawn up by Captain Irwin."

"Oh, *Irwin* ..." Thomson said, waving his hand dismissively.

"I did ask the Air Ministry—which comes down to the Air Vice Marshall here—for permission to reduce the test durations," Colmore said.

Dowding shifted uncomfortably in his chair. "The problem is, I'm not fully in the picture. As you know, I've only just assumed this position. I must be guided by the experts at Cardington."

Colmore explained, "We agreed that if Major Scott felt satisfied, there'd be no objection to shortening the twenty-four hour test to sixteen."

"And forgetting about the forty-eight hour?" Thomson asked.

"Providing *Scott's* comfortable. The test durations are really arbitrary. This'll allow us to depart Saturday—providing you still want to proceed, that is—" Colmore said.

They were interrupted by a knock at the door. Brancker popped his head in. "Ah, CB, I didn't realize you were in conference. I've been trying to reach you all day. It's important I talk to you," Brancker said.

Thomson waved him off. "Not now, Sefton. Come back about eight-thirty this evening. I should be free by then." Colmore and Dowding appeared uncomfortable. Thomson had skillfully avoided Brancker all day and didn't want him hanging around—he'd be eager to join this meeting and knew he'd have far too much to say. Brancker nodded and closed the door.

Thomson picked up exactly where they'd left off.

"Well, of course we're going to proceed. We can't delay the voyage any longer. I need to be back by the twentieth!"

"We'll make preparations, then," Colmore said.

"Can we get away on Friday, instead of Saturday?"

"That wouldn't be possible. It'll take until Saturday to get the ship prepared, fueled and gassed up. And the crewmen need rest. They've been flat out for weeks."

"Yes, yes. Of course they do," Thomson said.

"It's important we arrive in Ismailia around sunset—we need the smoother air," Colmore explained. "If we leave Saturday evening, everything should work out just right."

"Look, I don't want to rush things, Colmore. I bow to your superior judgment." Thomson glanced at Knoxwood, to make sure he was taking all this down. "Where are we with the documentation?"

Knoxwood held up the paperwork triumphantly. "The Airworthiness Certificate and Permit to Fly are here, Lord Thomson," he said.

Dowding had been thinking. "About these tests: Would it be possible to complete some of them around Cardington when you leave the mast on Saturday evening before heading south?"

Nobody spoke. On the face of it, it seemed like a daft idea. Thomson turned to Colmore. "Let me consult Scott," Colmore said.

Thomson slipped on his spectacles and shuffled his papers. "Let's go through the passenger list." He ran his finger down the names. "O'Neill. Who is he again?"

"He's the new Deputy Director of Civil Aviation in Delhi…Sir Sefton requested—"

"Oh, yes, and Palstra?"

"The Australian."

"Yes, right. I don't see Buck's name here," Thomson said frowning.

"Buck! Who is Buck?" Colmore asked.

"My valet, of course."

Colmore became flustered. "I didn't know anything about a valet, sir."

"I can't do without Buck! And what about the blue carpet?"

Colmore grimaced. "Yes, sir. We had to remove the parachutes and cut down the crew's luggage limit to ten pounds to accommodate that —in part, anyway."

"Colmore, we've just spent thousands on installing a new bay. Now you're fussing over a bit of carpet and my valet!"

Colmore kept his mouth shut.

"Okay, let's talk about the banquet. As you know, I'll be entertaining the King of Egypt during our stopover in Ismailia. No refueling operations will be allowed in Egypt—understood?"

Colmore couldn't hide his astonishment. His eyes popped and his jaw dropped.

Dowding came to the rescue. "You planned to carry *only* enough fuel to reach Egypt and then refuel there, Wing Commander—is that right?"

"Yes. Of course. It's a weight issue."

"Impossible! You will not be permitted to refuel in Egypt. The stench of diesel fuel would be intolerable—we're entertaining the King of Egypt, man!" Thomson snapped.

"I'd need to s-stand down the whole third watch crew to s-save that kind of weight, sir," Colmore stammered.

"Right. Then do it!"

Colmore slumped back in his chair, dazed.

"One more thing. I want you to arrange for my luggage to be picked up Saturday afternoon. I'm bringing a Persian rug to lay down for the banquet. Send a couple of crewman with a van."

"I'll make arrangements, sir," Colmore answered weakly.

"Everything's settled then!" Thomson said, jumping up and rubbing his palms together. He shook hands and dismissed them.

As Colmore trudged out, he looked as though he had the weight of *Cardington R101*, including the fuel—now increased by 100%, the crew—reduced by 33%, *plus* Thomson's valet, on his shoulders.

9

THE ALMIGHTY BLOODY ROW

Thursday October 2, 1930.

At 8:30 p.m., Thomson was still at his desk. The light had faded and the table lamps had been switched on. He was writing comments on the draft minutes of his meeting with Colmore and Dowding, which Knoxwood had left before going home. There was a gentle tap at the door.

Must be Brancker. Damn! I'd forgotten about him.

"Come!"

Thomson continued scribbling. Brancker approached his desk.

"Something on your mind, Sefton?" Thomson said, without raising his head.

"Yes, as a matter of fact, CB, there is."

Thomson continued writing. "And what is that?" His tone disinterested, patronizing.

"It concerns the airship."

"Which one?"

"*Cardington R101,* of course."

Thomson finally raised his head. Brancker appeared fidgety and nervous. Thomson, being calm, had the edge.

"Ah, *Cardington R101*—what about *Cardington R101?*"

"I'm very concerned. I've been trying to speak to you all day," Brancker said.

"I heard you've been chasing around after me. So, here I am. What's the problem?"

"The airworthiness of that airship."

"Whatever do you mean? They've issued an Airworthiness Certificate and a Permit to Fly. What *more* do you want?"

"Bits of paper issued by a department under your control—that's meaningless!"

"I don't make these people do things. I'm guided by *them*."

"Look CB, the R.A.W. and the officers don't have confidence in that ship."

"How do you *know* that?"

"I hear things."

Thomson got to his feet and drew himself up to his full height.

"From *whom?*"

"The ship's overweight."

"I was informed the lift and trim tests were satisfactory."

"She's *still* heavy," Brancker said.

"It's got forty-nine tons of lift now."

"Your own requirements were sixty tons. *Remember?*"

"*Howden R100* had only fifty-four," Thomson said.

"But that ship was still much lighter!"

"Well, their *engines* were lighter."

"It doesn't matter why. It's still a lighter ship. *Cardington R101* is too heavy."

"I'm guided by the R.A.W.," Thomson said, his voice trailing off.

"The gas bags were full of holes."

"They've all been fixed."

"And they'll be full of holes again before we reach the English Channel. They're still rubbing against the ship's frame."

"They're all padded now," Thomson said.

"They're *still* rubbing!"

"The inspector's satisfied."

"I don't think so. He only confirmed the padding installation is complete. He's dissatisfied with the method of addressing the problem. Then there's the cover—"

"They've assured me that's been taken care of."

"Not a hundred percent."

Thomson grunted in annoyance.

But Brancker kept on. "Their biggest concern is that the ship's untested—and is therefore unfit for this journey."

"I've just had a long discussion about the tests with Dowding and Colmore."

"Dowding knows absolutely *nothing* about airships. He'll be the first to tell you that—and as for Colmore, bless his heart, he'll do whatever you ask of him."

"They put the testing business to Scott and he's perfectly satisfied —that's *his* domain."

"*Scott!* You can't rely on Scott! He's not the man he was."

"What do you mean?"

"Did you read the report on the flight to Canada?"

Thomson looked vague.

"No, I *thought* not. Read it and you'll see why you can't rely on his judgment. The man's *totally* reckless!"

"They tested the ship yesterday," Thomson said.

"For sixteen hours? Sixteen hours!—before going off on a ten thousand mile voyage. That's insane!"

They stopped speaking and stared at each other. Thomson's jaw was set, his face grim, his eyes like lead bullets.

Brancker spoke softly now, coaxing. "CB, people confide in me— tell me things they're afraid to tell you."

"This is Irwin!"

"As a matter of fact, I did speak to Irwin, amongst others. Irwin is an excellent skipper and a very fine man with an *impeccable* record."

"He's a *whiner* and a *complainer*. He's spread dissatisfaction and discord throughout the ranks. *He's* the one responsible for the breakdown in morale."

"I know you're angry. All this doesn't change the fact that the ship is untested. You must think about postponing this voyage."

"I will not even *consider* it. We'd become the laughing stock. I've announced this ship will leave on her maiden voyage to India on October 4th—and leave we shall!"

"That doesn't make it a reason to leave. Just because you've announced it—you can *un-announce* it! You also announced to the world the ship would be adequately tested. Face the fact—the ship is unfit until it is given a clean bill of health by its captain."

Thomson leaned over his desk on the palms of his hands.

"Listen to me, Brancker. I know what's been going on. If you don't want to go, or you lack the courage, then don't. Show the white feather! There're many others who will jump at the chance to go in your place."

"I will go, CB—and I'll tell you why," Brancker said evenly. "I encouraged people to fly on this airship—people like O'Neill and Palstra—believing it'd be built and tested properly. I believed all your rhetoric about 'safety first.' I didn't think you'd use this airship for your own personal aggrandizement, for your own personal agenda, set to meet your own personal schedule. People like O'Neill put their faith in me and my word. I will *not* abandon them now."

Thomson sat down and resumed his scribbling. Brancker turned and left, silently closing the door behind him. But Brancker had shaken him.

10

A DAMNED GOOD BOLLOCKING

Friday October 3, 1930.

T he next day, at 7:50 a.m., Irwin found himself waiting in the
reception area of Thomson's outer office. He sat with a fixed
stare, his dark uniform accentuating his pale, drawn face.
Thomson marched in at 7:59 a.m. and swept past Irwin, into his office.

"You and I need to have words," he growled as he went by.

Irwin got up and followed. He stood before Thomson.

"You've become something of a liability, Irwin."

"I don't know what you mean, sir."

"You're insubordinate—getting way above your station."

Thomson sank into his chair, glowering.

"I'm not sure—"

"You've been speaking to Sir Sefton Brancker—the *Director* of
Civil Aviation!"

"Sir, I only—"

"You're a man with no confidence in what he's doing," Thomson
sneered.

"Sir, I'm responsible for my crew and my—"

"I don't need a lecture from you about your responsibilities, Irwin.
Keep your mouth shut and listen. Everyone who comes in contact with
you leaves with a bad case of melancholia!"

"Sir, that's not—"

"You've spread malicious rumors about *Cardington R101*. You've attempted to sabotage the inspection procedure, delay the Howden ship's voyage to Montreal, and thus put off your own flight to India. Well, you haven't succeeded. All you've done is cause a breakdown in discipline and morale. You think I don't understand what's been going on? If you lack the courage to fly this airship—*resign!* I don't believe you've got the guts—that's the crux of the problem."

"Sir—"

"An inquiry is underway regarding the brawling and drunkenness caused by the general breakdown in discipline—which may result in a court-martial. And *you* might be next for insubordination, insurrection, mutiny and cowardice!"

Irwin's eyes opened wide in horror and his jaw dropped.

"What—"

"If this flight to India isn't a success, there'll be no more funding for airship development—none will be asked for! That'll be the end of it. Do you get that?"

"Yes, sir."

"You've never understood, Irwin. There are careers to be made. Honors to be won."

"I do understand, sir. But for me, my crew and my ship always come first."

"*Wrong*! Your country comes first. This whole country's honor is at stake. ...If that means anything to *you!* ..."

Thomson let that barb sink in.

"Yes, it does sir."

"Get a grip on yourself. Do your duty. You're dismissed."

Irwin marched stiffly from Thomson's office to drive back to Cardington. He appeared to be in a state of shock.

11

FIXING SCOTT

Friday October 3, 1930.

That morning, Lou got word that Colmore would like to meet with him. Lou was at the tower checking on the ship's preparations with Atherstone and Steff. He went straight to Cardington House on his motorbike. He was a little surprised to see an RAF man on guard at the door. The pretty, blonde receptionist smiled at him and told him Wing Cmdr. Colmore was expecting him. Lou proceeded to his office, where Colmore was in conference with Scott. The partition between Colmore's room and the secretary's didn't reach the ceiling. He could hear voices. Doris, put her finger to her lips and gestured for Lou to sit. They listened.

"I want to make this perfectly clear. Your role will be limited," Colmore said.

"To nothing in particular, I suppose," Scott answered.

"*Irwin* will be in control as the commander. You'll be a passenger."

"I seem to be the one who always gets blamed."

"You'll have no significant role—symbolic only—that of Executive Admiral, pertaining to route and the time of departure. I hope you understand that, Scottie?"

"Executive Admiral! Is that supposed to make me feel good? A meaningless title!"

Lou and Doris exchanged glances.

"I was the first man in the world to fly the Atlantic and land on American soil—and return—as pilot in command! I was awarded the Air Force Cross."

"Yes, yes, Scottie—and it was well-deserved."

"Alcock and Brown did it the easy way, a month earlier, *from* Canada and landed nose first in an Irish bog. One way! And *they* got knighted for that!"

"Yes, there was no justice."

"No justice! You got *that* right."

"Scottie, my dear fellow, we'll give Thomson what he wants. He can impress his girlfriend. He'll be set for life. And so will *we!*"

"Yes, yes—"

"He's promising the world, so you never know …keep the faith. Oh, and yes, one other thing—no uniform."

"What do you mean, *no uniform?*"

"You're *not* to wear your uniform under *any* circumstances. You'll be a civilian on this flight, just like me."

"Look, the mishap on the Canada flight was just bad luck—"

"Yes, yes, Scottie, leave everything to Irwin. *He's* the commander, not you."

They heard Scott's chair scrape the floor as he got up.

"I want to tell you—I don't like what you're doing. You told the Secretary of State the fitness of the ship was up to *me*—whether the flight testing could be shortened, or waived. You put those decisions on *me*. Now you're telling me I don't have a role. So, I'll be the scapegoat when things go wrong. No, sir. If Irwin's in command, you should have made those decisions *his*. But you didn't. You made them *mine!*"

There was a long silence until Scott came rushing through the outer office and went storming off down the corridor. Doris glanced at Lou and raised her eyebrows.

"Not a happy camper," she said.

"Commander Remington's here," Doris called.

Colmore came and stood in the doorway. He appeared bashful, realizing Lou had heard everything. Colmore glanced at Doris. "Do you mind organizing some tea for us, Doris?" he said. She got up and went out, closing the outer door, realizing he wanted privacy.

"Lou, thanks for popping over. I have a favor to ask you in a minute, but first, I wanted to say, you don't have to make this voyage, you know."

"Yes, I know—but I'm committed."

"Are you *sure?*"

"Yes, of course, sir."

"How do you feel about the ship now?"

"From what I can tell, they've done a good job, but I would've preferred it if they'd completed the tests as laid down by Captain Irwin," Lou answered. "It would make more sense."

Colmore ignored this. He leaned forward earnestly and lowered his voice.

"How are things with you, Lou? At home, I mean?"

"Not particularly good, sir."

"Not giving up?" Colmore asked.

"No, of course not."

"You don't have a death wish or anything like that?"

Lou laughed. "No, no."

Who knows, perhaps I do.

Lou realized the implication of Colmore's question.

"Sir, will you please think about what I just said about testing?"

It was as if Colmore hadn't heard. "Was the guard at the door when you came in?"

"Yes. Never seen that before, sir."

"We've had the pilot's wife here again. Wants to meet with me."

"Mrs. Hinchliffe?"

"She's trying to get the flight stopped."

"So, you're not going to meet her?"

"Lord no, I've got enough problems."

Lou nodded, understanding; she'd probably push him over the edge again.

"Lou, you'll probably be in command of your own ship soon. I think you should stick around here with me tomorrow—it'll be good experience. Come in early and we'll check the weather and make the final decisions." Colmore paused and looked at Lou, his eyes skittish. "I was told by Thomson to stand down the third watch so we can carry a full load of fuel."

"Why?"

"He doesn't want us refueling in Egypt. I've asked the new AMSR to appeal the decision. If Thomson won't budge, we'll stand them down tomorrow."

Lou didn't comment, but thought the situation totally ridiculous.

"You mentioned a favor?"

"Oh, yes. Would you mind taking a van over to Lord Thomson's flat in Westminster tomorrow afternoon with a couple of your best men?"

"Sure. What does he need?"

"He's got a carpet he wants picking up, and his luggage."

"Sounds heavy."

Colmore winced, putting his hand to his temple, as though this hadn't occurred to him. "Dear God," he said.

"I guess we'll find out, won't we," Lou answered. Things were becoming more absurd by the hour.

"Sorry, but I don't want to send them unsupervised in case they muck it up—you know how he is," Colmore said.

"Fine. I'll take Binks and Church."

"Thanks, Lou. That's another load off my mind."

The phone on Colmore's desk rang and he picked it up. Lou heard Knoxwood at the other end. "Weggie, it's Wupert ..."

Colmore listened and turned deadly serious.

"Yes, I'll let them know ...forty minutes ...Right. I'll make sure they're standing by and ready to go ...Goodbye." Colmore put the phone down.

"That was Rupert Knoxwood. Thomson is sending his chauffeur. He wants to see you, Richmond and Scott. He'll pick you up then bring you back. He said it's going to be a very short meeting."

"What the heck about, sir?" Lou asked.

"Blowed if I know. It's weird. Sounds to me like he's got the wind up—but that wouldn't make sense—all I know is, Irwin looked dreadful when he came back from seeing him earlier."

Lou already knew that to be true. Perhaps they were going to get an ass-kicking, too.

The driver appeared on time and the three men were whisked off to Gwydyr House where Thomson was waiting for them. Knoxwood hustled them straight into Thomson's office without delay. Each of them glanced at the painting of the Taj Mahal as they filed in. They understood its significance, and that of its airship, at this moment.

"Ah, gentlemen, I apologize, but I felt it important to lay a few things to rest."

"Will you need me to take minutes, sir?"

"No, no, Rupert, no need. This is just an informal chat, thanks anyway."

Knoxwood went out and closed the door. Lou, Scott and Richmond made furtive glances at Thomson wondering what was coming. Thomson graciously ushered them to the easy chairs arranged around the fireplace where an electric fire glowed in the grate. He went to the sideboard. He was at his most benign.

"Scottie, my dear chap, what'll it be? Gin, whisky ...? I thought we ought to have a little drink and a talk."

"Er, make it a whisky, straight, sir, thank you," Scott said, unable to hide his relief.

Lou watched Thomson reach for a bottle of Macallan.

Nothing but the best. Must be a special occasion.

Thomson began pouring. "And you, Richmond and Remington, what'll it be?"

They asked for the same to keep it simple. Thomson poured three more out and handed them out. He took his own and held it up.

"Your very good health, gentlemen."

"Yes, sir, good health," they all said.

Lou took a sip.

Very nice—as good as Granddad's—the man from Moray!

Thomson sat down. "I didn't get you down here to discuss the pros and cons of *Cardington R101*. All I want to know is this: Are you fellows comfortable and confident we can make this voyage without undue risk? I want the unvarnished truth. I thought it only right and proper you should be given the opportunity to let your feelings be known. I've been hearing all sorts of scuttlebutt and I want to get it all cleared up and out in the open." Thomson looked from Richmond to Scott. "After all, you, Richmond, have been responsible for its design and you, Scott, are in charge of flying operations ..."

Scott and Richmond sat looking at Thomson with stony faces. Not sure what to make of it all. They'd had the jitters on the way down. Lou sat there astonished. Surely Thomson wasn't going to let them call it off? He'd soon get his answer.

Thomson went on. "I want you to both reassure me that this airship is capable of flying to India and back. I want to know you both have full confidence. And you, Remington, I brought you here as a highly experienced airshipman—I thought it worth hearing what you had to say about it all as you are, in way, an unbiased outsider—a *trusted* one, I might add."

Richmond put his drink down and was about to speak, but Thomson continued.

"We must all understand what's at stake: the country's honor. *Cardington R01* has become something of a symbol of the British Empire itself. Naturally, I want this voyage to be a rip-roaring success. It's absolutely imperative. The world is watching. Also, I should mention that the rewards will be huge for everybody. …What were you going to say Richmond?

Richmond sat up primly. "I was going to say that I believe the airship is now in tip-top condition … or, well almost. We've had our problems, now with the extra bay and all the padding …" Thomson waved his hand. He didn't want to hear about all that. "I think this journey can be accomplished quite safely, sir," he said.

"So you have *absolute* confidence?"

"Yes, sir, I do."

Thomson turned his gaze to Scott. "What about *you*, Scott? Do you feel the same way? Please understand, I'm not trying to put you chaps on the spot."

Scott boosted himself with another slug, draining his glass. "I do sir, yes. I see no reason to feel anything but confident now. We just ran her around the countryside for sixteen hours and she performed magnificently."

"What about the rest of Irwin's tests? Do you feel we're running any risks here? You know we're talking about people's lives and I feel very much responsible?"

"Oh, I think she got through a lot of tests last year and we took care of all the issues. I don't think we've got anything to worry about, not really, sir," Scott said. "And look at it this way: the Howden ship made it to Montreal and back without too much fuss in their bare-bones machine. I'm sure we can do the India run without a problem in *R101*."

That made Lou smile. He was unimpressed with this whole performance. Did Thomson think he was going to reinforce all their statements? Thomson got up and refilled Scott's glass and handed it to him.

"Now, what about you, Commander? I value your opinion."

"My feeling is this ..." Lou paused for some moments, moistening and licking his lips. "You're right, I *am* an outsider. And I see things from a much different perspective."

Their eyes were riveted on him.

"I don't share your urgency to get this voyage accomplished. I see the risks as being too great—for your long-term goal. I'd urge you to slow down and carry out the full schedule of tests Captain Irwin has proposed. With so much riding on this voyage, I think you have far more to lose than to gain. You're maximizing the risk of failure by *not* doing them. You're putting all your chips on black, Lord Thomson."

Richmond and Scott were stunned and extremely irritated. Thomson showed no emotion, keeping his eyes in a fixed stare at Lou.

"I see... That's one way of looking at it, I suppose," he said. "Now, here I have you disagreeing with my two most senior men."

"I'm sorry, sir, you asked me and I gave you the *unvarnished* truth, the way I see it." Thomson turned away to Richmond. "Can I get you another, Richmond?"

"Oh, no, sir, I don't usually imbibe during the day, thank you."

Thomson stood up; their cue to leave. "Well gentlemen, this has been useful. I'll think on what you've said." He turned to Lou. "Commander, you are under no obligation to make this journey, you know. If you're uncomfortable ..."

"Sir, I'm committed to the ship, to the crew and to our captain."

Thomson put his hand on Lou's shoulder. "Admirable, sir! Admirable! First class attitude, if I may say so."

They left Thomson's office and made the silent journey back to Cardington in just over an hour. Thomson sat back down in his easy chair and contemplated the situation. The young commander might be right. His two yes-men had said what he wanted to hear. He derived no comfort from their words. Lou's only worried him further.

... But he's young.

12

CELEBRATION & FAREWELL AT THE KINGS ARMS

Friday October 3, 1930.

A smoky haze hung over the excited crowd of well-wishers in The Kings Arms opposite the green, on Church Lane. The place was full of airship construction workers and crewmen with their families and girlfriends. Their frenzied chatter over the honky-tonk was deafening to any sober person, of which there were few. Lou entered around 9 o'clock and fought his way to the bar where Potter, Billy, Cameron, Binks, Disley, Church and Irene were tightly gathered. Among the crowd, Lou noticed a lot of faces he'd never seen before.

Probably press and spectators.

He was surprised to see the piano player was George Hunter from the *Daily Express*. Hunter gave him a wink. He was one hell of a pianist, presently knocking out "Putting on the Ritz." Church and Irene looked especially happy, with goofy grins on their faces.

"What are you two looking so pleased about?" Lou shouted.

Irene shyly buried her head in Church's shoulder and then held her left hand up in the air displaying a tiny diamond ring.

"Irene and me are getting married as soon as I get back!" Church proclaimed.

The room erupted into cheers and applause. "This calls for a drink," Lou said. He ordered another round and a bottle of champagne. The barman poured the champagne and they raised their glasses.

"You're a lucky man!" Cameron shouted. He looked down in the dumps. The incident with Rosie and Jessup on the ship had been the last straw. His marriage was over.

"Here's to you both," Lou said.

Three girls in the bar had their eyes on Lou, including the busty blonde from the Cardington House reception desk. They knew he was a free agent and on the market, or hoped he was. He smiled pleasantly at them, but kept his distance. Then he noticed Mrs. Hinchliffe loitering next to Hunter at the piano. She glanced over at him and he suspected she wanted to talk. He wasn't in the mood. Life was much too complicated as it was.

Hunter broke into "I'm Sittin' On Top of the World" and everybody sang at the top of their lungs—everybody except Lou and Cameron. Lou glanced at the door and imagined Charlotte walking in —just like that—kissing him on the lips and telling him how much she loved him, and asking him not to go, and he would say, 'Okay honey, I'll quit right now.' Even Colmore would understand …But Charlotte *didn't* walk in.

After half an hour of trying his best to look happy, Lou decided he needed some air. He walked out the door as Hunter was transitioning seamlessly into "Blue Skies." On his way through the smoky haze, he nodded politely to the three girls who gave him yearning glances. He left the pub and walked across the cobblestone road onto the damp, grassy field toward the fairground.

The sound of the out-of-tune honky-tonk drifted through the mist behind him with sounds of laughter, singing and chinking glasses. Soon, the carousel drowned out the pub sounds, reminding him of Freddie and the clown's head. He stood for a few minutes staring at the ominous shape riding at the tower bathed in searchlights. He heard rustling footsteps behind him in the grass and then a woman's voice.

"Do you think she's beautiful?"

Lou turned around. *Mrs. Hinchliffe* was beautiful. She had long, blond hair and deep blue eyes. She reminded him of Julia. There was something about her face he could only describe as spiritual. She was around his own age and as tall as Charlotte.

"No, I wouldn't call *that* beautiful," he said.

"*My* husband flew away, too."

She paused and stared sadly into the night sky, as if remembering the last time she'd seen him. "Every day since then I've wished I'd stopped him." She closed her eyes, reliving the awful pain. "Oh, how I've wished it!" she said.

Lou felt her regret. "Do you really think you could have?"

"That's a good question." She stopped to consider. "I think so." She paused again. "But I didn't even try." Lou sensed her self-blame. "He was so confident and to me, he was invincible."

"Now you warn others?"

She glanced down at his hand.

"Yes. I see you're not wearing a wedding ring. Aren't you married?" she asked.

He automatically raised his hand and looked at his ring finger. It came as a shock to see his ring missing. "Technically, I suppose I am."

"Then give this up for her sake."

"I would, but it's too late."

"I'm sorry."

"I met you and your husband just before he left," Lou said.

"Yes, I remember you. We were all right here in this pub."

"It must be tough for you to set foot in the place," Lou said.

"He wants the Airship Program stopped," she said.

"Your husband, you mean?"

"You must think I'm crazy?"

"I'm not sure what to think."

"Take it from me. I'm not crazy," she said.

God, what grief does to people!

"Mrs. Hinchliffe, I must go. I have a busy day ahead."

"I suppose I'm wasting my time?"

"I don't think you've a snowball's chance in hell of stopping that thing taking off tomorrow."

She took his hand to shake it and then clasped it with the other.

"I'll be here to see you all leave," she said, looking into his eyes.

"Goodbye, Mrs. Hinchliffe."

Lou sensed, like him, she was a lost and lonely soul. He put his arms around her and they hugged. She put her lips to his.

"Are you going back to the pub?" she asked.

"No, I think I'll call it a day."

She kissed him again, her lips soft and wet.

"Come with me," she said, her voice an urgent whisper.

"You want to save me from all this, huh?"

"Yes, I do."

"Perhaps we'll meet again, Mrs. Hinchliffe," he said.

"Yes, I hope so. Good luck, and may God be with you … And next time we meet, please call me Millie."

"So, you're confident I'll make it back?" Lou asked, with an amused grin.

"I don't know, but I pray you do, Commander," she said.

Lou nodded. "Okay, Millie."

He left her and walked across the field toward the fairground. The music and laughter grew louder, the lights more dazzling. Hundreds were milling around, enjoying the fun of the fair.

Minutes later, Lou reached the gypsy's tent. The old woman was standing outside. "I've bin waitin' for you, my lucky lad."

"To tell me my fortune, right?"

"Cross me palm with silver and I might give yer something."

He followed her into the tent, breathing in the familiar, musty smell of damp hay. Being dark this time, the place seemed more ominous. Flickering candles lent a sinister atmosphere. He laid a silver half-a-crown on the table. She stuffed it in her apron and gazed at him intently.

"I see you've used up more lives." She chuckled wickedly. "You might have one left. I ain't sure."

Lou's mind flashed to *Howden R100's* two mishaps over the St. Lawrence. His brush with the Klan. Did that count? And then Cameron nearly put them all in the drink on the way home. That was close. The old crone's crackly voice brought him back.

"She left yer, didn't she? The woman you brought to me last year. Your wife, wasn't it? Longing for a baby she was. I don't see 'er around you anymore. She had things she couldn't share. There was much troubling her—another victim of war—she was a very brave girl, that one. It all just got too much for 'er."

Lou had no idea what the woman was babbling about and though it sounded curious, he didn't answer. He really didn't want to know.

Yes, and probably you had a lot to do with it, dammit!

"But I do see another woman who patiently waits. I see her in your family." Her eyes opened wide as if looking at a portrait held up to her. "Another beautiful woman! My, oh my, you do attract the lovelies, doncha!"

Lou knew exactly who she was talking about. Still, he kept his mouth shut.

"You're wonderin' about this journey. Well, you will go, sunshine. And you deserve what you get! But just know this: The impatient one you all follow blindly is ruled by fire. He's surrounded by it. Always has been. So beware! Those who don't heed my advice, do so at their peril. Curses shall be 'eaped upon 'em!"

Lou stared into the gypsy's penetrating, watery eyes. In the flickering supernatural light, they appeared luminous green, flecked with red. He felt energy radiating from that old body into his like an electrical current. He became paralyzed, sensing her strange and powerful force, not sure if she was good or evil, or neither.

"Now, there's one who seeks to do you harm," she went on.

Lou realized she must be talking about Jessup, but then she looked away into a dark corner and dismissed that image with a flick of her bony fingers and a sneer.

"A message of ill and one of truth—these two shall be conveyed. At the end of the day, that's what this saga's about." Suddenly, her head slumped with her eyes closed. She was spent. She sat motionless for a few moments and then opened her eyes as though from a deep sleep. She seemed surprised. "Oh, you're still 'ere. Did you get what you wanted?"

Lou smiled. "Yes and no. You talk in riddles, lady."

"Have an interesting trip—might be good for yer soul," she said, getting to her feet with a sly grin.

At 10 o'clock, Thomson and MacDonald emerged from MacDonald's study on the second floor at No.10, having gone over the agenda for the Imperial Conference of Dominion Prime Ministers, scheduled to begin later that month. They stood on the wide landing overlooking the grand staircase. MacDonald put his hand on Thomson's arm, his eyes intense.

"Forgo this trip. I need your wise council for this conference. Do this for me, CB."

"Are you *ordering* me not to go, sir?"

"No, I'm asking you as my dearest friend."

They held each other's forearms and Thomson looked into the Prime Minister's face. "How can I not go? I'm committed. And besides, the troops are expecting me. I need to rally them." Thomson moved to the top of the stairs. "Don't worry. I'll be back for the conference—have I ever let you down, Ramsay?"

MacDonald's eyes, moist earlier, now glistened. Thomson saw this before he started down the stairs. When he got to the bottom, he stared up at MacDonald and waved. Thomson crossed the black and white checkered floor, stopping at the door.

"Farewell, my good friend," MacDonald called down.

Thomson's voice echoed up the stairway. "Don't look so glum, my dear chap. Don't you remember? Our fate is already written."

MacDonald stood hunched like a man watching his brother going off to war. He wiped his eyes with a handkerchief. "Yes, I do," he whispered. "Yes, I do."

"Ramsay, if the worst should happen, it would soon be over."

As Thomson left, the door slammed behind him, the sound echoing around the great hall like thunder.

Thomson left Downing Street and crossed Whitehall to Gwydyr House. He passed the nightwatchman, giving him a curt nod. His office was in darkness. He switched on the picture light over the huge oil painting of the Taj Mahal and sat down, staring at the airship he'd had superimposed upon it by Winston Churchill. He hoped for some sort of divine affirmation. But he got none. He got up and went to the window and peered out over the river, faintly glimmering under the dim street lamps. The bitter taste and the feeling he had was something akin to buyer's remorse. Brancker's words continued their stinging assault:

I will go CB—and I'll tell you why. I encouraged people to fly in this airship—people like O'Neill and Palstra—believing it'd be built and tested properly. I believed all your rhetoric about 'safety first.' I didn't think you'd use this airship for your own personal aggrandizement, for your own personal agenda, with everything set to meet your own personal schedule. People like O'Neill put their faith in me and my word. I will not abandon them now.

Then he heard the young American's voice like an echo, depressing him further.

You're putting all your chips on black, Lord Thomson... You're putting all your chips on black...

Then to cap it all, Wallis's words from six years ago gave him a jolt. *You're planning to build airships by committee?*

What if all these people were right? Did they have justification for being nervous? Were there indeed things he didn't know? Was he pushing them too hard?

He tightened the knot in his tie.

Come, come man—it's your destiny! No, I mustn't fall victim to negativity. Stay positive ... But ... no reason not to be cautious.

He went back to his desk and sat down again, opened the drawer and took out his address book. He picked up the phone and dialed the number. Knoxwood answered.

"Ah, Rupert, I'm so glad you're home. I want you to do something for me. Call Colmore immediately and tell him I've reconsidered. He *may* refuel in Egypt, but only after the banquet. If it delays taking off the next day, so be it. Tell him to stand the third watch down anyway—that'll be a double saving in weight."

Thomson replaced the phone and sat back for a moment. He pulled the drawer open, revealing Marthe's photograph. He stared at it wistfully. What was she doing? Was she with anyone? Were any of those damned American professors still hanging around? Had she got shot of them? He hoped so. He pulled out a sheet of paper and placed it on his blotter. He stared at it for a few moments then wrote forcefully in the shadows from the picture light behind him.

Air Ministry
Gwydyr House, White Hall, London.
Last Will and Testament
On this Friday, Third Day of October, Nineteen Hundred and Thirty, I declare that in the event of my death during my return voyage to India aboard HMA Cardington R101, I leave all my worldly goods and possessions to my brother Colonel R. Thomson, currently residing in Widdington, Essex.

Christopher Birdwood Thomson,
Brigadier General Lord Thomson of Cardington,
Secretary of State for Air.

After signing his will, Thomson thrust it into an envelope and put it in the top drawer. Knoxwood would find it and know exactly what to do, if required.

13

GO BREAK A LEG

Saturday October 4, 1930.

L ou woke with Fluffy beside him. He missed Charlotte most just before he closed his eyes and again when he first opened them at dawn. The bed was empty and, at times like this, he wondered what the hell he was doing in this place. The thought of flying to India no longer excited him and feelings of futility haunted him. He grieved for her. Soon, he'd be grieving for his father. He'd get this voyage over with and return to the States, immediately.

He'd enjoyed having Norway around, but he'd gone back up north. He rolled over and switched on the bedside lamp. His kitbag, already packed, lay on the floor. Mrs. Jones had helped him and Billy get their clothes ready.

While he boiled the kettle, he heard the letter box snap and the newspaper hit the mat upstairs. After pouring himself a cup of tea, he sat down and opened the *Daily Mirror*. Under a photograph of *Cardington R101* at the mast, the headline read:

GIANT AIRSHIP'S MAIDEN VOYAGE

The newspaper was full of praise for *Cardington R101*—previous negative stories forgotten. This was a great moment in British aviation history and the press was not about to spoil things. A knock came at the front door. Mrs. Jones appeared with her shopping bag.

"I've come to cook breakfast for you lads," she said, pushing her way down to the kitchen. "Can't have you boys going off to India on an empty stomach."

Lou poured a mug of tea and took it up to Billy, who had a thick head. The smell of eggs and bacon permeated the house. When they'd finished, Mr. Jones arrived to wish them well. Time was getting short. They hurriedly put on their uniforms and said their goodbyes, leaving Mrs. Jones to clean up. Before leaving, Lou picked Fluffy up and kissed her nose. Mrs. Jones would take good care of her.

They grabbed their kitbags and, after wiping off the wet saddle, set off on the motorbike in the rain at speed. As they approached the junction at the parade of shops, a painter's van, laden with ladders, turned out in front of them. There was nothing Lou could do. The bike skidded and they rammed the side of the van. The riders sailed over the hood and landed in the middle of the road. The van driver, realizing his error, swerved to the right, causing the vehicle to flip over and its doors to burst open. Paint and ladders were scattered everywhere. Lou came down on his left side, not badly hurt, except for a few bruises and a grazed hand. Billy lay groaning, his right leg bent at a sickening angle. Hearing the crash, corner store owner, Alan Rowe, rushed out. He recognized them and knelt down beside Billy.

"Well, *you* won't be going anywhere, sunshine. It's Bedford Hospital for you."

After checking on Billy, Lou went to see the driver of the truck, a middle-aged man in painter's whites. He sat on the curb holding his head, rambling incoherently—perhaps he had a concussion. Lou inspected the motorbike. The front tire was blown out, the headlight broken. He suspected the forks were twisted. He removed the kitbags from the carrier and put Billy's under his head and sat down beside him.

"Rotten luck, Billy," he said, holding the boy's arm.

"Damn, Lou, I was looking forward to going," Billy said. He winced in pain and then threw up.

So much for Mrs. Jones' breakfast.

"I'll have to go, but I'll call your mom and tell her what's happened."

"What about the bike?" Billy asked.

"I'll put it behind the shop," Alan said. "I'll take care of it 'til you get back, don't worry."

He got up and wheeled the motorbike down the alley. Lou stayed with Billy until the ambulance arrived. He watched them load Billy onto a stretcher and put him inside the ambulance with the painter. Before they closed the doors, Billy held up his hand.

"Lou, Jessup's out to get you. Everyone knows it."

"I'll be fine, Billy. I'll send word to Mrs. Jones and Irene. They'll come up and make sure you're okay."

"I wanted to be around to guard your back. He's been bragging all week—he's gonna kill you."

"You don't need to worry, Billy. His crew's gonna be stood down —but keep that to yourself—okay!"

"Good," Billy said.

He laid his head down thankfully as the ambulance doors were closed. Lou stood on the curb until Billy had gone before walking to the bus stop. He felt a twinge in his guts. Was this the 'Wiggy thing' all over again? He went and stood behind four waiting crewmen. Lou nodded and smiled at them. Pretty soon, a green bus arrived with the same cheery bus conductor Lou had come to know.

"Hell, you must live on this bus, Luke!" Lou said.

"I do indeed, sir, and I know where *you're* going."

The bus rattled and groaned its way along the country lane in the drizzle to the next stop, where more men in uniform were standing in line. Sam Church was among those waiting, with Irene, his mother and father, Joe Binks and Fred McWade. The men carried pith helmets and small bags. The bus conductor rang the bell after they boarded.

"Next stop, Cardington Gate, then Cardington Tower, then Ismailia," he said. He went around taking fares, stopping beside Binks. "Hello Joe, where you off to—the Kings Arms is it? Bit early for a pint, isn't it, mate?"

"No, I'm off to India with this lot."

"I know you are, lad—otherwise I'd need another penny," he said, and then with a grin, "Just don't pith in your helmet that's all!"

Lou glanced at McWade, who turned away with a scowl. He had the look of a condemned man. Lou had seen a few of *them* lately. The bus drew up to Cardington Gate and a crowd got off.

"This is it, ladies and gents—'ave a lovely time," the conductor shouted.

As they walked toward the gatehouse, Irene turned to Lou. "We're seein' Sam off in case we don't see him later. We'll be back this evening."

Church grabbed Irene and gave her a passionate kiss and the crewmen walking by clapped and cheered. Lou laughed. Even McWade cracked a smile. Lou glanced over at Binks and Church.

"We're going on a mission this afternoon. I'll tell you about it later," he said. He looked at Irene, "Irene, Billy and I just had an accident on the bike."

Her face fell. "Are you all right?"

"*I* am, but Billy's broken his leg. Could you tell my neighbor, Mrs. Jones, what's happened and ask her to go and see him in hospital?"

Everyone listened, shocked.

"We'll go straight up there, won't we, Mum?" Irene said. "Poor Billy."

"*Lucky* Billy, if you ask me," McWade mumbled.

When they arrived at the gate, the gatekeeper called to McWade.

"Got a message for you, Fred. Wing Commander Colmore wants a word."

"*Now* what?" McWade groused.

"I'll walk up with you," Lou said.

Two cars entered the gate. The first contained Capt. Irwin in his Austin Seven, his face deathly white, and behind him, Scott in his Morris Oxford, in full dress uniform. Lou wasn't surprised, especially after yesterday's meeting with Thomson. When Lou and McWade got to Cardington House, Scott and Irwin had already gone inside. An RAF man was still posted on the door. Lou and McWade went in and made their way to Colmore's office.

"Ah, Fred, do come in," Colmore said. "Come in, Lou. Bad news I'm afraid, Fred. I'm standing you down. We have to cut down on weight."

McWade appeared insulted at first, then visibly relieved.

"Standing me down? It's no disappointment to me, I can tell you that. Standing me down, indeed! Saving weight! I think you need to stand the whole bloody lot down!"

"Yes, Fred. Thank you," Colmore said, in his gracious manner.

"And I'll tell you something. If left to me, they'd *never* have got that Permit to Fly!" McWade left the room and went down the corridor muttering to himself. "Standing me down! Saving weight! I've never heard such nonsense in all my life. ..."

"I do love old Fred," Colmore said. "Hey, what've you done to your hand?"

"Had an accident on the way here. That's why I was late—sorry."

"Anybody hurt?"

"My passenger broke his leg."

"Who was that?"

"Billy Bunyan."

"He was in the crew?"

"Yes," Lou answered.

"Better inform Sky Hunt."

14

THE THIRD WATCH

Saturday October 4, 1930.

Lou and Colmore headed down the corridor in the north wing to the office of Giblett, the meteorologist on this flight also. Irwin, Johnston and Scott were already there, talking with him. Lou watched Colmore for his reaction to Scott showing up in uniform. Colmore did a second take, but said nothing.

Maybe he'll talk to him later.

Lou peered out of the window into the gardens. The wind was picking up. Giblett had chalked up weather graphics on a blackboard on the wall. Next to that, he'd pinned up a map of Europe and Asia. This showed the route Johnston had marked in black, dotted lines, from Cardington to London, over Kent to the town of Hastings, across the Channel, north of Paris, west of the Rhone Valley, Toulouse, then over the sea at Narbonne, along the Mediterranean to Ismailia, Egypt.

"How are things looking, Mr. Giblett?" Colmore asked.

They gathered around the map. "Right here, in the Newcastle area, there's a shallow depression moving into the North Sea and over here an associated cold front moving east, across France. I'd say, at present, things are looking pretty good," Giblett said.

"Okay, I'll report this to Lord Thomson's personal secretary. What time are we casting off, gentlemen?" Colmore asked, eyeing Scott and Irwin.

Scott glanced at the time. "No later than nineteen hundred hours. You can tell him his Lordship should be here an hour prior to that."

Back in Colmore's office, Lou and Colmore sat behind closed doors. Colmore dialed Knoxwood's telephone number in Gwydyr House and put on the speakerphone.

"Rupert, Good morning to you—it's Reginald."

"Morning, Weggie—big day!"

"Yes. I have Commander Remington with me. We've just been to the met room and checked the forecast."

"How's it looking?"

"Pretty good, they think."

Colmore repeated what Giblett had told them.

"So, it's definitely on?" Knoxwood asked.

A sudden wind gust shook the windows and Colmore turned in surprise. "Yes. Unless anything unexpected occurs with the weather."

"What time shall I tell Lord Thomson to be at the tower?"

"We're scheduled to depart at 7 o'clock," Colmore said. "Tell him to be here an hour earlier."

"His lordship won't like to be kept waiting. I'll tell him 6:15."

"Just as you wish, Rupert."

"Have you arranged for a van to deal with the luggage?"

"Yes. Thank you for dealing with the fuel issue, Rupert. I feel much better about that situation."

"Think nothing of it, Weggie," Knoxwood said and hung up.

"I need to call Billy Bunyan's mother in Goole and tell her what's happened," Lou said.

"Perhaps she'll be relieved," Colmore said.

"Then, I'll get over to the ship, if you don't mind. I want to set myself up in a cabin and talk to the crewmen I'm taking to London with me," Lou said.

"Let's meet again in the met office at noon. We can have lunch in the officer's mess after that," Colmore said. Before Lou left, Colmore had Doris type a bulletin for him to post in the crew's locker room.

Lou went to his office and called the hospital in Goole.

"Fanny, it's Lou Remington."

Lou heard Fanny gasp. "Is Billy all right?"

"Billy's fine. We had a spill this morning on the bike and he broke his leg. He's in hospital."

"So, he's not going to India today, obviously?"

"No."

"Thank God for that! If you want to know the truth—I'm glad. I've been worried sick. What did Charlotte say about it?"

"She doesn't know yet," Lou answered. Technically, it wasn't a lie, but Fanny had told him what he had wanted to know—Charlotte hadn't contacted her, either. He needed to get off the phone before Fanny asked any more questions.

"Look, Fanny, I'm sorry. I have to go. Just wanted to let you know about Billy. Please don't worry. He's gonna be fine."

"Oh, er, how is Char—"

"Bye for now, Fanny. I'll call you when I get back from India."

"Yes, er, all right. Good luck, Lou—"

Lou hung up and sat thinking. He rested his chin in one hand and drummed his fingers on the desk. Charlotte hadn't contacted John and Mary, or Fanny, her closest friend. And Charlotte's parents wouldn't open the door. *She must have gone off with some other guy.*

Ten minutes later, Lou picked up his kitbag and hopped on a bus from the main gate down to the tower gate and went into the customs shed for kitbag inspection. He put it on the table.

"Hello, sir. Let's see what you've got here, shall we?" the customs officer said, pulling everything out: a pair of work trousers, a pair of soft-soled shoes, four sets of clean underwear, four pairs of socks, three clean shirts, a bag of toiletries and a small, gold picture frame.

"It took me all morning to pack that bag!" Lou said.

"No lighters or matches, sir?"

"No, and no *parachutes*, either," Lou said with more sarcasm.

"Let's hope you won't be needing 'em, eh, sir."

Lou noticed Potter's accordion on the table behind the customs officer. "What's *that* doing there?" he asked.

The customs man shook his head. "Too heavy. They won't let him take it on board. All right, sir, this bag's cleared," he said, marking the bag with a chalk cross.

Lou went to the elevator at the foot of the tower, where Bert Mann, the operator, was supervising food and drink being loaded by a steward and galley boy. First, it had to be weighed, and then logged in by the R.A.W. chief storekeeper. The provisions included barrels of beer, cases of champagne and wine, an assortment of huge cheeses wrapped in cheesecloth and different types of biscuits in big tins.

"Won't keep you, sir," Mann said. "We're just getting the booze and grub aboard for the banquet. Hurry up, lads, make room for the commander."

"No, it's okay. I'll use the stairs," Lou said.

Lou eyed all this stuff. It looked heavy. Mann shut the concertina gates with a crash and Lou watched it travel up the tower before he started up the stairs. At the top, he found Scott standing with his hands on his hips, glaring with red eyes into the elevator.

"Just been doing the lift calculations with Captain Irwin. I need to lose four tons." He waved to the stewards. "Put this, this, and this on," he said, pointing at the beer, wine and champagne, "but take the tins and throw them out. It's all unnecessary weight. Put all these biscuits in paper bags."

Lou grinned.

This man's got his priorities right.

Leaving the biscuit tin dilemma in safe hands, he went on board and found Sky Hunt in the crew's mess giving instructions to the riggers about stowing materials and luggage. Lou took him aside and told him about Billy. He also mentioned Thomson had ordered the third watch stood down and that he'd be posting the bulletin in the crew's locker room. Hunt told him he'd meet him there, as some might make trouble.

Lou went to his assigned cabin. *Cardington R101* felt much different from the Howden ship. Odors of recently applied dope to the cover and overpowering diesel fumes combined with a strong smell of Axminster carpet to assault his nose. He'd miss Norway—but not pumping fuel by hand every few hours! This time, he'd brought a photo of his family taken at Remington's Farm. He stood it on the small table and smiled cynically to himself. It was the frame that used to hold the photo of him and Charlotte at the five bar gate.

'I no longer love you'—welcome home, pal!

He held up the frame for a closer look. Tom was smiling, Anna shading her eyes, Dad forcing a smile with his arm around Mom— more like *holding on* to Mom, he realized now. And then there was

Gran, sweet and kind—*but don't mess with me!* Julia was smiling demurely, classy as always. And last, at the edge of the photo, Jeb with Alice and their two kids, a sad weariness in Jeb's eyes. Lou wondered if Jeb would forgive and forget. He replaced the frame on the table and returned to the tower where Scott was in conversation with a reporter.

"Ah, Lou, this is Major Robertson with *Flight Magazine.* He's an old friend of mine. Major, this is Commander Lou Remington. I brought Lou on board in 1924. He survived the *R38* crash," Scott said, slurring.

Robertson stuck out his hand. "Indeed. Yes, of course. Honored to meet you, Commander."

"We lost so many of our finest airship people on that ship. We were lucky to get him. He'll represent the United States on this trip. We also have others representing India and Australia."

"You don't say," Robertson said.

"I'm going to show the major over the ship. He's writing an article about us. Why don't you come, Lou?" Scott said.

"Sure thing, sir."

Scott led them around from bow to stern, through the passengers' quarters, the chartroom and then down into the control car. They stood at the windows studying the overcast sky. The ship rolled and shifted with the wind.

"I must say she's most impressive. Are you satisfied with her since the modifications?" Robertson asked.

"She's a very fine ship now and I'm sure it's going to be a marvelous flight," Scott answered.

"And what will your role be on this flight, exactly, Scottie?" Robertson asked.

"I'm *officer-in-charge* of the flight. That's why I'm in uniform, of course."

Lou glanced at Scott's hat, which sported 'R101' stitched in gold, set crookedly on his head. Lou couldn't believe what he was hearing.

"I decide such matters as time of departure, course, as well as speed and altitude. The captain will command the crew and maintain discipline—carrying out my orders, you understand."

Robertson shook hands with them. "Well, gentlemen, I wish you a safe flight and look forward to a full report. Thanks for showing me around."

"We'll meet again when we get back. We'll celebrate," Scott said, beaming confidently. Robertson glanced dubiously at Scott as he left.

Lou left the ship and went over to the locker rooms, where crewmen were awaiting orders. When they saw Lou they stampeded to the bulletin board and gathered around. He posted the notice. Someone at the back shouted. Lou wasn't sure who, but suspected it was Binks.

"Well, somebody read it out then!"

Lou took the bulletin down and faced them. "Okay, guys: 'A demonstration flight will commence today, the 4th of October 1930, at 1900 hours GMT with a return flight to Karachi, India via Ismailia, Egypt. Dress uniforms shall be worn at all times when embarking and disembarking and for all official functions on board. Riggers and engineers of first and second watches shall report for duty at 1300 hours today. Note: The third-watch crew has been stood down. Luggage is restricted to ten pounds per man.'"

Pandemonium broke out among third-watch crewmen, led by Jessup, with much shouting and slamming of locker doors. The disgruntled men were about to leave as Hunt entered. He leapt up onto a bench. Everyone stopped to listen. "Don't you go anywhere, Jessup. I'll be needing you tonight, my lad," he growled.

Jessup, his confidence shattered, sat down sullenly at the back of the locker room. Lou glanced at him. He'd need to watch his back tonight, after all. Hunt pointed at the third watch crewmen. "All right you lot, be on your way. The rest of you, listen up! You heard the commander. Go home and get packed, if you haven't already done so. Ten pounds is all you're allowed to carry. That amounts to a change of underwear and a toothbrush. Catch an hour's shut-eye—you're gonna need all the rest you can get."

Lou went over to Binks. "We're going to London. Where's Church? Ah, there he is. Church!" Church came over. "You're both coming with me. We're taking the Air Ministry van to London to pick up the Air Minister—"

"I'd 'ave thought he would've come in 'is limo—" Binks said.

"Let me finish, Joe, —to pick up the Air Minister's luggage. I'll come and find you on the ship. Gas up the van and bring it to the tower. We'll leave at 2 o'clock."

"Have we got to be in uniform, sir?" Church asked.

"Wear your work clothes."

Lou returned to the administration building, where he met Colmore in his office.

"I see Major Scott's in uniform, then sir," Lou said.

Colmore shook his head wearily. "Yes, I know. Silly damned fool!" But, of course, Lou knew Colmore had seen him earlier.

"He's just been telling Major Robertson he's in overall command of the ship."

Colmore shook his head. "He's just sounding off, I expect. I'll keep an eye on him. If I send him home to change, he won't come back."

"That might be a good thing, under the circumstances, sir, don't you think?" Lou said. Colmore didn't respond.

Lou realized just how reliant Colmore was on Scott, for all his faults; like a broken crutch. They headed to the meteorological office, where they met Atherstone. Giblett reported conditions had deteriorated somewhat. A low pressure trough was moving from western Ireland, bringing winds of ten to fifteen mph, and expected to increase up to thirty mph across northern France, accompanied by heavy rain.

After lunch, Lou and Colmore returned to Colmore's office. Remembering Colmore the night he boarded *Howden R100*, he seemed a different man.

"I must say, you look very well, sir."

"You mean compared to the Canada trip? Yes, Lou, I must tell you, I feel much better this time. I think if we could survive the St. Lawrence, we can survive anything—especially in *this* ship with all her improvements! And thank God Thomson relented on the refueling. I'm *fairly* confident everything's going to be all right."

"You seem to have convinced yourself. But look, there's still time to postpone this voyage, if you're not one hundred percent sure. Finish all the testing—do things right—stand up to him. You'll have Brancker and Irwin standing behind you, and the other officers, and me, of course."

Colmore considered for a moment and then shook his head sadly.

"It's just not possible, dear boy—besides standing up to Thomson and the Air Ministry, we'd be up against Scott and Richmond—both have their eyes set on knighthoods—and then there's the Treasury. I just have to have faith in the ship. We've addressed all the problems, after all—at least, I think we have."

Lou looked at him skeptically, knowing they sure as hell hadn't.

Colmore took out a piece of paper from his drawer and gave it to Lou.

"Here's Lord Thomson's address."

"Thank you. I have a map. It'll be no problem."

15

THE MAGIC CARPET

Saturday October 4, 1930.

Lou headed back to the tower to locate Binks and Church. Binks had gone to his engine car—No. 5. Lou made his way there and descended the ladder as Binks was pouring a drum of oil into the engine. All parts of the engine, its pipes and valves, gleamed.

"You're a thirsty girl, ain't you," Binks was saying.

Lou raised his eyebrows. "Talking to the engine now, are we, Joe?"

Binks turned, embarrassed. "Oh, sorry, sir, I didn't hear you comin.' I already put one drum of oil in and she still needs more." He was about to stop.

"Take it easy, Joe. Finish what you're doing. We've got plenty of time. Meet me by the van when you're done. Seen Church?"

"He's in the crew's quarters, having a fry up."

The crew's quarters was a mess hut at the foot of the tower, where crewmen could cook something to eat. Church was finishing a 'bacon sammy.' Seeing Lou enter, he got up and wiped the grease from his mouth with the back of his hand.

"Can I get you one, sir?" he said.

"I've just eaten, thanks. Ready?"

"Ready when you are, sir."

With Lou giving directions, they motored from Cardington through the country lanes to Shefford and then on through Henlow, Hitchen, Welwyn Garden and onto Potter's Bar.

"Have you decided on a wedding date, Sam?" Lou asked.

"Irene wants to get married at Christmas at St. Mary's," Church answered.

"That'll be a wonderful time."

"And you're invited, of course, sir."

"D'you remember what that old gypsy told yer, Sam?" Binks said.

Church choked. "Yeah, I remember."

"You didn't tell Irene, did you?" Binks asked.

"Nah, 'course not. I told her after this flight, I'm only gonna work in the shed. But this one voyage will 'elp pay for the weddin'—then that's it."

They continued south through Barnet, Whetstone, Swiss Cottage and past Lord's Cricket Ground.

"What about you, sir? Are you staying in England?" Binks asked.

Lou knew they must be wondering. They'd been upset when Charlotte cleared off.

"Not sure. My life's a bit up in the air."

"Nicely put," Church said.

"We all loved Charlotte, sir," Binks said, shaking his head sadly.

Lou didn't respond. He stared out the window wondering what she was doing. Was she thinking about him? Probably not. He reached for his map of London. They passed Regent's Park and drove down Portland Place toward Regent Street. At the end of Regent Street, they moved through Piccadilly down the Haymarket, passing His Majesty's Theater, and around Trafalgar Square.

"Take a good gander, guys. We might pass over this way tonight," Lou told them.

"I love London," Binks said.

They drove slowly down Whitehall, the mounted guardsmen in their red tunics at the Horse Guards Parade on their right. Church studied them in awe. "There's somethin' about this place ..." he said.

They passed Gwydyr House. "That's Lord Thomson's office in the Air Ministry Building," Lou said. They stared at the brick and stone mansion.

"Hey, there's Big Ben and the Houses of Parliament," Binks said, gleefully pointing at Westminster Palace.

"And here, in front, is Westminster Hall with Westminster Abbey across the street," Lou told them. "Okay, we're here. Turn here. This is Ashley Gardens."

At 3 o'clock precisely, they drew up outside Block No. 9 and parked the van just as Knoxwood arrived in Thomson's chauffeur-driven Daimler. The three men got out and went through the lobby, where Knoxwood joined them. Knoxwood motioned them to the birdcage elevator, with its black iron concertina gate and brass pull, just big enough to carry four.

They crammed themselves in. Lou felt uncomfortable and began to sweat. He closed his eyes. They traveled up the open, steel-framed elevator shaft to the third floor and found flat 122. The Great Caruso's voice was belting through the door from Thomson's gramophone. Knoxwood rang the bell. Thomson opened the door himself immediately, dressed ready for off: dark, pinstripe trousers, grey waistcoat, white dress shirt, wing collar, black and white-spotted tie. Gwen the housekeeper, Daisy the parlor maid and Buck the valet, hovered behind him. Lou sensed an atmosphere of excitement as they stepped inside. He felt sorry for the staff—Thomson must have run them ragged all day.

"Ah, here you are, gentlemen. Good day to you all," Thomson said grandly.

"Good afternoon, Lord Thomson. How are you, sir?" Knoxwood asked.

"I'm in superb shape! We'll need all hands. It's in the living room. Follow me."

Lou had never seen Thomson so exuberant. Knoxwood went first, followed by Lou and the two crewmen. The furniture had been pushed back against the walls to make room for Thomson's pile of belongings —cases, trunks, leather bags, bulky canvas bags, packing cases and cardboard boxes. Alongside the luggage, was a roll wrapped in brown paper, tied up with string. The ends were visible, showing part of its vivid red and black pattern and fringe. A dress sword sat atop the mountain.

Lou, Binks and Church stood motionless, unable to believe their eyes.

"My good Gawd!" Binks mumbled in a daze.

"And this must be the magic carpet, sir?" Lou said.

Thomson's magic carpet had become a legend around Cardington. Lou wasn't sure why.

"Yes indeed, *that's* my famous Persian rug—all the way from Sulaymaniyah. We'll lay it down for the banquets in Egypt and India."

Sammie, the big black cat, padded into the room and rubbed itself against Lou's uniform trousers, mewing mournfully. It was the biggest cat he'd ever seen. Like a damned panther.

"Could be good luck, I reckon," Binks said, eyeing the cat.

"Yeah, looks like you've got a new friend there, sir," Church said.

"Sammie can't resist a man in uniform," Thomson joked.

"That cat might be a bit queer. I'd watch out, if I were you, sir," Binks muttered.

"Actually, you're perfectly safe. We used to think it was a 'he', but we recently discovered 'he' was a '*she*'. Hence, we changed her name from Samuel to Samantha," Thomson explained.

"Well, I'm glad we got that one sorted out, sir," Binks whispered.

They spent the next hour taking everything down in the elevator to the van. Knoxwood, Buck, the chauffeur, Gwen, Daisy and even Thomson himself, pitched in. The two trunks took four men to carry. The Persian carpet was manhandled by all six down the stairway, being too long and too heavy to go in the elevator. Finally, it was pushed into the van alongside cases of wine and champagne and Thomson's dress sword. Binks closed the van doors with a big sigh.

Lou stood catching his breath with his crewmen, Knoxwood and Buck, waiting for Thomson to reappear. Finally, he emerged from the building in a black overcoat and matching trilby, carrying a brown leather case, his walking stick hooked over his arm. He was followed by Daisy and Gwen, who held the cat in her arms. Thomson said his farewells and rubbed the cat's nose with a gloved finger.

"Now, I want you to be a good girl, Miss Samantha, do you hear?" Thomson whispered. The cat wriggled from Gwen's grasp and ran under a hawthorn bush. She glared at Thomson and mewed wildly, scolding him. Binks was unnerved and glanced at Lou for reassurance.

Before climbing into the car, Thomson handed the case to Lou.

"Here, Commander. Guard this with your life. This is part of my personal record collection. We shall have music on the ship to brighten our spirits throughout the voyage."

Knoxwood climbed in with Thomson. Buck sat in front with the chauffeur. Thomson gave a royal wave to the two women and the

Daimler set off with the van behind. Thomson told them he had two stops to make on the way. On Victoria Street, the convoy drew up at the post office. Thomson marched up to the clerk at the counter.

"I'd like to send a telegram to Romania, please."

"Romania!" the clerk exclaimed, handing him a telegram form.

Thomson scribbled a few lines.

Princess Marthe Bibesco, Posada, Par Comarmic Prahova, Romania En route to board Cardington R101 for India STOP The Persian accompanies us STOP As always I am thinking of you STOP Yours ever Kit

Thomson handed the message to the clerk.

"When will this be received?" Thomson asked.

"Monday, I should think, sir."

"Thank you. You're very kind."

Thomson next requested the chauffeur to stop at the florist's shop a few hundred yards up the street. He jumped out and went inside. Thomson was a regular customer and the florist greeted him warmly.

"I'd like you to arrange to send fifteen roses to Paris, if you please," Thomson said

"*Fifteen,* sir? You'd have to pay for two dozen, I'm afraid."

"Yes, yes, that's okay. The number has significance."

"Certainly sir, I quite understand. Any particular color?" the florist asked.

"They *must* be red *Général Jacqueminot,*" Thomson answered.

"Ah, yes of course, sir, *the usual.* They might be a bit hard to come by."

"You'll have plenty of time, my dear fellow."

Thomson solemnly wrote a note for the card to accompany the bouquet. When finished, he handed it to the florist with Marthe's address and delivery instructions. After paying by check, he bade the florist 'good day' and strode out. In the car, Knoxwood was waiting with the red box full of ministerial documents.

"Now, what have we got?" Thomson asked.

"Here's a cable from Egypt confirming the High Commissioner is coming to the banquet on Monday night. As are the other ten you invited."

"Excellent."

"The secretary of the Royal Aeronautical Society, the chairman of the Royal Aero Club and a few others all send their good wishes."

"How nice."

"You have a message from the Prime Minister wishing you a safe journey."

"Good. Please reply. Say: Thank you for your kind wishes. I'm confident this voyage will be a great success and I look forward to seeing you on the twentieth."

"And here, sir, is the latest weather report from the Air Ministry."

Thomson took it from Knoxwood and read it aloud, nodding as he did so.

"Anticyclone centered over Balkans. ...Depression over Eastern Atlantic moving east. Occluded front running from shallow low centered near Tynemouth to South of France moving east. ...Winds tonight over France likely to be west or south-west moderate strength over Northern France light over Southern France. Weather mainly cloudy. ...Western Mediterranean: light and variable or south-west winds probable tomorrow with fair weather. ...Central Mediterranean: light easterly or variable winds. Weather fair. ...Eastern Mediterranean: winds northerly or easterly Athens to Crete lighter toward Egypt. Weather mainly fair perhaps local thunderstorms."

Thomson handed the report back to Knoxwood. "Well, that doesn't sound too bad."

"That's a blessed relief, sir," Knoxwood said.

Thomson peered outside. The weather over London was cloudy, but calm. They continued the journey northwards, retracing Lou's route down.

In the van, Binks and Church were anxious to find out what recordings Thomson had brought. Lou allowed them to take a peek. Church held the case on his knees and pulled each record up and read the label. The first three were operas, which he'd never heard of. He was disappointed, but then he got excited.

" 'Ere look at this! "I Wanna Be Loved by You", "Bye, Bye Blackbird", "Happy Days Are 'ere Again", "Puttin' on the Ritz", Wow, ee's a gay old dog!" Church exclaimed. "Who would have thought? And here's "Somebody Stole My Gal" and "Singing in the Rain"—"

"Sounds like we're gonna have a party," Binks said. "Yes, sir!"

The lads in the van continued on with new respect for the Minister of State for Air.

They reached the village of Shefford as light was failing. Thomson checked his watch.

"Ah, we're running early and I'm dying for a cup of tea. What say you fellows?"

"I don't see why not, Minister," Knoxwood said.

"Look here. Teas and Hovis," Thomson said, pointing at a small inn. Its black and white façade, tiled roof and soft, warm lights looked inviting.

"The White Hart Inn. How quaint. Let's stop here, driver," Thomson said.

The Daimler pulled into the gravel carpark with the van behind.

"Bring all those chaps, Buck. Least I can do is buy everyone a cup of tea. I expect they could do with one."

At dusk, they reached the top of Hammer Hill on the Bedford Road. Thomson asked his driver to stop again. They were still early.

"Let's see how she looks from up here," Thomson said, climbing out of the car.

He walked to the crest of the hill. Everyone followed him. Two hundred and fifty feet below, the colossal, silver airship was a dazzling sight. She floated head to wind at the tower, bathed in light. Faint thumping sounds of a brass band were carried on the increasing winds from the west.

Thomson turned to Lou. "Now, *there's* our magic carpet, Commander! It's taken almost a decade to fulfill this dream. But there she is in all her glory. Look at her. See how the light catches her—how she sparkles!"

"You must be proud, sir," Lou said.

PART TWO

Passengers board *Cardington R101* from the tower.

INDIA

16

GRAND FAREWELL

Saturday October 4, 1930.

Thomson's Daimler slowed at the gate on the road to the tower. A cheer went up from the crowd. He waved grandly to everyone while the brass band hammered out another inspiring march. Today, he felt almost like royalty—perhaps this was the beginning of greater things to come. The airfield was surrounded by vehicles of every description, the atmosphere was one of celebration, despite the blustery weather.

The multi-colored lights of the fair grew vivid in the falling darkness and carousel music added to the gaiety, as it competed with the *um-par-par* and *thump-thump-thump* of the brass band. Thomson glanced up and listened to laughter and screams from girls on the Ferris wheel.

Their view of the ship must be wonderful.

Thomson scanned the multitudes huddled along the fence, bundled up in overcoats, scarves and hats, backs to the wind. Those lucky enough to have cars remained inside, wrapped in blankets. Some dozed, having traveled many miles. Small clusters gathered around vendors selling hot chestnuts and jacket potatoes cooked on steel braziers over glowing coals. The tasty aroma wafted across the field, filling Thomson's nostrils. It was comforting, and for a moment, he was reminded of his mother's kitchen in Devonshire.

Other vendors, unfortunate souls without the comfort of heat, attempted to sell mementos from tables or boards lashed to the fence. "Postcards! Postcards! Come an' get yer postcards 'ere. Two for threepence, ten for a bob," one cried.

"Keyrings and flags, only a shillin'. Come and get 'em!"

"Lovely souvenirs, commeneratin' this 'istorical event!"

Thomson sympathized with the poor wretches. In this chilly wind, they were having a devil of a time preventing their wares being blown away. And in such hard times, few spectators had money to fritter away on souvenirs. Clowns mingled with the crowd, handing out flyers, enticing people into the fairground. One, in a bowler hat high above the crowd, wore colossal, billowing, black-and-red-striped trousers over stilts. Flowing white locks blew around his head. Thomson admired the man's skill in such awful conditions.

The Daimler slowed while the gate was opened and the clowns gathered around the car, laughing and waving at Thomson. Amongst them, Thomson spotted Mrs. Hinchliffe, barging her way to the car. Obviously, she had something to say to him. He was irritated.

"Driver, *don't stop!*"

He glanced at Knoxwood, who'd seen her, too.

"I don't want to talk to *that* woman!" Thomson grunted.

The driver put his foot down and they sped through the gate. Another cheer went up.

A BBC crew was waiting under the tower for him to make his appearance, ready to do a commentary on the departure of the airship and ask for his comments. Many in the nation were glued to their radios and millions around the world were following this extraordinary event.

The car drew up. Thomson pulled out his wallet and took out a ten shilling note. "Here, Buck. Go back to the gate and pick up a few souvenirs. Get a couple for yourself, too," he said. And then as an afterthought, "And don't speak to that Hinchliffe woman, whatever you do."

"Right you are sir, absolutely."

Buck scampered off, clutching the money. The chauffeur opened the door and Thomson got out and waved to the crowd. Binks parked the van. As Thomson walked toward the BBC crew, his hat flew off and rolled on its rim across the field. Embarrassed, Thomson watched ground crewmen chase it down. He received the hat gratefully and replaced it on his head. He stood close to the BBC van and leaned on his walking stick. The reporters moved in.

"...Lord Thomson has emerged from the limousine and many reporters are gathering around. We'll listen to some of their questions ..." the commentator said, moving closer. He thrust the microphone out toward Thomson and press photographers took pictures for tomorrow's Sunday newspapers.

"How do you feel about the flight, sir?"

Thomson gazed up at the airship. "All my life, I've prepared myself for this moment."

"Any second thoughts?"

"Absolutely *none*. There's certainly nothing to fear," Thomson answered.

"The weather is kicking up, sir. Sure she can take it?"

"This airship is as strong as the mighty Forth Bridge!"

"Do you think your departure will be delayed?"

"The experts will be looking at the weather. They'll make that determination."

"Will you be making the whole voyage, bearing in mind you have a tight schedule?" George Hunter asked.

"The Prime Minister has given me strict instructions to return by the twentieth of October. Yes, I'll make the entire journey in this very fine airship."

Ground crewmen gathered around Lou, Binks and Church behind the van. Church flung the doors open.

"Gordon Bennett!"

"Cor blimey!"

"S'truth!"

"Bloody 'ell!"

"Holy smoke!"

"I don't believe it!"

"Someone's gotta be jokin'!"

Lou knew he'd better inform the captain—this would affect all his calculations. He climbed the tower steps, carrying Thomson's case of records. He went to the lounge, where he locked it in the gramophone cabinet, then proceeded to the chartroom.

Since early that morning Irwin, Atherstone and Johnston had been busy working on the ship's lift calculations. Its lifting capability had to be weighed against many complex issues which constantly affected it:

air temperature, atmospheric density, purity of gas, fullness of gasbags, gas bag leakage, fuel load and projected rate of usage, ballast requirements and usage, likelihood of collecting water ballast (from rain) en route, duration of journey, altitude and the airship's relation to terrain they'd be crossing, and of course, the weather. The task was daunting.

Lou entered the chartroom as the three men poured over their figures. "Captain, we've just returned with Lord Thomson's luggage. It's quite a load. He's brought everything but the kitchen sink."

Exasperated, Irwin threw down his pencil, went down the steps into the control car and glared down at the van. "Get all that stuff weighed. Don't load anything before you let me know the *exact* weight and *I* give you permission," he said.

"Yes, sir."

Lou went down the gangplank to the tower, where Sky Hunt leaned on the rail watching the activities. The ground crew laid Thomson's carpet down on a tarpaulin. Buck stood keeping an eye on it as though it were the *Shroud of Turin*.

"*That* could be the straw that breaks the camel's bleedin' back," Hunt muttered, shaking his head. Lou nodded in agreement and descended the stairs. He went to the stores foreman making out the load sheet.

"Don't put anything on board until it's weighed and cleared by Captain Irwin," he said. "*Nothing!*"

On the ground, Lou found himself surrounded by much hugging and kissing and tearful goodbyes. It made him sad and a little bitter. He looked for Charlotte's face in the crowd, even though he knew that was futile, but then a young RAF man came to speak to him.

"Sir, are you Commander Remington?"

"Yes."

"There's someone at the gate asking for you—says he's your father. Should I let him in, or will you come out? We know most of these people," he said, gesturing to the crewmen's families, "but we haven't seen this gentleman before and he has a north-country accent."

"I'll come and talk to him," Lou said. Obviously it wasn't his dad, but maybe it was Charlotte's father. His spirits soared as he marched quickly toward the fence. It was John Bull. He couldn't help feeling disappointed, but didn't allow it to show. The two men hugged.

"John, you shouldn't have driven all this way down here," Lou said.

"I had to come. I've been brooding all week. Mary said 'Go on, John, you go and see him off.' So here I am."

"That was thoughtful of you—you know I'm pleased to see you."

"Charlotte isn't here anywhere, I suppose, is she?" John asked, peering around.

"No, she's washed her hands of me."

"I can't believe that. I hope you'll try and see her when you get back."

"I tried. I went to her parents' house, but they wouldn't open the door."

"Oh, no ..."

"I'll definitely visit you when I return. Then, I guess, I'll head back to the States."

John was heartbroken. "God, I'm so sorry. Look, if anything changes—the cottage will always be yours, you know that."

"Thank you, John."

They shook hands and hugged again. John's eyes filled with tears.

"Good luck, son. Make sure you come back safe," he said and then, turning away abruptly, he disappeared into the crowd.

God, I'll miss that man!

A familiar voice spoke up behind him. "Good evening, Commander."

Brancker magically appeared next to Lou in John's place. He carried a small case and held a pith helmet under his arm. With the flat of the other hand, he tried valiantly to hold down his toupée while screwing up his face to keep his monocle in its socket.

"Sir Sefton!" Lou said, forcing a smile.

Then, to his surprise, among the crowd near the gate, Lou spotted her dark, shining hair—no mistaking those long, flowing locks down to her waist. She stood next to a young man about Lou's age and build, her arm through his. Lou's heart raced.

Damn, she's been in Bedford all this time!

"Excuse me, Sir Sefton, I'll be right back as soon as ..." Lou said, marching over to where she stood.

"Charlotte!" he shouted as he approached.

Her companion at first became confused and then hostile. The girl turned—she was nothing like Charlotte. In fact, her hair was auburn when he got up close—the light was wrong. He was bitterly disappointed, but relieved. Then he remembered—Charlotte had cut all her hair off.

"I'm sorry, no offense. I thought you were my sister," Lou said, holding up his hand.

He returned to Brancker and they were joined by Mrs. Hinchliffe, who stepped out of the crowd. "Good evening, gentlemen," she said.

"Millie. What on earth are you doing here?" Brancker said. "I'd give you a hug, but my hands are rather full."

"Then I'll kiss *you*," she said planting a kiss on his cheek. She smiled at Lou and kissed his lips. "I've come to tell you what Ray— " she began.

Brancker exploded. "Millie, Millie, don't! Just go home! The ship will leave tonight. Thomson has decreed it." He turned away from her. "Come, Lou, we must go. *Goodbye*, Millie!"

Lou gave Mrs. Hinchliffe an apologetic smile. He'd not seen Brancker so on edge and the poor woman didn't deserve it. He took Brancker's case and they marched off through the gate to the tower with others who ambled trance-like toward the great beast. Maybe they were all under its evil spell. A clown appeared with a handful of flyers and stuffed one in Lou's hand. Lou couldn't help grinning as he read it.

LET THE GREAT CLAIRVOYANT

MADAM HARANDAH

THE ROMANIAN GYPSY

TELL YOUR FORTUNE

PSYCHIC READING

PALM READING

TAROT CARDS

3d each

"What's that?" Brancker asked.

"It's an invite to talk to a fortune teller from the Elephant and Castle," Lou said. "Would you like to meet her?"

"No, I don't think I would."

"Mrs. Hinchliffe mentioned Ray ...that's her—"

"Dead husband. I love Millie dearly, and she may be right, but we have our duty to do. Can't be listening to all that stuff tonight. I'm depressed enough already."

"I guarantee you don't need a session with Madame Harandah, in that case," Lou said.

"I had my fortune told in Paris once ..." Brancker began. He stopped in mid-sentence, seeming to think better of it.

"What did they say, sir?" Lou asked, but Brancker didn't answer.

They walked to the tower, passing Thomson, who was just finishing his press conference. His well-wishers were gathered around him shaking his hand. In that group were Dowding and his predecessor, Higgins, Richmond, Scott, members of the press, Knoxwood and many from the R.A.W. Colmore stood apart with his wife, seeming more relaxed than she. Lou moved to the elevator with Brancker where Bert Mann, the elevator man, waited with a cheery smile.

"Good evening, Bert. I'm expecting a lady friend any time now— Lady Cathcart. When she arrives, show her to the gangplank. Tell her to follow the blue carpet, would you? Inform her I'll be waiting. We're having a little leaving party," Brancker said winking.

"I can do that, Sir Sefton. No problem at all, sir."

"Before I go up, I'd better have a word with Lord Thomson," Brancker said. But Thomson had already spotted Brancker and was approaching with hands outstretched. They greeted each other like long lost brothers.

"Ah, Sefton, good evening! Lovely to see you, my dear chap." The two men stood smiling and shaking hands while photographers' cameras flashed.

"Come on, everyone. Gather round. Let's get some nice group pictures. Get as many crewmen in as possible," Thomson instructed.

While they were taking a third picture, eight ground crewmen trooped past with Thomson's Persian balanced on their shoulders. Irwin appeared from the tower staircase, his face contorted with anger, vividly pale in the searchlights' glare. Thomson was quick to spot him marching stiffly toward the men with the carpet. Thomson raised his voice above the wind, spiking Irwin's guns.

"Ah, there you are, Captain Irwin. Please join us."

"What the hell is *this*?" Irwin demanded, gesturing at the heavy roll in disbelief.

"Why, this is my talisman. It flies with us. We'll lay it down for the banquet in honor of the King of Egypt. We'll do things in style. Now come and stand next to me Irwin, there's a good chap."

Irwin fumed, but did as he was told. Everyone dutifully gathered around for more photos. In the next few hours, Lou would come to fully appreciate what a truly intimidating presence Thomson could be and what a skilled manipulator he was. Brancker picked up his belongings and headed for the elevator.

Lou stood posing until he could slip away. He went over to Colmore and his wife, who had her arm linked through his. Colmore grinned. "Not sure if you've met Mrs. Colmore, Lou," he said.

"You were in church last year—for the blessing," Lou said.

Mrs. Colmore smiled. She had a sweet face and she obviously doted on her husband. Her eyes shone with love each time she looked at him.

"I'm always relaxed when *this* man's around," Colmore said.

"I know you are, my darling." She glanced at Lou, seeming almost convinced.

"He's my special assistant and our third officer. He's also our American observer, as Zachary Lansdowne had been on Scottie's voyage to America."

"And where is Mr. Lansdowne these days?" Mrs. Colmore asked innocently.

Lou bit his tongue, remembering.

Killed on the Shenandoah with Josh.

"Er, if you'll excuse me, I think I'd better check on that girl over there. She'll have news of my injured crewman. It was good seeing you again, ma'am," Lou said, with a slight bow, touching his cap. Irene and Church were locked in a tearful embrace, while Church's mother and father stood by. Irene noticed Lou approaching and tore herself away.

"Lou, I went and saw Billy this morning and this afternoon. He's got a compound fracture, but he'll be okay. He said to tell you not to forget what he said to you this mornin'—especially now. He said you'd know what he meant. His mum's coming down from Goole tomorrow morning."

"Thanks, Irene," Lou said.

Someone must have told Billy that Jessup had been picked as his replacement. He thought about Fanny again and how she'd rather her son had a broken leg than be on this flight tonight. Suddenly, he remembered and his stomach turned over. What was it Madame Harandah had said to Billy a year ago?

Go break a leg!

Lou was shaken. Church kissed his mother and shook his father's hand.

"We'll be back by the twentieth. I'll see you all then," Church said. Before heading to the ship, Church grabbed Irene and they kissed passionately. "I love you, my darlin'," he said as he let her go. He turned toward the tower and as he retreated he raised his arms triumphantly, shouting at the top of his voice. "You're gonna be the most beautiful bride in all of Bedford, my darlin'!"

Once again, Lou felt uneasy.

What else did that old gypsy crone say?

While the Churches waved to their son, Sky Hunt was saying his own goodbyes. His wife held a baby in her arms and their son stood beside her. "Albert, if anything happens to me, you must take care of your mum and the baby. You'll be the man in the family, son," Hunt said, kissing each of them. He stood and watched them troop off to the gate.

For Lou, this was tough; never had he felt more alone. All around him were similar scenes: young men in uniform kissing their wives and girl friends; Richmond and his wife; Atherstone and his wife; Olivia Irwin looking earnestly up into her husband's face.

Harry Leech's wife tucked a piece of heather into his lapel while he smoked a last cigarette. "Here you are, Harry," she said. "For luck." She patted his chest and kissed him.'

"I'll be all right now then, won't I? You go on home, love," Leech said, peering up at the swirling clouds. "Goodness knows what time we'll leave—that's if we leave at all."

He stamped out his dog-end on the ground. Mrs. Leech agreed and, showing not the slightest sign of anxiety, kissed Leech again and made for the bus stop.

Leech glanced over at Lou. "No point in 'er hangin' around 'ere," he said.

Lou agreed. Binks arrived at his side.

"Where's your missus, Joe? Isn't she coming?" Lou asked.

"Nah. I told 'em to stay home. I don't wanna go through all this rigmarole. I told 'em I'd be back in a couple of weeks."

But Binks seemed upset.

"What's up, Joe?"

"Sir, some of the blokes have been talkin'. Jessup's carrying a bloody great stiletto. He 'ad it in customs. Jessup told 'em a lot of old bollocks about needin' it for emergencies."

"He's got a point, Joe."

"Sir, everybody knows he's got it in for you."

"All right. Thanks. I appreciate it—but don't worry."

"Oh and sir, they weighed the old geezer's stuff. It was over two hundred and fifty pounds."

"Jeez! Thanks for your help today, Joe."

"Welcome, sir."

Lou re-joined the main group just as Thomson was ushering them into the elevator.

"Come along, everyone. We'll have a farewell drink on board," he said.

While they were piling in, Knoxwood handed Thomson a telegram. Thomson stopped to read it, waving the group on. He thought it might be from Marthe. Mann slammed the accordion gate shut. The wives stood watching their husbands sadly.

"Keep the old flag flying, Florry, my dear," Richmond called to his wife. Standing behind the steel bars of the elevator doors, they reminded Lou of men on death row.

Thomson tore the telegram open.

A word to wish you good luck on your historic flight STOP kindest regards Burney

"That's decent of him," Thomson said, disappointed.

He handed the telegram back to Knoxwood.

"Send him a reply."

Knoxwood pulled out his notepad.

"Thank you for your very kind wishes. Indeed, this is a wonderful day. We're looking forward with excitement to flying down Marco Polo's ancient route—sign it CBT."

Lou was about to take the stairs when he spotted a chauffeur-driven Rolls-Royce approaching the tower. Perhaps it was Sir Sefton's lady friend. The limousine stopped and a pair of elegant legs stepped out. The finely-dressed woman made her way toward Lou, clutching her long, dark coat tightly to her breast.

"Lady Cathcart? Lou inquired.

"Yes, I'm here to wish Sir Sefton Brancker *bon voyage*."

By now, everyone was onboard the ship. Feeling obligated, Lou led her to the elevator gate. "This is the lady who Sir Sefton is expecting. Please take us up, Bert," Lou said.

"Right you are, sir."

Lou closed his eyes as the elevator ascended.

17

ON BOARD RECEPTION

Saturday October 4, 1930.

When Thomson had arrived at the tower gallery minutes earlier and climbed the gangplank, he was reminded of that New Year's Eve of 1923, on the train crossing the Firth of Forth on his way to meet MacDonald—a truly wicked storm. He listened to the intermittent rain beating on the ship's cover and felt the wind's fury.

I survived that night and I shall survive this one.

Thomson made his entrance into the lounge with great fanfare—shaking hands, giving nods of encouragement and expressions of thanks. Tables had been set up for a brief farewell celebration. R.A.W. passengers had gathered, along with Higgins and Dowding and the Deputy Director of Civil Aviation for India, Squadron Leader Bill O'Neill and his wife. Thomson sensed Mrs. O'Neill was in serious distress about this flight. He couldn't abide such feelings of negativity and, with a stony look, moved away to speak with Squadron Leader Palstra and his colleague from the Australian Embassy.

Lou led Brancker's terrified visitor up the gangplank and then past a group of crewmen struggling to stow the Persian carpet at the bow, between Frames 1 and 2. Lou and Lady Cathcart continued unsteadily along the main corridor, over the blue carpet. The ship rocked and rolled from side to side to the sound of rain, belting down in torrents. Lady Cathcart found all this unnerving and took hold of Lou's arm. The deeper into the airship they got, the more uneasy she became.

At last, they arrived at the entrance to the magnificent dining salon, its brass wall sconces casting light onto slender, white columns, each with its own shining, gold leaf ornamental head. Lady Cathcart peered around helplessly, not noticing or caring about the beauty of the room. Brancker came rushing over.

"So good of you to come, my dear," he said, taking both her hands and gallantly kissing her on both cheeks.

"Oh Branks, will you be safe in this *bloody thing?*"

"Safe as houses, my love. Don't you worry—old Sefton's going to be all right."

"Dear God—are you sure? I'm scared to death."

"Let me get you a glass of bubbly and we can go and have a little chit chat." Brancker left Lady Cathcart with Lou and nipped off to the table. He returned with a tray and four glasses of champagne and a few brandies. "Come along, my dear, let's go this way, where it's quiet. We'll have a drink and you'll feel so much better," Brancker said. He gave Lou a smile of thanks and another of his little winks as he led the lady off to his cabin. Lou grinned.

Not the most private place in the world—what the hell—it could be The Last Supper.

In the lounge, the stewards came round with trays of champagne. Thomson took one and moved to the center of the room.

"Ladies and gentlemen, well-wishers and fellow travelers. Please take up your glasses. Here's to this historic voyage—to our success— *to India!*"

"To India!" everyone repeated, and swallowed it down.

With that, Thomson went over to Colmore. "What's the latest on the weather?"

"We're waiting for Mr. Giblett, sir. He'll have the updated weather report in his hands shortly," Colmore replied.

"Good. We'll meet and discuss it after the reception—somewhere private."

"The chartroom would be the best place, sir. We can just about squeeze in there."

"Schedule that meeting in half an hour," Thomson said.

After Brancker and the woman had gone, Lou poked his head in the lounge. Colmore stood in the corner talking to Thomson, Richmond and Scott. Scott was drinking heavily. Colmore still appeared relaxed. He smiled at Lou and beckoned him over.

"I've told Lord Thomson that we'll have the latest weather report any time. Would you tell Captain Irwin we'll meet in the chartroom in half an hour?"

"I'm on my way there now, sir. I'll relay your message," Lou said.

Lou headed along the corridor passing the passenger cabins. Sounds of passion were coming from what he guessed had to be Brancker's cabin.

God bless the old dog!

When Lou reached the end of the corridor, he ran into Jessup lurking with two others, listening to Lady Cathcart moaning with delight.

"Oh Sefton ...oh Sefton ...oh, oh, oh, yes, yes, *yes, yes, yes!* ...Aaaaaaaaaahhh!"

The crewmen laughed and sniggered.

"Okay, you lot. Get away from the passenger quarters. Immediately!" Lou said.

"Yes, sir. Sorry, sir," one of them said. "We've just been turnin' down the beds."

Jessup gave no lip, but he had a glint in his eye. The three slouched off toward the bow. Jessup turned back to Lou and with a crooked smile said, "See you later ... *sir.*"

After they'd gone, Lou went to the chartroom overlooking the control car. Although doubling as the control room, it was usually referred to as the 'chartroom.' It was from here the ship was managed, including the production of weather charts, navigation and load calculations. Johnston was studying the weather charts with Giblett. Irwin had returned and was going over the load sheet with Atherstone, inputting additional data—Thomson's luggage.

"Two hundred seventy-four pounds," Irwin said.

Atherstone entered the number onto a load sheet.

"We'll have to adjust the ballast for that," Irwin said.

Irwin continued with the figures. As he called them out, Atherstone repeated them and wrote them down.

"Okay, fuel 25.3 tons ...lube oils one ton ...water ballast 9.25 tons ...drinking water 1.1 tons ...crew and passengers 3.8 tons ...food and provisions .33 tons ...luggage .53 tons ..."

"Including Thomson's?" Atherstone asked.

"Yes. Crew kit .8 tons ...furnishings and equipment 1.25 tons ..."

"That bloody Axminster carpet weighed more than half a ton," Atherstone muttered.

"We'll call it permanent ballast. We'll tear it up and throw it in the Channel, if we have to," Irwin said. Lou knew Irwin meant what he said. "Okay, so, lift available, with bags filled to ninety-six percent, is 161.75 tons. Lift needed is 162.1 tons. We'll need to dump 1.35 tons of ballast to slip," Irwin concluded.

"All very nice, but we have no margin for safety," Atherstone said.

Irwin glanced up at Lou for a second, giving him a nod. Lou went to the rail and peered down into the control car. Steff stood on watch, his face frozen. These men were under almost unbearable stress. Lou had seen faces like this before aboard *R38*. His uneasiness returned.

"Lord Thomson wants to have a conference before we leave," Lou said.

"Where?"

"Right here," Lou answered.

Irwin nodded again. "Okay," he said absently.

While Lou was in the control car, Thomson walked along the corridor with Buck to his cabin. Thomson was mystified by grunting and moaning noises coming from one of the cabins. He said nothing.

Surely that can't be what it sounds like!

Buck was impassive as he stopped and held the curtain of Thomson's assigned cabin open, although Thomson detected a hint of a smile at the corner of Buck's mouth and mirth in his eyes.

"This one's *yours*, sir," Buck said. "I'm next door."

Thomson surveyed the cabin. It was double size, having had one partition removed. A large desk and a comfortable chair had been installed for him to work on affairs of state.

"This one's bigger than the others, sir," Buck said. "So's the bed."

Thomson nodded with satisfaction. Buck had laid out a clean shirt and underclothes for a change before dinner. Although it was chilly without heating, Thomson removed his overcoat and Buck hung it in the closet behind the curtain.

Thomson picked up the postcards Buck had bought from the souvenir vendors and left on the table. He browsed through colored pictures and photographs of the airship floating at the tower. They were emblazoned in red letters with *Cardington R101* alongside the Union Jack. Each had been date-stamped: 4th October 1930. Pleased, Thomson laid them back on the table. He picked up the two key rings, each of which had a chain and the metal shape of an airship attached with HMA *R101* pressed into the metal—one red, one blue. Thomson nodded with satisfaction and handed Buck the blue one along with three postcards.

"Here, some mementos for the trip," he said.

"Thank you, sir. I shall always remember this," Buck said, genuinely grateful.

Thomson slipped the red keyring into his trouser pocket.

18

THE WEATHER CONFERENCE

Saturday October 4, 1930.

Fifteen minutes later, everyone trooped into the chartroom. Five chairs had been placed at the bow end, where Thomson, Knoxwood, Colmore, Scott and Richmond sat, with Thomson at center. This left the officers and Rope standing. Lou stood next to Irwin at the back with Atherstone and Johnston. It was cramped and oppressive. There was no sign of Brancker, still in his cabin recovering from Lady Cathcart's '*bon voyage*'.

Colmore stood up. "Minutes ago we received a new weather forecast. Why don't you give us an update, Mr. Giblett?"

Giblett leaned against the chart table holding the latest information, his eyes darting back and forth across it. "Around one o'clock today, the occluded front over France moved eastwards, leaving a trough of low pressure off the Irish coast to move in, causing rain to spread over England this evening and throughout the night. Therefore, we can expect increasing southwesterly winds over the south of England and northern France."

"And the velocity of these winds, Mr. Giblett?" Thomson asked.

"They're forecasting surface winds of ten to fifteen miles an hour, freshening later. Upper winds above two thousand feet are expected to be from twenty to thirty miles an hour."

"At what altitude will we be flying?" Thomson asked, looking at Scott.

"Between one thousand and fifteen hundred feet, sir," Scott answered.

Giblett continued, "On the basis of what we're being told, we don't expect a huge increase in wind strength tonight—but I must stress, we *can't* rule that out."

"So you're saying it *could* increase … and if it did, by how much?" Thomson asked.

Brancker entered the room, soaking wet, embarrassed, and a little the worse for wear. His toupée was askew and his monocle splashed with rain. Lou wondered if he'd been wearing it in his bunk with Lady Cathcart. He couldn't help grinning at the thought.

I'd like a snap of that!

"Ah, Sefton, it's so very good of you to join us," Thomson said.

"I'm terribly sorry, Minister. I didn't realize you'd called a conference."

Thomson looked down his nose. "I don't suppose you did. We were discussing the weather. Mr. Giblett has been telling us of the possibility of the winds increasing."

"I just saw someone off to the elevator—it's *bloody awful* out there!"

"I asked Mr. Giblett how much the winds might increase and he was

about to tell us." Thomson turned to Giblett.

"That's not possible to predict, sir, but—"

"Might they increase to, say, thirty or forty knots?" Thomson pressed him.

"It must be blowing twenty-five knots *right now!*" Brancker announced.

"I have to tell you anything's possible. I can't give you the odds. Weather forecasting is not an exact science, sir," Giblett said.

"All right. Let's suppose the winds do increase to 40 knots." Thomson's eyes fell on Richmond. "Would that be too much for this airship, Colonel Richmond?"

"No, Lord Thomson, not at all. She's proved herself on that score."

Thomson's gaze was transferred to Scott, whose red face became animated.

"No, sir. *Absolutely not!*" Scott affirmed.

Irwin's voice projected from the back of the room. All heads turned in his direction. "I must remind you this airship has *never once* been flown in foul weather and its tests have *never* been completed," Irwin said. He sounded almost detached.

"So, Captain, you don't have confidence in your ship. Is that it?" Thomson snapped.

"That's *not* what I said, sir. I was merely pointing out the fact that this ship has *never* flown in anything more than a ten-knot breeze—and *never once* under full power."

"Captain Irwin—" Scott started, but Irwin stubbornly continued.

"And I should mention the gas valves are pumping out gas at an alarming rate every time the ship rolls. The gas bags are rubbing on the padding, which will wear holes in them in no time …and the cover was never completely replaced."

"So, are you proposing that we postpone this voyage, Captain?" Thomson asked.

"I'm saying we should definitely consider that possibility, yes," Irwin replied.

Scott tried again. "I don't think—"

"You *do* realize we'd become the object of ridicule. Thousands are camped out around this field—people who've come from all over England, Scotland and Wales to witness history in the making—not to mention the distinguished passengers we have on board. The eyes of the world are upon us and on British engineering. If this flight is postponed due to the weather, we'll be announcing that airships are fair-weather aircraft. I should also remind everyone here that the Treasury is looking for a glimmer of hope—some small success."

"Sir, I think—" Scott began again.

"So, I ask you: Is it to be that the government's revered airship *Cardington R101*, which has cost millions of pounds, cannot match the splendid performance of the men at Vickers, who did *what* they said they would, *when* they said they would—for a fixed sum of a mere three hundred and fifty thousand pounds—despite efforts to coerce them into a postponement."

"Sir—" Richmond began. Thomson cut him off, too.

The tirade was over. His voice became soft and cajoling. "I will say just this, gentlemen: Reward for success will be great and honors bestowed. Careers and reputations will be made with financial rewards beyond your wildest dreams …" Here Thomson paused. Everyone in the room waited while the wind howled and rocked the ship. Then came the knife, silent and smooth. "...But there will be no reward for failure. No more government funding—none will be asked for."

Richmond leapt to his feet followed by Scott.

"I'm completely confident this airship can handle it, sir," Richmond said.

"I agree," Scott said.

"What about the gas bags and valves and the cover the captain is referring to?" Thomson asked.

"All airships lose a certain amount of gas. It's to be expected," Scott said.

"The cover was thoroughly inspected and approved. We've been over this time and time again, sir," Richmond said.

Another long pause.

"So, from what you're saying, we have *nothing* to be concerned about?"

Brancker stirred himself, stepping forward from the back of the room. He'd composed himself somewhat, his toupée now on straight. All eyes turned toward him. He carefully finished wiping his monocle with a handkerchief and stuck it back in his eye. "Lord Thomson, I'm going to make a suggestion, if you'll allow me, sir. We depart on schedule and flight test the ship around this area of Bedford. And then, if, and only *if*, Captain Irwin and Major Scott are satisfied—we *then* strike a course for London and France."

"Oh, yes, I heartily agree," Richmond said.

"And if not?" Thomson said.

"Then we'll return here to the tower," Brancker said.

"That certainly sounds like a pwudent plan, sir," Knoxwood said brightly.

Suddenly, people were smiling and nodding—but not Irwin, Atherstone, Johnston and Lou. Colmore's mood had deteriorated over the last thirty minutes, but now he was perking up again. Lou had paid attention to Irwin while Brancker was putting his suggestion forward.

"Easier said than done." He'd muttered to Atherstone beside him.

"Why can't this test be done en route to London? It all sounds like a waste of fuel," Thomson asked.

"It'll give us a chance to test her on all headings under full power, sir," Scott said.

"I do remember Dowding suggesting this at our meeting," Thomson said, glancing at Colmore. "But won't people be wondering why the dickens we're flying around in circles?"

"Everyone'll think we're making a grand tour—in honor of the city," Scott said.

Thomson peered at the wall clock.

"What time do you propose getting started, Major Scott?"

"Immediately, sir. Immediately!"

"*Splendid.* I'm going to sit in the lounge with Wing Commander Colmore. Carry out your testing and keep us informed."

Knoxwood stood up and shook hands with everyone. "I wish I was coming with you," he said. "Bon voyage!"

While the meeting was breaking up, Hunt entered and whispered into Irwin's ear. Irwin became concerned and left. Lou followed. Irwin raced down the corridor and down the gangplank. Lou heard the captain's rapidly descending feet on the steel stairs. Lou stayed on the upper gallery and looked down. He could see Olivia Irwin some distance away, standing beside their small black car. She was dressed in a long, hooded, black cloak, which swirled around her in the wind, her face stark and white in the floodlights.

Lou watched Irwin rush out of the tower and into her arms. She hugged him to her, crying and speaking into his ear—pleading. He laid his head on her shoulder, doing his best to hold back his own tears. He drew back, obviously trying to reassure her, perhaps telling her of Brancker's plan, which Lou knew he had no faith in at all.

Olivia didn't appear convinced, but finally seemed resigned. They kissed again and he helped her into the car. Irwin stood and watched her drive slowly away, the wind churning the autumn leaves as she went. He turned and trudged back to the tower and up the staircase. Lou noiselessly retraced his steps, his heart heavy for the captain and his wife.

19

SALUTE TO BEDFORD

Saturday October 4, 1930.

Lou checked the wall clock: it was 6:32 p.m. On this day, the 4th of October, the clocks were scheduled be set back one hour at 1.00 a.m. Irwin had posted a duty schedule on the wall in the control room:

CARDINGTON R101 DUTY ROSTER INDIA FLIGHT:
FIRST LEG TO EGYPT

WATCH	HOURS	DUTY OFFICER
Evening	_16:00 – 20:00_	_F/O M. Steff_
1st Night	_20:00 – 23:00_	_Lt. Cmdr. Atherstone_
Middle	_23:00 – 02:00_	_Capt. C. Irwin_
Morning	_02:00 – 05:00_	_F/O M. Steff_
2nd Morning	_05:00 – 08:00_	_Lt. Cmdr. Atherstone_

Lt. Cmdr. L. Remington Relief Duty Officer and Navigator
This rotation will continue throughout the voyage.

Steff had been officer of the watch since 4 o'clock with Potter as height coxswain. Lou leaned on the rail overlooking the control car, alongside Johnston, Brancker and Scott.

Irwin's face was grim, his jaw set. "Start engines," he ordered.

"Start engines," Steff repeated.

Steff relayed the order via the telegraph, first to engine car No.1 and then through the others to No. 5, where Joe Binks was located with Ginger Bell. Atherstone was also in the control car, shining a flashlight on the propeller of engine No.1 to check it was turning. It wasn't. The two coxswains were ready at their wheels. Suddenly, everyone's attention was diverted by a woman's scream carried on the wind across the field from the gate. Irwin beckoned Lou down.

From the control car, they recognized Rosie, rushing toward the tower, waving something in her hand. Some distance behind Rosie, a policeman was in pursuit, blowing a whistle, his black cape gleaming in the rain.

"Lou, go down and find out what's going on," Irwin said calmly. "Looks like she's got a letter for her husband. Take it to him."

"We don't have time for this nonsense," Scott shouted.

Irwin glared at Lou. "Do as I say!" he snapped.

Lou left the control car as the first propeller began to turn on engine No. 2. The crowd cheered. As each engine was started, a cloud of black smoke spurted from its exhaust into the floodlights, sending a greasy, diesel odor across the field. Lou rushed down the corridor to the gangplank three hundred and fifty feet away. Church was about to assist another crewman in pulling up the gangplank.

"Hold it, Sam. I've gotta go down. Something's going on," he said, dashing out into the steady rain. He bounded down the stairs to the bottom where he found the now obviously pregnant Rosie Cameron pleading with Bert Mann. She was a sorry sight; her clothes, hair and face, soaking wet. Lou's heart went out to her.

"Please, Bert, let me go up and talk to Doug," she sobbed.

"No, 'course yer can't, Rosie. Ship's about to leave," Mann said.

Seeing Lou, Rosie turned to him, her eyes imploring. "Oh, sir. Can you get Doug for me? Please, I beg you. I *must* talk to him."

The out-of-breath policeman arrived on the scene. Lou held up his hand.

"It's all right, officer, we can deal with this." He turned back to Rosie. "That's not possible, Rosie. What you got there?"

Rosie grabbed Lou's arm, burying her face in his shoulder. "It's a letter for Doug. Can you give it to him—*please, please?*"

"Sure I can, Rosie."

She handed over the soggy letter. Lou put it in his inside pocket.

"I'll make sure he gets it. Don't worry."

"You must go home now, Rosie. You can't stay here," Mann said.

"Come along, miss," the policeman said.

Rosie nodded and walked off toward the gate, the policeman following. Lou glanced up at the ship. A bright, amber light shone down from the long windows of the promenade deck and her red navigation lights flashed on the port side where he stood. Three engines were up and running now, their blades spinning. Torrents of water ran down the ship's outer cover and spilled to the ground. A black cloud shot from engine No. 4. He bounded up the stairs. At the top, Mann followed Lou to the gangplank where a concerned Capt. Ralph Booth stood bundled in rain gear.

"What are you doing here, Ralph?" Lou asked.

"Just wanted to wave you fellas off. Take care of yourselves," Booth said, shaking Lou's hand.

"You wanna trade places?" Lou shouted above the wind and engines.

"Can't tonight—gotta wash my hair."

Lou went aboard. Church and Hunt pulled up the gangplank and closed it from inside.

"You might save a marriage, sir," Church called after Lou.

"I think it's a bit late for that, Sam," Lou replied.

Lou went to the crew's sleeping quarters, passing Jessup in the crew mess having his evening meal of bread, cheese and cocoa. He'd missed the commotion with Rosie, which Lou figured was a good thing. Lou found Cameron on his bunk reading a magazine. He handed him Rosie's letter.   Cameron screwed up his face. "What's this?"

Lou spoke kindly. "Rosie's been here. She asked me to give you this. She wants your forgiveness, Doug."

Cameron snorted with disgust and threw the letter down on his pillow. "Stupid bitch," he muttered.

By the time Lou got to the control car to report what had happened, all engines except No. 1 were running smoothly, their propellers whirring in the sparkling raindrops. Lou went back up to the chartroom.

In the control car, Irwin glanced across at Atherstone. "Take over the elevators from Potter. Let me know how she feels."

Potter went up and stood in the chartroom beside Lou with Johnston, Brancker and Scott. The speaking tube whistle sounded and Steff put it to his ear. "They're having trouble with No.1, sir. Hunt says they can't get the starting engine going," Steff said.

"Tell them to keep trying," Irwin said. He raised his eyes and glared at Scott as if it was his fault. Scott stared back with bloodshot eyes as he paced back and forth along the rail. Finally, engine No.1 fired up with a shower of sparks in the blackness and all five engines were humming smoothly. Lou had concerns about weight, especially since the cover was totally saturated. The process of ballasting up began, so the ship could rise when they slipped from the tower.

"She's nose heavy. Drop two half ton bags at Frame 1," Irwin ordered.

This was done. A fine mist appeared in the floodlights.

Irwin wasn't satisfied. "Not enough. Drop two more at Frame 1 and two half tons at Frame 6," he snapped. That seemed to do the trick. Irwin appeared more comfortable the ship could rise. "Okay, slip now!" he ordered.

Lou marveled. This had to be the toughest getaway ever undertaken, lifting more men and dead weight into the air than any craft in aviation history—and in the foulest conditions. As the bow lifted and was released from the tower, the crowd roared. Pushed by engines 1 and 2, the airship drew backwards and rose above the tower, falling off to starboard.

"Cut engines 1 and 2 and convert to running forward. All engines at seven hundred rpm's." Steff telegraphed the instructions.

"She's still heavy. Drop another ton at Frame 6!" Irwin ordered.

The mighty *Cardington R101*, dangerously low over the crowd, slowly pushed forward, spewing water from her ballast tanks, wallowing into the night. From the control car, they saw signals from loved ones on the ground who were using flashlights. Car headlights flashed on and off and horns sounded nonstop.

"Okay, Captain, get all engines up to eight twenty-five," Scott ordered from the rail above. Irwin nodded to Steff who relayed the order by telegraph.

"How's she handling, Captain?" Brancker called down.

Irwin turned to Atherstone who muttered something inaudible.

"Heavy as hell," Irwin replied.

"Let's try her on another tack," Scott said.

"Turn ninety degrees to starboard. Steer forty-five degrees toward South End," Johnston called down.

"That's good, Johnnie," Scott said, pacing to nowhere.

The ship pitched and rolled. Nobody spoke.

"How is she now?" Scott asked finally, leaning on the rail again.

"Like the *Titanic*," Irwin replied.

The ship, traveling downwind, moved along a northeasterly track. Lou turned to the chart table. Johnston pointed to the map. "We're over the captain's house on Putroe Lane."

They'd barely reached six hundred feet. Lou wondered if Olivia had reached home and how she was feeling.

If she's watching this, she'll be horrified.

Irwin called up to Lou. "Take a look round the ship, Lou."

Lou passed through the lounge, where Thomson sat in silence opposite Colmore. Neither of them spoke as he went by. He walked into the dining salon. The tables had been set for dinner. Some had been pushed together, forming a head table at one end. Pierre entered and smiled nervously at Lou, hoping for his approval.

Lou nodded. "Everything looks good, Pierre."

"I'm waiting to hear if they'll be dining this evening, sir," he said.

"We'll know soon enough," Lou said, on his way out.

He headed out onto the catwalk where Leech and Rope were making an inspection. The wind had picked up. Rain beat like gravel on the cover in squalls, while the valves expelled gas in great puffs. Lou eyed the surging gas bags and wondered if they'd have any hydrogen left by the time they reached Egypt—*if* they reached Egypt! He got level with Leech, who no longer seemed so carefree. "She's pitching a bit, isn't she?" he said, glancing at Rope.

"She's bound to in this weather—but I'm not unduly worried," Rope replied.

They heard someone behind them and turned. It was Jessup. He stood on the catwalk holding the rail.

"What's up, Jessup?" Leech barked.

"Just making some inspections, sir," Jessup responded, glancing at Lou.

"Good man," Rope said.

Lou nodded and went to engine car No. 5 to check on Binks and Bell. The flap was already open. When he peered down the ladder, he noticed the propeller was still. He returned and got Leech, keeping an eye out for Jessup—but he'd disappeared. They made their way down, clinging to the slippery rungs. They could see by lights on the ground, the ship was turning a hundred and eighty degrees to port. They squeezed into the engine car.

"What's up?" Leech asked.

"She was running okay for a while then the pressure dropped—so I shut her down," Bell replied.

"All right, I'll let your foreman know," Leech said.

"Could be something wrong with the gauge," Binks said. "The engine sounded fine."

Lou and Leech left Binks and Bell to wait for their supervisors. Lou went back to the chartroom while the ship now traveled in an easterly direction—still within striking distance of the tower.

"What's going on?" Scott demanded.

"No.5's down. Oil pressure dropped, sir," Lou said.

"They'll fix it," Scott said.

Irwin scowled up at Scott. He raised his voice to Johnston. "Where exactly are we, Johnny?"

"We're over Marston Thrift Wood. Let's turn ninety degrees to port, Captain, while you decide what we're gonna do," Johnston said.

Just then, Colmore arrived from the lounge expecting a report. "The weather appears to be worsening," he said. "Are we going back to the tower?" He looked down at Irwin and then at all the other faces. Everyone ignored him.

Finally, he got an answer. "She seems all right to me. I suggest we make tracks for London. Anyone disagree with my decision?" Scott said.

Colmore looked forlorn. "But Scottie, what about the engine? I hate to start a voyage with one engine down already," he said.

"They'll get it back up, don't worry," Scott said.

"But the weather's—"

"You're right—it's getting worse. It's too dangerous to attempt a landing at Cardington now."

"Wait, Scottie, I think we should discuss this."

"What do *you* think, Captain Irwin?" Scott shouted down to the control car.

"It'd be much too dangerous. But let's face it, that was obvious from the start, wasn't it. Now, we have no choice," Irwin replied.

Lou glanced at Colmore. He'd been outwitted. He understood how both Colmore and Irwin had become virtually powerless. Scott had usurped them—enabled and sanctioned by Thomson, since their last-minute meeting with him in London.

Scott's mind was ticking over. "Look, Reggie, if anything goes wrong, we'll make contingency plans to land in France, that's all."

"Do you really think we could?" Brancker said.

"Oh dear," Colmore mumbled, wiping his forehead with his handkerchief.

Lou knew this was a false hope for Colmore to cling to—if they couldn't dock in Cardington, they couldn't possibly land in France in this weather without facilities or huge teams of trained men.

"What's the heading for London, Johnny?" Scott asked.

"One hundred and eighty five degrees," Johnston answered.

"Steer one hundred and eighty-five degrees. Full speed on all engines," Scott ordered.

"This is ridiculous. My ship's been commandeered from under me," Irwin muttered.

"Captain Irwin, I'm the senior ranking officer aboard this ship. You *will* obey my orders without question," Scott shouted.

Irwin glanced up at Lou. "Commander, inform the chief coxswain the flight test is over. Tell him to get down to scheduled watch-keeping routine."

"Yes, sir."

Over Clophill where the A507 crosses the A6, the airship turned south. Brancker and Colmore appeared beaten. "Come on, Reggie," Brancker said. "Let's grab a couple of stiff ones."

Thomson sat patiently in the lounge, staring straight ahead, listening to the rain beating on the ship and cascading down the promenade deck windows. He felt it gently pitch and roll. With the engines running, the heat was on, and it was nice and cozy. Thomson thought it amazing that even in weather like this, airships were smooth and comfortable. He had no qualms about imposing his will on these men.

They just need leadership.

Again his mind went back to the night on the Forth Bridge.

Well, the Tay Bridge came down, but not the mighty Forth. They'd learned by experience—as we did with the crash of R38. We'll sail on to victory through all the storms and torrents the gods can throw at us.

He smiled with satisfaction as Scott came bursting into the lounge. He was able to speak freely, since the passengers were out on the promenade decks, where Disley had dimmed the lighting so they could see lights on the ground.

"I've decided to press on, sir. I'm going to drive her hard. We'll outrun this storm."

"*Bravo,* Scottie! It's times like this when the men are sorted from the boys, momentous decisions are made, and great things are achieved."

"Nothing ventured, nothing gained, sir. That's my motto."

"I shan't forget this. You've shown leadership and courage tonight."

Colmore and Brancker entered the lounge.

"Scott informs me he's decided to push on to London and beyond. We shall ride the storm!" Thomson said, unable to conceal his pleasure.

"Yes, sir," Colmore mumbled.

"What time's dinner? I'm famished," Thomson asked, glancing at Colmore.

Pierre was hovering in the doorway. "We can be ready for you in thirty minutes, gentlemen," he said.

"I think it's time we had some music, don't you?" Thomson said.

20

EVENING WATCH: 16:00–20:00 HOURS (DOG WATCH)

Saturday October 4, 1930.

After Scott's announcement at 8:20 p.m., Thomson went to his cabin to change. Fifteen minutes later, with assistance of his valet, Thomson appeared—pressed and dressed in a new, lightweight, black evening suit made by Anderson & Sheppard. He'd also bought some expensive white shirts and splendid ties. With a blood-red rose in his lapel, tonight he looked fine indeed. He thought back fondly to the afternoon in July when Marthe had dragged him to Savile Row, insisting he had new clothes for the voyage. She'd helped him choose the materials—money he could hardly afford—but he was glad he'd splurged. Marthe would be proud of him tonight.

Thomson headed for the dining room. Buck went to the crew's quarters for bread and cheese. Thomson chatted with passengers on the promenade deck. They stared nervously out into the night, occasionally lit by a half-moon showing itself between squalls and scudding cloud.

Everyone had dressed for dinner. Pierre unlocked the record cabinet and showed the galley boy how to operate the gramophone. When the music came on, Thomson, Brancker and Colmore moved to the lounge for cocktails. Brancker appeared rigid—his way of masking his inebriated state—his monocle immovable, as if screwed into his head. Colmore was showing apprehension, but the alcohol had taken the edge off. Thomson didn't care how much they drank as long as the ship pushed on for India. Some would feel lousy in the morning—that was their prerogative. He anticipated enjoying the view of the Mediterranean with a clear head the following day. How beautiful that was going to be!

The first recording the galley boy put on (no one knew if it was intentional) was "Singing in the Rain", sung by Cliff Edwards. Everybody had a good laugh, which helped ease the tension. Most people sat down around 8:40 p.m., but it wasn't as formal as Thomson would have liked, since some of the officers were tied up with their duties. VIPs and special guests were served by the stewards as they arrived in the dining room—the more senior VIP's (including his 'Top Three'—Colmore, Scott and Richmond) sat at the head table with Thomson. Seating had been designated with white cards embossed with silver lettering, bearing their names at each place setting.

The first course was a tasty oxtail soup with crusty bread rolls, followed by meat cold cuts. Now Miss Helen Kane was giving her all on the gramophone with her smash hit, "I Wanna Be Loved By You."

In the chartroom, Irwin, Johnston and Lou studied the maps while Steff remained on duty below them. The evening watch would be over in half an hour. Potter had taken back the elevator wheel from Atherstone.

"What's the elevation of the ground ahead?" Irwin asked.

They checked the maps. They were coming up on Bendish, a small hamlet on rising ground just east of Luton, west of the A1.

"Four hundred feet above sea level," Johnston answered.

"After that, we've got the South Downs to contend with," Irwin said.

The ship was still dangerously low.

"Bring her up as much as you can, Steff," Irwin shouted over the rail.

"Aye, aye, sir," Steff said and then, "You heard the captain, Potter."

Potter turned the elevator wheel. "She's heavy, sir. She's stayin' right where she is."

"We're going to have to dump ballast and quick, sir," Steff shouted to Irwin.

"Do it! Right now!" Irwin replied.

While Thomson and his fellow passengers were enjoying their first course, Church was keeping an eye on Jessup, who was still on the prowl. Church had checked the duty roster and knew Jessup was scheduled to be on the next watch. The villain was snooping around at the bow for no apparent reason—he had no business there.

Church and the others were very concerned about Lou. While the big shots had been having their conference, a few of the crew were having a conference of their own. They knew Lou was capable of snapping Jessup's neck in a second. Jessup would only get one chance —they reckoned he'd lie in wait and strike from behind. They'd taken turns watching him ever since leaving the tower. The time had come to put their plan into action. Jessup approached amidships toward Church. Church put two fingers in his mouth and gave him one of his own wild whistles from the lower catwalk. "Hey Jessup, I got something for you, me old cock," Church yelled.

Jessup was outraged. He stared down, his hateful eyes narrowed. "Who you whistling at, you little shit? What's that you got there?"

"A letter for you from Charlotte Remington. She sent someone to the ship with it tonight. Must be stuck on you, eh! Who would 'ave thought?"

Everyone knew there'd been a bit of a 'to do' over a girl at the tower earlier, but not the details. Jessup's infatuation with Charlotte was common knowledge.

"Give it 'ere, you little punk," Jessup shouted, rapidly climbing down a ladder.

Church ran off toward the oil storage room, laughing like a crazy man with Jessup in pursuit. Church slipped inside, closing the door behind him. Catching his breath, he leaned against the door, taking in the smell of lubricants and sacking piled in stacks. Jessup pounded with his fists, throwing himself against the door. Church stepped away and Jessup came stumbling in. Clearly, it wasn't what he'd expected. Church stood at the other end of the room waving the envelope in the air, taunting him. Church sang the words.

"Oh, Jess ...up ...come ...and ...get ...it."

Then too late, Jessup spotted the others. With the sounds of "boo hoo beloo" drifting from the dining room above, he realized he'd been set up. He took in the faces of Disley, Binks, and now, closing the door behind him and blocking his escape—Cameron. Jessup turned toward him in time to see the high-speed blur of a lead pipe coming toward his head. The pipe connected with his front teeth with a sickening crunch.

"You won't be smilin' at my wife again, boy," Cameron said.

Jessup spat his teeth on the floor mixed with gobs of blood and phlegm. Cameron hadn't finished. He brought the pipe back, swinging it up into Jessup's groin, crushing his testicles.

"Nor will you be doin' her anymore," Cameron whispered.

Jessup sank to his knees holding his crotch and groaning, his face contorted in agony. His eyes rolled up in his head and he threw up. Cameron reached to his back pocket and pulled out Rosie's letter. Cameron held it up, glaring at Jessup, his eyes murderous.

"*This* is the letter delivered tonight—you destroyed my Rosie. She's really buggered now, and so are you—you piece of shit!"

Cameron unhurriedly and methodically stuck the envelope back in his pocket. He swung the pipe high in the air and brought it smashing down on Jessup's skull. His head exploded. Blood, brain and bone fragments flew in all directions and Jessup went down like a side of beef.

"Dammit Doug, you've gone and killed 'im now!" Binks said incredulously, wiping splatter from his face with his sleeve.

"Yer don't say," Cameron said.

"You weren't supposed to *kill 'im*, were yer," Disley said.

"The plan was to put him out of action—not *this*," Binks said.

"Shit—now what are we going to do?" Church said.

"You've made a right mess of 'is 'ed, look," Binks said, standing over Jessup.

"Drag him over here while we figure this out," Disley said, stepping out of a pool of blood that had soaked one of his canvas shoes. They pulled Jessup across the room and pushed him up against the shelving stacked with cans of oil. They wiped up the blood from the floor with sacking and covered Jessup's torso with it.

"We're gonna have to get rid of 'im," Binks said.

"We'll have to dump him overboard," Church said.

"He might land in someone's back yard," Disley said.

"Or on somebody's roof," Binks said.

"Come *through* somebody's roof, more like," Church said.

"That wouldn't be very nice," Binks said.

Church took a rag and wiped blood from his face, jacket front and sleeve and then his hair, now an unruly mess. He took out his comb, put his foot up on Jessup's chest and began combing his hair back into place, while Jessup's demonic eyes stared vacantly up at him. When he'd finished, he threw a sack over Jessup's face.

"You're such an *ugly* sod!" he muttered.

Moggy Wigglesbottom loved cats, hence her nickname. She sat in her 15th century cottage in the quaint hamlet of Bendish finishing the last of her delicious baked trout. On a chair beside her, a majestic, white Persian, named Queen Isabella, sat watching and licking her lips. Moggy was a contented woman. Her tranquil life had never been better.

Suddenly, to her bewilderment, a bloodcurdling scream emanated from the kitchen. The cook and the maid must surely be under some kind of attack. Without hesitation, Moggy jumped up from her upholstered antique chair, snatched up the white ball of fluff, grabbed the poker from the fireplace and raced to the kitchen. She found both women staring, trance-like, out the garden picture window over the sink. Moggy couldn't believe what she saw.

Coming toward them, up her garden path, was the largest object she had ever seen in her entire life—a monster with flashing red and green eyes and yellow rays spilling from its sides. All she had worked for was about to be erased from the map and she, Queen Isabella, and her staff faced certain death.

"Come on! We can't stay here," Moggy yelled. She dropped the poker and rushed to the back door clutching the cat, the cook and maid close on her heels. All three ran full gallop down the path and leapt over the fence—a remarkably clean effort, worthy of a trio of Olympic hurdlers. They landed together in a heap on the other side in a pile of the gardener's horse manure. The area was suddenly lit like a stage set by an eerie, amber glow and flashing, green lights that made it even more surreal. The once white Persian howled in disgust.

"Oh, bugger!" Moggy exclaimed, surely echoing the Persian's thoughts, while picking manure out of her hair.

The women stared up in horror as His Majesty's Airship *Cardington R101* sailed over their heads. They were mesmerized by the sound of thumping railway engines accompanied by "I Wanna Be Loved By You". More annoying was the sight of men in dinner jackets and bow ties casually moving around the promenade deck as if they were in some swanky hotel bar, oblivious to the plight of Mrs. Wigglesbottom and her staff.

Then came another unwelcome sound—gushing water—two tons of ballast released by Steff. The beleaguered women were saturated by the freezing deluge as it spilled down upon them. They struggled to their feet, shivering.

"Shit and bugger!" shouted Moggy. The maid and the cook were shocked. They'd never heard such profanity fall from the lips of their mistress, church deaconess, Moggy Wigglesbottom.

The airship passed over, just clearing the thatched roof. It did, however, scrape the clay pot from the ancient chimney stack, which crashed onto the driveway on the other side of the cottage and smashed into tiny pieces.

"Damn you!" Moggy screamed at the dirigible's rear end. The twinkling lights, the roaring engines and Helen Kane singing her song faded gently into the night. She took a deep breath, her teeth chattering in the howling wind. It could've been worse. Much worse—they could all be dead and her beloved cottage destroyed. She would get down on her knees tonight and thank God her home had been spared and, after that, she'd write to the Air Ministry. She'd read earlier, with mild excitement about the airship leaving for India—but didn't expect to actually set eyes on it, let alone get close enough to be touched by the diabolical thing!

Dinner jackets indeed!

In the oil storage room, the crewmen were still debating the situation.

"We'll have to dump 'im in the sea," Disley said, at last.

"How long before we're over the Channel?" Church asked.

"I dunno. We'll 'ave to find out," Binks answered.

"It's gotta be a couple of hours," Disley said.

"I'm on watch in ten minutes," Church said.

"So am I," Binks said.

"Me, too," Cameron grunted. Until now, he'd remained mute.

"You gonna be all right to go on duty?" Binks asked.

Cameron didn't answer.

"Yeah, it'll be better if he does," Disley said.

"We'll 'ave to do it after 23:00, when we get off," Church said.

"We could dump 'im from the hatch above No. 5," Binks said.

"We'd have to lower 'im down the ladder on a rope, so he doesn't hit the car or the prop and make another bloody mess," Disley said.

"There's plenty of rope over 'ere, look," Church said.

"We'll have to wait till they've fixed my engine," Binks said.

"Won't they spot us from the control car?" Disley asked.

"They're usually looking where they're goin,' not backwards," Binks said.

"As long as the navigator ain't there, buggering about," Church said.

"We'll have to make sure the coast is clear," Disley said.

"And time it just right," Church said.

"Gettin' 'im to the 'atch without anybody seein' is going to be difficult," Disley said.

"We'll need more help. He's a big bugger," Binks said.

"I'll get Potter. He hates the bastard," Church said.

"They'll hang the lot of us for this, you know," Cameron said.

"Shut the hell up, will yer? No one's gonna find out," Binks said.

"Besides—you were the silly arse what clobbered 'im," Church reminded him.

"What 'appens when they can't find 'im?" Binks asked.

"He's on the next watch. They'll be lookin' for 'im," Church said.

"They'll think he's hiding somewhere," Binks said.

"We can say he must've committed suicide. Jumped out or got blown away," Church said.

"Here, grab this tarpaulin," Disley said.

They pulled out a folded tarpaulin and wrapped Jessup into a bundle, tying it with rope.

"A nice, tidy package," Disley said.

"He's humming a bit," Church said.

"What if people come in 'ere for oil and stuff?" Binks asked.

"Let's hope no one notices," Church said.

"We'll have to keep an eye out," Disley said.

In the control car and the chartroom, the officers had had a few nervous moments approaching Bendish. They'd heard the control car strike Moggy Wigglesbottom's chimney pot. They'd managed to gain altitude, but it was insufficient and too late. Lou realized the captain was worried about dumping more. The ship would get lighter and they could rise too high over the following days as the weight of fuel diminished. Then they'd be forced to valve off gas and not have enough to last the voyage. It was a vicious circle, but in this weather, the ballast tanks were being replenished with rainwater for the moment.

"Make a note, Johnny. We owe somebody a new chimney pot," Irwin said.

"Better than a new house," Lou said.

"We should go in to dinner. His Lordship will be expecting us," Irwin said. Lou, Irwin, Giblett and Atherstone trooped off to the dining room, leaving Johnston and Steff in control.

Dinner was well underway when they arrived. The diners were finishing their first course, oblivious to the near catastrophe just beneath their soft-soled shoes, which they all had to wear. The mood was upbeat and Brancker was relating tales of his world travels and wild affairs, his face flushed with the four glasses of wine added to the whisky, brandy and champagne. Everyone laughed and enjoyed his stories, or appeared to—Lou put it down to nerves. He'd seen all that before.

"…so there we were, stranded on the bloody lake in Jinja with the lady standing on the plane's floats in the most delightful pair of the shortest shorts with the damned crocs and me eyeing those beautiful legs. I think they were thinking about lunch—"

"And you were a tad hungry yourself, I suspect, Sefton, what!" someone said.

"Yes, I was getting hungry all right. Damned hungry!"

The room erupted. Thomson smiled at the four officers who'd just arrived.

"There you are, gentlemen. Is everything under control?" Thomson peered at Irwin, who was trying to suppress a yawn. Atherstone appeared just as tired.

"Yes, sir," Irwin answered.

"Will we be showing ourselves over the West End?" Thomson asked.

"Over the city, actually."

"What a pity."

"If you like, I'll ask Johnston if we can divert course slightly," Irwin replied.

"Would you? That would be such a wonderful gesture. It's Saturday night and the revelers will be out. It would give them such a thrill," Thomson said.

"I'll see what we can do, sir," Irwin said.

Irwin explained they didn't have much time and the stewards rushed off and brought the three late arrivals soup and bread rolls. The officers refused wine for water and tea.

"I wonder, will we be passing over Beauvais?" Brancker asked, looking at Irwin. "Treacherous place!"

⌐ "Ah, Beauvais. I made an unscheduled stop near there last year," Thomson said.

"An emergency, sir?" Richmond asked.

"Yes, the weather was rough and we couldn't get into Paris due to fog."

Thomson related his adventure of landing near Allonne in the dark and being taken to shelter by a funny little rabbit poacher named Rabouille, while they waited for transport to take them to the station.

"So, will we be passing that way, Captain?" Thomson asked.

"The navigator has us maintaining a safe distance from the ridge."

"We must be careful," Thomson said.

"They will be, sir, I'm sure," Scott said.

The officers finished their soup.

"We must go. It's time to change the watch," Irwin said, getting up.

"Yes. I'm on duty," Atherstone said, following Irwin back to the control car. Lou remained behind to finish his coffee. Pierre switched off the gramophone and put the wireless on. The BBC News came on after the sound of Big Ben striking the hour and the familiar signal.

Beep Beep Beep Beep Beep Beeeep.

'*This is the BBC Home Service. Here is the nine o'clock news. This evening, at seven thirty-six, precisely, His Majesty's Airship Cardington R101 left the tower in Bedfordshire to begin the first leg of her maiden voyage to India. The airship will travel across France toward Paris and then down to the Mediterranean and on to Ismailia, where a banquet will be held aboard in honor of King Fuad—the King of Egypt. From Egypt, the airship will fly across the Arabian Desert to Karachi in Northern India. A number of dignitaries are on board for this historic flight, including the Secretary of State for Air, the Honorable Lord Thomson of Cardington, Sir Sefton Brancker, Director of Civil Aviation and Major Herbert Scott, the first man to command an aircraft making its return flight to America. Also on board, are other high-level staff members of the Royal Airship Works along with representatives from Australia, India and the United States. The weather forecast for the first leg of the journey promises a stormy passage, but it will be plain sailing once the airship reaches the Mediterranean tomorrow ...'*

21

FIRST NIGHT WATCH: 20:00–23:00 HOURS

Saturday October 4, 1930.

Atherstone had taken over the watch and was busy writing up the hourly report when Lou returned to the chartroom. Pierre followed him, bearing a plate of roast beef sandwiches. He placed them in front of Johnston at the chart table with a mug of tea. Johnston thanked him and ate ravenously. Leech came and reported that the pressure gauge had been replaced and No. 5 was running smoothly once again.

"What's our position, Johnnie?" Irwin asked. Lou leaned over the map with Irwin. Johnston continued eating. Pierre hung around. He liked to be aware of their position so he could inform Thomson, if asked.

"We've covered thirty-nine miles over the past hour. We're up against a virtual head wind varying between twenty and thirty miles per hour. We're over Hadley Common, approaching Alexandra Palace —after that, we'll be looking for the Cattle Market."

"His Lordship wants to fly over Soho. What do you think?" Irwin asked.

"What's he wanna wave to his old girlfriends?"

"Be nice, Johnny," Irwin chided.

"Okay, since it's his show, we'll continue down to the West End and make a left turn at Big Ben and Westminster Hall, then along the river toward Greenwich," Johnston said.

"Johnny, you really are the best," Lou said.

"Yes, he's lovely," Pierre agreed, before returning to the dining room with Johnston's plate.

"I'm gonna lie down," Irwin said. "Come and get me if you need to."

"Aye, aye, sir," Lou said.

Five minutes later Atherstone called up from the control car. "We're coming up to the Cattle Market, Johnnie."

"All right. Time to change course. Steer 210 degrees. That'll take us over Piccadilly and down to Westminster."

Johnston marked the time down on the chart—9:15 p.m.—as he'd been doing throughout the flight. The rudder coxswain brought the nose round onto the new heading. The ship 'crabbed' against the weather to stay on course. As they closed in on London, Hunt arrived in the chartroom to make a strange announcement.

"Excuse me, gentlemen. We seem to have lost a crewmember. He's supposed to have come on watch, but no one can find him. I had to put someone else in his place."

"Who's gone missing?" Atherstone asked.

"Jessup. No one's seen him, I suppose?"

Everyone shook their heads.

"Wait 'til I find that bugger, I'll kill 'im. He's ruining my kip," Hunt muttered, as he left to resume his search.

Lou was suspicious. Maybe Jessup was lying in wait somewhere.

The whistle on the speaking tube sounded. Atherstone listened, exasperated. "Damn! The bloody oil pressure on No. 5's dropped again."

Lou left the control car to inspect the engine himself. He climbed down the ladder in the atrocious weather and entered the engine car. It was warm and quiet—too quiet. Binks had taken over from Bell and stood glaring at the engine with Leech and another charge hand.

"What's up now?" Lou asked.

"There was nothing wrong with the gauges. We're gonna have to inspect the big end bearing and main bearings. After that, we'll check the relief valve," Leech said.

In cramped conditions, Binks began removing the eight inspection covers. Lou wished them luck and climbed back up the ladder into the ship to give Atherstone an update. After that, he walked the ship from stern to bow, moving around carefully on the catwalks in case Jessup was lurking somewhere. There was no sign of him.

In the dining room, Thomson and his party were finishing their coffees and enjoying brandy and port chasers. Their stimulating conversation covered aviation, war, women and horses. Pierre came and stood beside Thomson.

"Sir, I've been informed we're coming up to the West End, if you and your guests would like to remove to the promenade deck."

Thomson jumped up. "Oh yes, mustn't miss *that!*"

With "Blue Skies" belting out by Al Jolson from the gramophone, everyone followed Thomson's lead. Colmore, Scott, Brancker and Richmond stood with Thomson.

"We'll have blue skies when we get to the Med, sir," Scott said. "That, I can promise you."

"Champion, Scottie!"

They stared from the windows into the bright lights of London, startled to see the roof tops so close. On the glistening streets of Piccadilly, cars were stopping to get a better look. People peeped at them from under umbrellas in swirling rain. Hundreds sheltered in doorways gazing upward while the airship pushed on relentlessly. Thomson caught sight of His Majesty's Theater. He knew *Bitter Sweet* was still playing. He couldn't read the billboards, but he knew what they said. Marthe had so enjoyed that musical. He'd been by the theater many times and read them since—treading the precious ground she'd walked on. Sadness seized him. He smiled wistfully—such fond memories, and yes, they were indeed bitter sweet! What was she doing at this moment?

Those Romanians like to stay up half the night!

He glanced at his watch: it was 9:22 p.m. They were two hours ahead in Bucharest. He knew she'd now be back at Mogosoëa. He doubted she'd be in bed yet—she may be entertaining. So many admirers! The thought depressed him, but he fought it off as he usually did. At times like this he thanked God she wasn't the over-sexed siren they made her out to be.

Maybe she's writing—who knows, perhaps to me.

Over Trafalgar Square, Thomson peeked out at the wet lions guarding the fountains. And then at his idol, Lord Nelson, standing high on his column, looking in their windows.

Oh, that I would someday be as revered as thee!

A red double-decker stopped below for the passengers to get a good look. The conductor stared up from its exterior, curved staircase. He was, no doubt, excitedly announcing that *Cardington R101* was overhead on her maiden voyage to India!

How rapidly the world is changing! Thank God I can play my part.

The ship traveled down Whitehall toward the luminous, white faces of Big Ben standing mute next to Westminster Hall, his most favorite Gothic room in all of England!

Just before 9:30 p.m., Lou and Giblett composed a message to Cardington using the ship's call sign.

CROW: 20:21. GMT. Crossing London. All is well. Rain moderate, heavy at times. Low cloud. Base ceiling 1500 feet. Winds 25 mph at 240 degrees.   On course for Paris via Tours, Toulouse and Narbonne.

Lou showed the message to Atherstone. After taking it to Disley for transmission, he rejoined Atherstone in the control car where Johnston was giving Atherstone the new course for Greenwich. Lou winked at Cameron, but he didn't respond.

Poor guy's still upset about Rosie.

Lou figured Cameron had read Rosie's letter. The envelope was sticking out of his back pocket, its flap ripped open, its edges stained with blood. Lou was puzzled.

Must have cut himself.

The time had come to gain altitude. The ship turned over Westminster Hall and flew east toward Greenwich, along the river. They passed over Greenwich Observatory and the Royal Naval College, then Greenwich Park, where they turned onto a heading of one hundred and ninety-five degrees, toward Blackheath Park Station. Atherstone ordered Lou to dump a ton of ballast from Frame 6. They'd replenished plenty from the rain now. The ship became lighter as they burned fuel. They dropped another ton and Cameron brought the ship up, keeping an eye on the altimeter. They were soon up to twelve hundred feet. The North Downs, Johnston told them, would rise to eight hundred feet. Their concentration was high and intensifying—there'd be no room for error.

Twenty minutes after leaving Greenwich, they thundered on toward Eltham and Crockenhill. Over Lullingstone Park, Johnston had them turn the ship through forty-eight degrees to starboard and from here they traveled along the Darent Valley through the Downs. Lou marveled at Johnston's navigational skill as they wove their way between the Kentish hills—especially in such foul weather with little or no visibility.

Lou returned to the chartroom, where Disley came in with a message. Giblett read it and laid it down silently in front of Lou and Johnston. They leaned over reading the contents together with growing alarm.

To: CROW. From: Met Office, Cardington.

A trough a low pressure along coasts of British Isles is moving east. Ridge of high pressure over southern France forecast for next 12 hours. SE England, Channel and Northern France Wind at 2000 feet will be from 240 degrees at 40 to 50 mph. Low cloud with rain.

Johnston scowled. "I wish we'd known this three hours ago."

"These winds will be double what we were told," Giblett said.

"What's going on up there?" Atherstone called up.

"They're now telling us the winds are going up to fifty miles per hour," Johnston replied. Fear showed in the coxswains' faces.

Atherstone winced. "You'd better inform the captain," he said

Lou went to the captain's cabin adjacent to the chartroom and called from behind the black curtain at his door.

"Come in, Lou. What's up?"

Lou pulled back the curtain. Irwin was lying on his back, wide awake.

"A weather report just came in, sir."

"I presume it's bad news."

"The winds are expected to kick up to fifty miles an hour."

Irwin swung his feet down off the bed and sat up. He rested his head in his hands, rubbing his eyes and sighed. "This is turning into a full-fledged gale," he said. Lou knew he must be thinking about Olivia. "There's not much we can do—we're stuck."

"'Fraid so, sir."

Lou returned to the chartroom where they were still engaged in negotiating their way across the Weald through the Downs. He went back down to assist Atherstone in the control car. As soon as they reached Sevenoaks, they made a right-angled turn to fly due east, passing Kemsing on port. The ship was turned again to pass through another gap between Borough Green and Ightham and then onto a southerly track for Tonbridge.

Atherstone turned to Lou. "D'you mind checking No. 5 again, Lou?"

"Not at all. I *love* it out there."

Lou put on his topcoat and disappeared along the gangplank toward the problem engine. He climbed down the cat ladder. It felt like the winds had increased a lot. Inside the car, Binks had removed the inspection covers. Leech was examining the big end bearings and main bearings. Lou waited for Leech to speak.

"Can't tell you anything yet, sir," Leech said. "Might know something in another hour."

"I'll come back later," Lou said.

Back in the control car, Lou attempted to see through the rain.

"Where are we now, sir?" he asked Atherstone.

"We're passing Tonbridge on starboard."

Lou looked across at the lights, but ascertained little in the blinding rain. He checked the altimeter. They'd dropped to eleven hundred feet. Atherstone spotted it, too.

"Cameron, bring her back up to twelve hundred. *Concentrate!*" he snapped.

Lou stayed in the control car on watch, while Atherstone took a break. When Atherstone returned, Lou checked with everyone and then went to rest in his own cabin. He'd be back and forth as relief watch and navigator for most of the night. Irwin remained in his cabin and as Lou passed by, he noticed light under the door curtain. He worried about the captain. He thought he heard a sob.

Lou lay down with a light on over the night table. He'd dreaded this. It reminded him of the Canadian voyage. He'd been so euphoric then. All those times while he'd lain in his bunk thinking of her and making plans, she'd been cleaning up and getting the hell out—but God, how he still loved her. The agony of being separated was too much to bear—especially tonight. He wondered what she was doing— if she'd listened to the 9 o'clock news. Maybe she's out with someone else—perhaps this Robert guy. The thought was intolerable. He felt like a failure—he'd not measured up.

Maybe she's got someone who can give her what she craves. A kid.

He glanced at the time: it was 10:20 p.m. They'd soon be coming up to Bodiam Castle. He could faintly hear the sound of the gramophone above. "Sittin' on Top of the World" was playing.

That's a laugh! She could be right, though. Perhaps this is the end. No—the thunderstorm over Montreal was worse. We survived that. I'll take John's advice and try to see her again when we get back—if we get back!

He glanced at the picture frame on the bedside table—the family, Julia, Jeb and Alice. Somehow, at this moment, the frame had more significance than the photo. Even the sight of it caused him pain. Why the hell had he used the same frame? He studied his father, trying his best to smile. He wondered how he was doing. What was it, six weeks since he'd seen him? Did he look worse? Many of Lou's boyhood days with his father had been rancorous, but they'd gotten closer that last day than during his entire life. Lou switched off the light and lay back.

The darkness accentuated the movement and sounds of the swishing, buffeting wind and rain. It sounded like the ship was being peppered with shards of glass. The engines were noisy, too—more intrusive than *Howden R100's*.

Ol' Nev and Wallis would love to hear that!

He missed Nevil and Billy being around. But at least Potter, Binks, Church, and Dizzy were on board. His mind wandered to Mrs. Hinchliffe. Perhaps he should have taken her up on her offer!

She's a beautiful woman.

He thought about Julia. He wondered if it was time to start taking an interest in other women. He didn't feel ready for that. His mind changed the subject. He thought about the American airships and the interest expressed in him in Washington. Perhaps he should retire from this crazy life and help his family make moonshine and grow carrots and corn—and keep the Klan at bay!

That'd be more sensible and probably a lot safer!

Lou missed Virginia. He lay there, finding it impossible to relax. Then the gypsy's words began tormenting him.

She had things she could not share ...Another victim of war.

After all her deceit, he figured cheating would have come easy. After half an hour, he got up and went back to the chartroom.

While Lou had been trying to rest, Thomson and his group were sitting comfortably in the lounge, most of them well oiled and quite numb. Pierre approached Thomson again.

"Sir, we're coming up to Bodiam Castle. They tell me we'll be crossing the English coastline in a just few minutes."

"Come on, Sefton—time to say goodbye to Dear Old Blighty," Thomson said, getting up from his floral-cushioned, wicker armchair. Everyone got to their feet. Thomson's choice of words upset Colmore and Thomson wished he'd been more careful.

The airship passed over Bodiam but they couldn't see much, save a light shining from a crofter's cottage. They flew over Ewhurst Green, crossed the River Brede, over Guestling Green and then the village of Pett. Everyone gathered at the windows on the promenade decks.

When they reached the coast, they passed over the *Olde Cliff End Inn*, its illuminated sign on the gable plainly visible. Outside, braving the weather, revelers stood wrapped in raincoats by their cars, under umbrellas—those that hadn't been blown inside out. Some waved mugs of beer up at them, to wish them luck. Now, "Blue Skies" was being repeated from the lounge and dining room speakers. Thomson hoped the inn patrons could hear it.

Our crabbing attitude must appear awfully strange.

The ship swept out over the raging sea at a weird angle, still minus an engine, its colored navigation lights reflecting intermittently on the turbulent water. The sound of music gradually faded. Soon, the throbbing engines were gone, the glints of red and green swallowed by the darkness. Now, only the pounding surf on the rocks and the vicious wind in the swaying poplars could be heard by the pub crowd at the cliff edge.

Thomson, surrounded by his entourage, stared back at England's receding lights, Hastings and Bexhill on starboard, Rye and the Dungeness Lighthouse on port. Colmore couldn't hide his gloom. "Perhaps the air will be smoother over the water," he mumbled, almost to himself.

"Don't you worry, Colmore, it'll all be here when we get back— and we'll get a rousing reception, the likes of which you couldn't possibly imagine!" Thomson reassured him. "Gentlemen, I think the time has come for a fine Cuban cigar to round off this very special occasion."

The thought of that only increased Colmore's depression.

"Good idea, sir," Scott said.

"*Rather,* CB," said Brancker.

A party of six, including O'Neill, the Indian representative, went with Thomson to the smoking room, led by the reluctant chief steward. Richmond and Rope excused themselves, needing to make another inspection. Colmore went back to the lounge with the Australian and a couple of R.A.W. officials for tea. Thomson shook his head.

That's what some British do to make themselves feel better—while the rest get drunk!

In the smoking room, everyone settled down in easy chairs around the perimeter. Brancker took off his dinner jacket and sat next to Thomson on the long couch against the wall. Pierre served yet more port and brandy in fine crystal glasses to everyone, except Thomson, who requested coffee. Once they had drinks, Pierre came round with the box of cigars, cutting the caps off and assisting with the lighter chained to the trolley. Soon, the room was filled with smoke, causing Pierre to cough and his eyes to stream as before.

The ship ploughed on toward mid-Channel and Johnston came down into the control car followed by Lou, who carried a box of flares. Johnston, his clipboard under his arm, also carried his sighting instrument. Lou put the flares on the sill and Johnston opened the window, causing a blast of cold air to rush in.

"Sorry, gentlemen," Johnston shouted above the howling—not sorry in the slightest.

"That's okay, these boys need waking up," Atherstone said, eyeing Cameron.

Lou threw the flares down into the thrashing sea at fifteen-second intervals, where they burst into flames on contact. Soon, a line of bobbing flames lay behind them, visible intermittently.

"Look at the angle we're flying at. *Bloody ridiculous!*" Johnston exclaimed.

"She's taking a beating all right," Lou said.

Johnston took his sightings, noted them on his clipboard, then closed the window.

"Are you done, Johnnie?" Atherstone asked.

"Yes, sir."

"Check how they're doing with No. 5, Lou. We need that engine," Atherstone said.

"Aye, aye, sir," Lou said.

Lou left the flares on the windowsill. He and Johnston went back upstairs. As Lou was putting his coat on, he glanced down at the altimeter. It'd dropped to nine hundred feet. Atherstone had also noticed.

"Wake up, Cameron! What the hell's wrong with you? You need some more cold air!" He took the wheel and brought the ship up to a thousand feet. "Keep her right here."

"Yes, sir, I'm sorry." Cameron looked more miserable than Lou had ever seen him, unaware he'd just committed cold blooded murder.

That boy shouldn't be on the wheel tonight.

Lou left the control car and went down the catwalk to engine No. 5, keeping an eye out for Jessup. Rope was still making inspections. They both nodded without smiling. Lou pulled back the flap to the cat ladder. The wind lashed his face and head. He clung on and climbed down. Inside the car, they were wrapping things up. Leech gave Lou a half smile, confident now. He leaned down and peered out the window.

"Blimey, look at them whitecaps. Who the bloody hell's on the elevators?"

"It's a bitch of a night, Harry," Lou said. "You guys done?"

Binks screwed the last of the inspection plates back on.

Leech answered, "Should be all right now. I'm going up to the oil storeroom. As soon we dump in some more oil, we'll crank her up and find out."

Binks jumped up. "Stay where you are, Mr. Leech. *I'll* get the oil," he said.

"That's damned good of you, Joe," Leech said. "I'll wait here."

Binks went out and up the ladder like a squirrel up a tree. Lou's eyes followed him.

"He's a damned good fella. So willin'," said Leech.

Lou nodded, wondering what Binks was up to and where the blood on his collar and sleeve had come from. A few minutes later, a shaken-looking Binks was back with drums of oil in a sack tied on his back. Leech poured oil into the engine. Binks got the starter engine going and cranked up the Tornado. After a few moments, the engine was running sweetly with its familiar, deafening rumble, the oil pressure perfect. Leech gave Lou and Binks the thumbs up.

"I'm going up for me cocoa," he shouted.

"Wish I could come," Binks said.

Lou checked his watch: 11:45 p.m. "You've only got fifteen minutes, Joe."

Leech and Lou climbed back up into the ship.

22

MIDDLE WATCH: 23:00–02:00 HOURS

Saturday October 4, 1930.

Lou got back to the chartroom at ten minutes to midnight. Irwin had arrived to take over the watch with two fresh coxswains, who'd already taken over the wheels. Cameron and the rudder coxswain hung around while they got the feel of the ship. Irwin looked positively ill. The voyage had hardly begun. Exhaustion was already taking its toll.

"Okay, time for cocoa and then a kip," Atherstone said.

"I hope *you* can sleep," Irwin said.

"I've just requested bearings from Le Bourget and Valciennes," Johnston told them. "As soon as I have them, we'll reset the course and I'll take a nap myself."

At 23:00, Cameron glanced at his relief coxswain who nodded to him.

"Okay, I've got it, Doug," he said. Cameron scuttled off. Lou thought everyone seemed too damned jumpy this evening.

At midnight, a wireless operator popped into the smoking room. The smoke-laden air and cigar odor was overpowering. "Gentlemen, would anyone like to send a message to friends or loved ones?" he asked, trying not to sneeze. He held up a notepad and pencil. Thomson was profoundly pleased.

This will delight Marthe. Why not, I'll send her another one.

He took the pad and pencil and wrote in his bold scrawl.

M Bibesco Mogosoëa Palace, Romania

Dearest M We are making good progress STOP Now over the English Channel en route to Paris STOP Thinking of you as always K

Brancker was next to take the pencil. He leaned close to Thomson.

"I must drop a line to my dearest love, Auriol Lee in New York. She's producing a play on Broadway, you know," he whispered.

Thomson gave him a funny look while Brancker scribbled a few lines. When he'd finished, O'Neill wrote a note to his wife. The wireless operator took the messages and hurried out.

Church was tense. He'd waited five long minutes for the others, who slipped in one by one—Cameron, Binks, Disley and then Potter who'd joined the party.

"About bloody time!" Church growled.

"Keep yer wool on," Binks said. "I came in 'ere twenty minutes ago for some oil an' there's two bleedin' riggers sitting on Jessup's carcass drinking beer." Everyone gasped. "I told 'em the foreman was comin' and they scarpered, right quick."

"Best get moving. We've only got twenty minutes. We're near the French coast," Disley warned.

"We gotta be careful. Where is everyone?" Church asked.

"No. 5's fixed now—Mr. Leech is out of the way," Binks said.

"Where is he now?" Church asked. "He's always making the rounds."

"He's 'avin' his supper in the mess," Disley answered. "Where's the navigator? Has he finished with the flares, Doug?"

"Yes, he left the control car," Cameron mumbled.

"What about the chief?" Church asked.

"Sky Hunt's asleep in his bunk," Potter said.

"What about them two officers with the R.A.W.?" Binks asked.

"They're up in the tail, climbing around," Church said.

"Let's hope they stay out the way. Sammy, make sure the coast's clear. We'll get him ready," Disley said.

Church went to the door and switched off the light before opening it. After poking his head out, he moved stealthily along the catwalk and then amidships to the hatchway at No. 5. No one was around. He scampered back to the storage room and slipped back inside.

"Come on—it's all clear," he whispered.

They'd pulled Jessup into the center of the room, nicely wrapped, and tied ropes to his ankles, which were sticking out the bottom. The corpse was lifted among them and they carried it along the catwalk, Church holding the feet. Up ahead, Church spotted Richmond, approaching.

"Whoa! Watch it. Someone's comin'," he hissed.

"Quick, under here," Disley said, gesturing to an area off the catwalk. They laid the body down and threw a sack over Jessup's feet. They stood in front of the bundle until Richmond arrived.

"Evenin', sir," Church said, giving Richmond a sweet smile.

"Evenin', sir," the others said together.

Richmond was pleasantly surprised by so much respect. "Good evening, gentlemen," he said. "What are you fellows up to?"

"Just stretching our legs, sir, and saying what a wonderful airship this is," Binks said.

Richmond smiled. "And what's in the bundle?" he said, eyeing the tarpaulin behind them.

"We wrapped Lord Thomson's carpet and brought it up here from the bow to distribute the weight better, sir," Church answered.

"Excellent! I must confess that did concern me. Well done!" Richmond spotted drips of blood. "What's that trail of red liquid along the catwalk and down here?"

"Oh, that's just dope. Someone spilled some, sir. Horrible stuff," Binks said. "Don't worry, we'll clean it up."

"Dope, right. Ah, well, I'm off to the promenade deck to take a peek at the coast of France. Keep up the good work, chaps," Richmond said, walking off.

"Come on, we'd better hurry," Church said.

Around 12:15 a.m., one of the stewards reported the sighting of the French coast. Thomson waited while Pierre put out the last cigar in a pail of water, switched off the lights and shut the doors. Thomson followed them to the promenade deck. Some were in a bad state. Brancker, his jacket over his arm, was having difficulty negotiating the corridor. When they reached the promenade deck, they joined Colmore and the Australian at the window. Brancker collapsed into an armchair. Up ahead, the lights of France beckoned in the darkness.

"Gentlemen, the lights you are seeing ahead are on Point de Saint Quentin," Scott announced proudly.

"Bravo," someone said.

As soon as Richmond had disappeared, the five crewmen resumed their unpleasant task. They grabbed Jessup in his tarpaulin shroud and marched rapidly to the flap over engine No. 5. Church shimmied down the ladder to warn Bell and make sure the coast was clear. He checked the control car. Irwin and the coxswains were facing forward.

Church returned and they got themselves in position. Jessup's body was lowered head first down the cat ladder, while Cameron, Disley and Binks held the ropes tied to his ankles. Awkward to the last, Jessup became snagged between the engine car and the ladder and Church had to go down and push him out until he was clear. Soon Jessup was dangling free in space below the engine car. Church came back up the ladder.

"Okay, let him go," he whispered.

"Anyone gonna say a prayer for him?" Binks whispered.

"You're jokin', right?" Church asked.

"Yeah, I'll say a prayer for him, all right," Cameron said.

They unraveled the ropes from their wrists and let go. The bundle and rope was gone in a flash. They heard nothing but howling wind.

"Go straight to hell, you worthless sack o' shit!" Cameron shouted down the ladder.

"*Amen!*" Binks echoed.

At 12:20 a.m., the wireless operator handed a message to Johnston in response to his request to Le Bourget and Valciennes for bearings to fix their position. Lou and Johnston referred to the chart, calculating an adjustment to the course. Johnston drew a new line.

"We need to steer two hundred degrees. This'll bring us nine miles southwest of Abbeville and four miles west of Beauvais," Johnston said. He wrote the heading down and gave it to Irwin.

Scott entered the chartroom a little unsteadily. "Commander, do you mind coming with me? I need your assistance." Lou followed Scott past the dining room, now laid for breakfast, to the lounge.

"Have a seat. We must write a communication to Cardington," Scott said. He had some *Cardington R101* stationery on the table. Lou sat down.

Scott held out a pencil. "Here, your writing's better than mine."

"Okay, sir. What would you like to say?"

Scott sat thinking.

The passengers were still gathered on the promenade deck with Thomson, Colmore at his side with Richmond. Brancker remained slumped in his chair.

"Well, gentlemen," Thomson said, "having seen the welcome sight of France, I must now bid you all a *very* good night!"

Amid a flurry of 'good nights' and brimming with satisfaction, he drew himself up to his full six foot five inches and marched away—every inch a brigadier general. Tonight, he'd accomplished something great—this would go down in the history books. Thomson entered his cabin. He took out the red keyring from his pocket and put it on his desk. He then changed into his pajamas and put on his silk dressing gown. Before sitting down to write his journal, he picked up the keyring to examine it closely. Satisfied, he slipped it into his dressing gown pocket and began to write.

Saturday October 4th, 1930.

A successful day. Airship standing up to gale admirably. Having crossed the Channel, we are now heading toward Paris. Tomorrow, I anticipate enjoying sunshine over the Mediterranean. Today, we have put an end to the naysayers.

When Thomson had gone, Colmore appeared at Lou's table in the lounge, Pierre at his side. "Lou, please give Sir Sefton some assistance. He's a little bit under the weather," Colmore said, squinting as if to say, 'Let's not make a fuss.'

Lou went to Brancker and held out his hand. Brancker took it and Lou pulled him to his feet. "Can't seem to get my legs going, old man," Brancker mumbled.

Lou put an arm around Brancker's back and under his arm. "Quite all right, sir," Lou said. They walked crablike down the corridor, joined at the hip, with Pierre leading the way, holding Brancker's jacket.

"It's awfully good of you, Lou," Brancker said.

Pierre pulled back the curtain to Brancker's cabin and Lou manhandled him to the bunk and gently laid him down. Lou pulled off Brancker's shoes and stood over him. Colmore remained at the doorway. Brancker tugged at his tie and collar, revealing a St. Christopher on a silver chain. He pulled it over his head and held it out to Lou, smiling happily.

"See that? Belongs to Lady Cathcart. Took it off and gave it to me, she did. *Insisted* I wear it. Sweet gal—said it'd keep me safe."

"I'm sure it will, sir."

"Wants me to give it back to her when we get back," he said with a devilish grin.

"I expect she's making sure she sees you again soon, sir," Lou said.

Brancker grinned at that. He wanted to confide more, but speech was difficult and his eyelids were beginning to flutter. Lou was sure he wouldn't remember any of this in the morning. Brancker revived for a moment.

"Lady Cathcart is a close friend of Lord T's lady love—Princess Marthe, you know."

"Interesting, sir," Lou said.

"But you know *Auriol* is the one I love the most. Oh, how I miss my Auriol. She understands me …I'm not *perfect* you know …"

"That's nice, sir."

What came next stunned Lou. It was as if Brancker was merely continuing their earlier conversation and he'd just decided to answer Lou's question. "Yes, as I was saying, I had my fortune told once. The woman said she couldn't see a damned thing in my palm after 1930 …Precious little time left now, what!"

Brancker faded out and was sound asleep, snoring gently. He clasped the St. Christopher to his chest. Lou carefully removed his monocle and laid it on the side table.

Pierre hung Brancker's jacket in the closet. "You're such a good man, sir," he whispered. He took a blanket from the closet and covered Brancker with it. "I must be off to bed myself," he said with an impish smile. Lou came out into the corridor where Colmore shook his hand.

"That's why I switched to tea; otherwise you'd have been putting us *both* to bed," Colmore said.

"Maybe *I* should have 'one too many'," Pierre said playfully.

Lou ignored this and bade Colmore goodnight. He smiled at Pierre and returned to the lounge, where he found Scott waiting, brandy glass in hand and a bottle of cognac on the table.

"I think I've got it now," he said.

While Lou wrote, Scott spoke slowly—having difficulty getting his tongue around some words. "After a lovely dinner—"

"How about ...after a splendid supper?" Lou suggested.

"Yes, that sounds nice ...our important guests—"

"Our distinguished passengers?"

"Okay ...smoked another cigar—"

"How about ...smoked a *final* cigar?"

"Yes, that's good ...and having reached France—"

"What about ...having sighted the coast of France?"

"Right ...have gone to bed to rest—"

"Okay, sir."

"...after all the stress of saying goodbyes to their—"

"How about this ...after the excitement of their leave-taking?" Lou suggested.

"Right. And then ...all essential services are functioning," Scott said.

"You could say ...all essential services of the airship are functioning normally and the crew has settled down to their normal watch-keeping routine?"

"Yes, right, that's very good." Scott glanced at the time. "Show it to Captain Irwin and send it to Cardington. Everyone'll read it in the Sunday papers tomorrow. I'm off to bed." Scott yawned.

"Good night, sir," Lou said.

Lou showed the message to Irwin and then took it to the wireless room, where the radio operator was trying to decipher the messages

Brancker and O'Neill had scribbled earlier. Lou studied them and dictated what he thought they said.

Miss Auriol Lee Manhattan Hotel New York NY

Darling Auriol On board R101 to Paris Egypt and India STOP Just thinking of us in Jinja STOP Told my traveling companions about you STOP Love always Your Sefton

O'Neill's was easy:

Mrs O'Neill West London Hospital Hammersmith London

Wishing you the best for a speedy recovery STOP Cardington R101 progressing well STOP Love W O'N

Lou went to Irwin in the control car. "How are things now, sir?"

"She's at least three tons heavy."

"Should we dump ballast?"

"Running with the engines at full bore, she's developing enough dynamic lift like a plane, so it doesn't matter right now—unless we ease off."

Lou checked the altimeter. They were maintaining 1500 feet without too much problem. Outside, they were enveloped in darkness, no lights or landmarks to use for navigation. He hoped they were on course.

"Sir, something weird's happened," Lou said.

"What?"

"One of the crewmen disappeared earlier," Lou said.

"Disappeared? Who?"

"Jessup."

"Hmm. Must be on board somewhere," Irwin said.

"He was missing for his watch at eight o'clock. No one's seen him."

"Did you check the engine cars?"

"I'll ask Leech. He's been in and out of the cars all night."

Later, a groggy Johnston returned from his cabin. He went down to the control car and stared out. He spotted a landmark in the distance. He told Lou he was familiar with the area.

"This is Poix. We've been blown *way* off course again, damn it!"

Johnston returned to the chartroom and worked out a new course to make the correction. After a few minutes, he went back to Irwin and handed him the bearing.

"Here, you need to steer two hundred and ten degrees toward Orly," he said.

The coxswain reset their course.

In his humble cottage outside Allonne, in the gloomy half-light, Monsieur Eugène Rabouille, the button maker, sat huddled by the fireplace in a threadbare armchair. He smoked a rolled cigarette and stared into the dying embers of his log fire, listening to the din.

"God, I hate this weather," he muttered.

Violent gusts roared down the chimney, pummeling the tiny windows, making them whine and rattle and tree branches to scratch at them like ghosts' fingernails—a sound that had terrified him as a child living there with his mother. And it terrified him still. Adding to his misery, a violent clap of thunder shook the cottage and the tiny room was lit by lightning.

Lightning or not, he had no choice. There was work to be done, bellies to be filled. Rabouille wearily pulled himself up and donned his scruffy brown overcoat and flat cap. He picked up his sack of paraphernalia. The metal parts inside rattled as he threw it over his shoulder. He blew out the lamp and opened the front door. The wind blew the door open with such force it smashed against the stone wall, almost tearing it off its hinges. He had difficulty pulling it shut behind him. He trudged up the road and across the field toward Therain Wood. Oh, God, how he hated the struggle.

Rabbits by night and buttons by day—that's my miserable life!

Lou gingerly opened the smoking room door and closed it tightly behind him. He opened the second door and peered inside. The odor of stale cigars and brandy filled the air. Leech was lying on the couch previously occupied by Thomson, smoking a cigarette. Lou closed the door.

"Still wearing the wife's lucky heather, I see, Harry," Lou said.

Leech glanced down at his lapel. He'd obviously forgotten about it.

"I thought I was gonna get blown away once or twice, tonight—it must be powerful stuff!"

"Taking a break?" Lou asked.

"Yep, a fag before bed, sir," Leech said, taking a long drag.

He swung his feet off the couch, sat up and killed the dog-end in the ashtray. He picked up his glass from the floor beside him and took a sip.

"You having one, sir? I'm having a whisky and soda."

"You deserve it. No, I'll fall asleep. Seen anything of Jessup?"

"No. I expect that sod's hiding somewhere."

"He's not in one of the engine cars?"

"Definitely not. I would've seen him. I've been in all of them four times tonight."

"He'll turn up when he gets hungry. I'll say goodnight. Great job tonight, Harry."

"Thank you, sir."

Lou returned to the control car.

It was a beautiful day. The sun streamed in through the café windows. Thomson sat at his usual table, engrossed, watching the girl in the carriage. He couldn't see her face—her wide-brimmed hat obscured part of it and its shadow hid the rest. But somehow, he was able to imagine it, as though he knew her and had seen her beautiful face many times before—though perhaps not in this lifetime.

He hesitated, knowing if he rushed outside that damned coachman would snap the reins and she'd be gone. He studied the girl's slender, white neck and dark brown, almost black hair with tinges of red, tumbling around her shoulders. He caught a glance of her magnificent profile as she turned toward the shop next to the café. She was waiting for someone.

A short, dumpy, Slavic woman wearing a drab, brown headscarf came into view. She marched to the carriage carrying a large package tied with pink ribbon. She opened the door and clambered in. Thomson leapt to his feet, charged outside and sprang to the curb. The coachman leered down at him from his lofty seat with that sickening, cocky smile of his. The maidservant's back was to Thomson—she sat facing the girl. The coachman snapped the reins and called to the two beautiful, white beasts with long flowing manes.

'*En avant! Walk on!*'

The carriage moved toward Thomson in slow motion. He desperately wanted to take in the features of this girl—to know her, make sure that beautiful face was etched in his mind forever. As she drew closer, she looked directly at him. She'd never done that before. Her eyes lit up and she gave him the smile of an angel, moving her head as she passed, so they shared each other's gaze—a moment of pure love. It was *her*! No doubt about it. She could be no more than fourteen years old and so beautiful he was overcome. He cried out her name.

"*Marthe!*"

She lifted her white-gloved hand to her lips and blew him a gentle kiss as she passed, still smiling. He noticed her drop her eyes to his neck for a moment, taking in the insignia on his collar—the flames of the Royal Engineers.

The carriage gathered speed and she turned her head back toward him, not removing her eyes from his. The carriage turned the corner and she was gone. Thomson turned back and stared at the cloistered shop and read the words over the door from which the maidservant had come. He was devastated!

MADAME DUPREE
Haute Couture Bridal Gowns.

23

MORNING WATCH: 02:00-05:00 HOURS

Sunday October 5, 1930.

Head down, Rabouille pressed on across the sopping field toward Therain Wood, pulling his soaking overcoat around him. "It doesn't get worse than Beauvais Ridge," he grumbled, his words swallowed by the beastly wind and driving rain.

He became conscious of a distant droning behind him. He turned. A mile away, the dirigible glistened in the intermittent moonlight and lightning flashes. The sinister sight made him shudder. He stopped, open-mouthed, for a few moments, staring in astonishment. Even far off over the city, the horrible thing appeared enormous. The ship was struggling to make headway. He caught its green navigation light between fast moving clouds. Thunder rolled across the angry skies all around him. Rabouille turned and continued his tramp toward the woods, where he hoped it'd be less miserable, sheltered among the trees. He cursed as he moved through a bleating flock of terrified sheep suddenly lit up like day, bells tinkling and clanking around their necks.

Lou and Irwin stood side by side, staring at the beautiful city, which, under normal circumstances, they would have appreciated—but not this terrible night. The magnificent Cathedral of St. Peter of Beauvais with its tall, flying buttresses rose before them, glistening between lightning flashes. Too close for comfort! Lou checked the altimeter: twelve hundred feet. They had just adequate clearance over the rising ground. The winds increased the closer they got to Beauvais Ridge. He glanced at Irwin, who was shaking his head, not believing they'd arrived in *this* of all places! The town hall clock was striking two. It was time to change the watch. Steff and Hunt came down into the control car with two fresh coxswains, one of them, Potter.

"We're approaching the ridge," Irwin said. "You can take over once we're clear of this damned place. Hopefully, the wind's gonna die down once we get by." But for now, it was growing more violent by the minute. The four newcomers peered out of the windows over the city with concern.

"Okay, sir," Steff said. "I'll do the hourly report. Let me know when you're ready for me." He took the log and went upstairs to the chartroom. Hunt stayed in the control car and the fresh coxswains took over.

Binks was snoring in his bunk when he was awakened by his foreman.

"Come on, Joe, wake up! You should've been on watch by now. Bell's waiting for you." Binks sprang up and sat on the edge of his bed.

"Oh, bugger!" he exclaimed.

The foreman thrust a cup of cocoa at him. "Here, take this."

"I don't have time for that, Shorty. Bell's gonna be mad."

"You'd better drink it, mate, or *I'll* be mad!"

Binks swilled the cocoa down, nodded his appreciation and took off along the catwalk. He collided with Richmond, on his way to the bow to do another inspection. Apologizing over his shoulder, Binks ran to the hatchway and slid down the ladder. He clung on to prevent being blown away like a leaf, stunned to see the ground so close. He slipped into the engine car. Bell gave him a nasty look, eyeing the engine car clock, which said 02:03 a.m.

"I'm really sorry, mate," Binks shouted.

Bell shook his head in disgust. Then something caught Binks's eye out the tiny window.

"Oh, my God!"

"What?"

"I just saw a church steeple in the lightning—just *yards* away."

Bell pushed Binks out of his way and peeked out into the darkness. He saw nothing.

"You silly sod, you're still asleep!"

Just inside the tree line of Therain Wood, Rabouille was checking his snares. He came upon a trap with a creature caught in its jaws, its leg broken. He released the dripping animal and held it up roughly by the scruff of the neck. The sky lit up again. The rabbit shivered with fright.

"You'll do for dinner," Rabouille muttered.

His attention was taken from the rabbit by that infernal droning noise again—louder this time. He looked up in shock, believing *he'd* now become the hunted one. The airship was coming straight at him at about five hundred feet. The covering material at the front was torn and flapping wildly. Vicious winds were rushing inside the hideous contraption.

The shrill speaking tube whistle sounded in the control car. Irwin grabbed it and listened; his eyes widened in horror and the blood drained from his face. He shot a glance at Lou and winced, mouthing, "Oh, my God!"

Lou sensed his panic. Something catastrophic must have happened. Irwin listened a few more moments and then began yelling.

"We have an emergency! Richmond says the cover at the bow's torn and the first gasbag's getting destroyed and more are gonna be. Sky, go and see what's going on. Take some riggers with you. Try and close it up. We'd better get prepared for a crash landing—just in case. Be ready to warn all hands." Hunt dashed up the steps toward the crew's quarters and Steff came down into the control car. Irwin shouted, "We've got to try and save the rest of the gasbags. Lou, dump emergency ballast at Frame 2 and Frame 6. Steff, be ready to dump fuel."

"Aye, aye, sir."

Lou grabbed the toggles on the control panel and released emergency water ballast. At the same time, Irwin released additional ballast with the valves on his side. Now bow-heavy from the loss of gas and the breakdown of airflow over the nose, and aided by vicious downdrafts, the bow dipped violently.

When Thomson cried out "*Marthe!*" in the dark, the sound of his own voice woke him with a start. His mouth felt like sandpaper. He coughed, unable to swallow, trying to remember the dream before it was gone. He was brought back to reality by the buffeting wind, which caused the airship to buck and dive. Alarmed, he jumped out of bed and switched on the light. It was near impossible to maintain his balance. His watch said 2:07 a.m. He hurriedly slipped on his soft shoes and dressing gown and made his way unsteadily along the corridor to the chartroom. His feelings of satisfaction and well-being had evaporated.

Something must be seriously wrong!

Rabouille couldn't budge. He remained staring at the airship, which seemed to lose buoyancy, its nose dropping without warning. Suddenly, water spewed from its front end and it came back up, leveled out and continued to fly straight for him at about two hundred feet. He could see both the red and green navigation lights. The tear at the front had grown into a gaping orifice, like the mouth of a great fish. He clung tightly to the rabbit. Now, two sets of bulging eyes stared up at the monstrous creature coming to devour them. Rabouille prayed the damned thing would clear Therain Wood.

Thomson clung to the railing and hurried down the steps into the control car. He was thoroughly displeased.

During the dive, Irwin shouted to Potter, "Bring her up!"

Potter reacted immediately. He spun the elevator wheel forcefully, until it refused to turn anymore.

"That's maximum elevators, sir!" Lou shouted.

The speaking tube whistle sounded again. Irwin grabbed it and listened intently, his face ashen. He replaced the tube with resignation.

"What the deuce is going on, Captain Irwin?" Thomson snapped.

"That was the chief coxswain. The cover's failed completely at the bow. We have a massive hole. Un-repairable! He confirmed we've lost Gasbag 1 and Bag 2's deflating fast. Bag 3 is soaked and getting ripped away from its valves. Bag 6 has also ripped away at one side. He thinks more are coming loose due to the surging. We got caught in the vicious winds. It's all over."

"Is this Beauvais Ridge?" Thomson asked, desperately struggling to hold on as Potter tried to bring the ship back up to her original altitude. It felt like a roller coaster.

"Yes, it is," Irwin answered.

"But you *knew* this place was treacherous!"

"We got blown miles off course by the gale. We should never have left the tower—but you *all* overruled me, didn't you!" Irwin shouted, not hiding his contempt.

As the ship finally leveled out, a loud crack vibrated throughout like a harmonic chord. Potter swung the elevator wheel in dismay—all resistance gone.

"We've lost elevators," Potter yelled.

"That was the elevator cable," Irwin said calmly.

"What's happened to it?" Thomson asked, his eyes finally registering fear.

"It snapped under the strain of full elevators."

More unnerving noises followed, slowly at first—creaking, groaning, popping, snapping—sounds all too familiar to Lou. He could only think of Charlotte. The image of her when he'd last seen her standing on the front step in the moonlight filled his mind. A Greek goddess. He was brought back by Irwin.

"Now you're listening to the sounds of her back breaking," Irwin said, matter-of-factly. "Add an extra bay! Loosen the harnesses. Huh!"

Richmond jumped down into the control car in a state of panic.

"Ease off power! Some girders are buckling," he shouted.

"It's worse than that!" Lou shouted, pointing out of the windows toward the bow. Through lightning flashes, they saw the hull slowly sagging. When they turned to look at the stern, the same thing was happening—she'd gone limp from head to tail.

"Oh, no. She's done for!" Richmond cried.

"Her back's broken," Irwin said.

Thomson was speechless. He thought of Marthe—and all his carefully laid plans.

"Prepare for crash landing! Dump *all* ballast at the bow," Irwin ordered. "I'm gonna try and put her down."

Lou blew down the speaking tube. Someone answered. It wasn't Church.

"Where's Sam? Find him and tell him to dump the emergency ballast. *Right now*!"

"Bring her head to wind!" Irwin ordered.

The rudder coxswain swung the wheel, bringing her bow into the wind to slow her down.

"Signal all engines to SLOW," Irwin shouted.

Lou rang all telegraph bells, relaying the order to the cars. "Dump all fuel!"

Steff grabbed the emergency fuel tank cutters, emptying many of the diesel tanks instantaneously.

"Lou, go and wake Disley. Tell him to be ready to pull all breakers as soon as we're on the ground. Find Hunt. Tell him to warn all hands. Steff, go and warn Atherstone and the passengers."

"Can I send Potter? I'll stay with you, sir," Lou asked.

"No! Get out of this control car. Everyone above decks!" Irwin ordered, grabbing the rudder wheel from the coxswain and pushing him toward the stairs. The two coxswains rushed upstairs. Lou and Steff hesitated. Potter stopped at the chartroom railing above, to wait for Lou.

"*Go!* All of you! That's an order!"

Before following Steff upstairs, Lou turned to Irwin, making eye contact.

"Good luck, sir," he said. Irwin nodded. But Thomson wouldn't budge. He stared straight ahead through the window into the blackness of Therain Wood.

Irwin glared at Thomson. "And *you*! This is the most dangerous place on the ship—you'll have a chance upstairs." Thomson and Irwin faced each other, neither backing down.

Lou rushed upstairs to the chartroom where Potter was waiting.

"I'm gonna stick with you, Lou," Potter shouted.

"Come on then."

As the ship dived, Binks was thrown backwards against the engine.

"Oh, bloody hell!"

"Don't panic, Joe. It's only the storm. She's done this 'undreds of times," Bell said.

But then, stampeding feet and yelling above their heads increased Binks's fear.

"Something's very wrong, Ginger, I just know it. I'm really scared," Binks whimpered.

The ship leveled out again and as it did so, they felt the harmonic vibration and then the creaking and groaning as her keel compressed and other parts were pulled apart. The telegraph bell rang. They watched the indicator move to SLOW.

Bell grabbed the throttle lever and eased the power.

"Oh, no! What now?" Binks groaned.

Steff had already set off for the passenger cabins, having roused Atherstone. Lou rushed to the switch room, Potter on his heels. Lou burst in, finding Disley asleep on a cot, his chess set in disarray on the floor next to a blood-soaked shoe. Lou leaned over and shook him.

"Dizzy, wake up! We're making a crash landing. Be ready to pull the breakers as soon as we're down."

Disley leapt out of bed in a daze. Lou turned and ran off to the crew's quarters, Potter close behind. There, he found Hunt, who'd already begun rousing the sleeping crewmen.

"I took riggers to the bow, but it was hopeless. She's done!" Hunt said.

"Yeah, the skipper's putting her down, Sky. You felt it go, didn't you?"

Hunt nodded.

"We gotta warn all hands," Lou said.

Hunt hollered at the sleeping crewmen. "We're down, lads. Come on, shake a leg!" He turned back to Lou. "The bags are full of holes again and the valves have been puffing their guts out. We could never 'av made it anyway," Hunt said.

Crewmen began sitting up, bleary-eyed. Lou looked in cabins adjacent to the crew's quarters and roused the men inside. He rushed into Pierre's cabin. Pierre was snoring in his bunk, his hairpiece lying on the table beside him.

"Get up, Pierre. The captain's putting the ship down—try and save yourself. Run to the stern!" Pierre became wide awake immediately, springing bolt upright like a jack-in-the-box, shielding his balding head from Lou's eyes. He cried out in anguish, eyes wide with terror.

"Oh, no. God no! Save me, Commander, please save me!"

Lou suddenly remembered Leech in the smoking room and rushed off in that direction. Potter was slower off the mark this time. The ship dived a second time as Lou dashed down the corridor, his momentum increased by the ship's acute nose-down angle. He grabbed the railing and hung on, glancing back to see what had happened to Potter. Potter was twenty yards behind, also clinging to a railing, unable to move. Lou felt the bow gently touch the ground and heard the unnerving squeaking, squealing sound of the nosecone scraping the earth down to bedrock. It put his teeth on edge.

The floor fell away beneath Lou's feet, and then leveled out. The ship settled, while continuing to move forward. The hull shuddered and shook violently, as though in an earthquake, grating and juddering over the rocky ground, before telescoping into itself. The sound was deafening and the vibration rattled every tooth in his head.

We're down now, all right!

Just after the lights went out, massive explosions erupted at the bow and behind Lou (where Potter had been), knocking him to the floor. Stunned, momentarily blinded and almost deaf, he struggled to his feet, grabbing the railing again. He hung on, looking desperately for Potter, trying to see through the wall of fire. His face and body were seared by the heat and much of his hair burned away. His uniform smoldered, scorching his back, chest and legs. For a few seconds, a gap appeared in the curtain of fire and smoke. Potter was gone. At that moment, he realized how much Potter meant to him and how much Potter depended on *him*.

I must go back and find him.

Lou let go of the railing, which had blistered his palms and fingers, and started back toward the inferno. A hand roughly grabbed his shoulder, pulling him back.

"No, sir. This way!" a voice shouted behind him.

Leech had emerged from the smoking room.

"I've got to find Potter!" Lou cried.

"He's got to be dead. He couldn've survived that."

"I can't just leave him."

"No! You're coming with me."

Potter filled Lou's mind—aboard *R38* and at their wedding at St. Cuthbert's. Overcome by a sense of profound loss, he began to weep. He felt himself gripped in a bear hug from behind and dragged down the corridor. All the while, above the roaring fire and rolling thunder, he heard piercing screams that made his blood curdle. Lou was too weak and in too much pain to fight. Moments later, they were in the smoking room, lit by flames from outside. Utter chaos reigned. Most furniture had slid against the bow-end wall. The remaining chairs lay on their sides with the drinks trolley, from which glasses and bottles had been flung like missiles. Leech grabbed a soda siphon and sprayed Lou's smoldering clothes. Then he slammed the two doors shut, leaving them in pitch darkness. Once inside, the rumbling inferno surrounded them. Lou's heart pounded and unbearable panic rose in his chest and throat. The moment he'd dreaded all these years had come.

Moments earlier, Thomson had stepped up beside Irwin at the wheel, reconciled to his fate. "The fault is all mine. I stand beside you, Captain Irwin," he said. Nothing but bitter regret filled Thomson's heart.

Was all this for Marthe? Never will I see her again—not in this lifetime.

He looked at Irwin and saw terrible sadness in his face.

He's thinking of his wife. What have I done! Dear God, forgive me.

Irwin turned to him, and as if reading his mind, nodded his forgiveness. They shook hands. Thomson stared at the ground coming up to meet them. The bow gently kissed the earth and the ship balanced on its nose for an eternity, ploughing a deep furrow into the woods.

Perhaps we can survive this. Maybe God will allow us live, after all.

The hull settled slowly down—so very, very slowly, moving forward at a snail's pace. Everything unfolded in milliseconds with astonishing clarity. The forward port engine propeller made contact with the ground, causing the car to be twisted round on its supports and driven up into the hull. Its exhaust pipe was glowing red and shooting a spray of beautiful sparks, like the sparklers he'd had as a child in India during the Diwali Festival of the darkest night. The massive explosion that followed at the bow blew out the control car windows, the shards ripping flesh from their faces and bodies. The flares Lou and Johnston had left on the windowsill dropped to the floor.

The gigantic bulk gradually sank on top of the control car, pushing it into the sodden ground. Irwin went down with a moan and Thomson fell backwards to the floor beside him. He held up his arms to protect his bleeding head and face, but the structure came down upon them and the flares burst into vivid white flame as the ballast water mains over their heads ruptured with a great whoosh.

In that instant, Thomson's life played out before him. He heard his own first cries as he left his mother's womb in Nasik ...every word he'd ever uttered and every word spoken to him ...his early childhood in India and then England ...growing up with his siblings ... Cheltenham School ...the Royal Military Academy ...the Army ...the Retreat from Mons ...Ypres ...the girl in the carriage on Rue de Rivoli ...meeting Marthe at Cotroceni Palace ...his sorry attempts in her boudoir ...having dinner and blowing up oil wells with her husband, George ...Palestine ....Versailles ...campaigning for a Labour seat and failing ...riding the Flying Scotsman ...meeting MacDonald at Lossiemouth ...battling Lord Scunthorpe in the Lords ...witnessing the launching of *R101* ...his meetings with Colmore and Richmond ... all his bullying ...and all his arrogance. It all took less than a second before his chest was crushed under the collapsing structure. He gave himself up to the blinding white light.

In engine car No.5, during these last moments, Binks's terror had increased. Their car vibrated with the urgent, pounding feet of crewmen above.

"Oh, blimey, now what?" Binks sobbed.

Both men were thrown backwards a second time as the ship dived again. Hunt's voice above them in the crew's quarters reached them loud and clear.

"Oh, no, that's Mr. Hunt. We've had it now!" Binks cried.

Though it might have meant certain death, Rabouille stood rooted to the spot, paralyzed with fear. The monster moved toward him against the wind, balanced on its nose, carving its deep furrow and clearing a wide swath through the trees. The smell of diesel, spilling from the ship's belly, overpowered him and he was enveloped in a cloud of fuel and water vapor. With relief, he realized the ship was going to miss him—just barely, having turned away during the last moments. He could now only see the starboard green navigation light. It settled to the ground like a beached whale, still moving, the hull telescoping in on itself for a hundred feet. Sparks flew as the structure and the propellers tore at flints in the rocky earth. In horror, he watched the massive bulk settle onto the control car, squashing it like a tin can, along with the two doomed men he'd seen inside.

As with Thomson, Rabouille experienced events in slow motion. Engine No.2 hit the dirt, its propellers still turning, forcing the car upward into the envelope. The ship was ripped apart, the flaming cover torn to shreds. Broken guy-wires and cables whipped and lashed about. Sparks showered in all directions, from severed wiring torn from electrical devices and from smashed light bulbs. All went dark for some seconds after she'd come to rest and then a deafening explosion shook the ground and knocked him down. He sat clinging to the rabbit like a child with a stuffed toy, as flames burst hundreds of feet into the air, lighting up the French countryside for miles.

Rabouille wept uncontrollably as he watched screaming figures perform a terrible, macabre dance of death inside the inferno. The heat scorched his face. He choked on the smoke and acrid fumes of burning diesel, oil, carpet, wood and canvas. Brilliant white columns with golden heads withered away to ash, along with the poor creatures trapped within.

He tried to block out their screams, sticking his fingers in his ears, letting go of the terrified animal. He cried out in horror and his rabbit hopped lopsidedly away, leaving him alone. The ship's cover blazed from stem to stern, revealing the grand lounge and dining room, fine furniture and upholstery gutted with vivid intensity. Curtains to the passenger cabins were aflame, along with bedding and bodies, giving off suffocating, black smoke and the odor of burning flesh. High on the stern, the scorched red and blue ensign fluttered defiantly in the howling wind.

Rabouille watched a flaming super-human struggle out of the blazing structure, jump down and run toward him, falling at his feet, screaming in agony. He heard the poor wretch cry out a woman's name as he fell: "Florry!"

Rabouille leapt to his feet and dashed through the forest like a madman chased by the devil, wet branches tearing and lashing his face. He ran out into the tussocked field, tripping and stumbling among the wildly bleating, clanking sheep and crossed the Meru Road. He didn't stop until he reached the cottage, where he barricaded the door and fell down on his knees beside the bed. He prayed he'd forget the horror of this night. He crossed himself and climbed into bed, pulling the covers over his head, listening to the rolling thunder dying away over the ridge. There, he remained for the next three days, his bed becoming like him, grubby and smelling of diesel fuel and acrid smoke.

Binks stared out of the window of the car from the center of the inferno. No sooner were they hearing the commotion above their heads and the signal given to SLOW, than the ship became a blazing wreck on the muddy, wooded plateau. For them, there was no jarring crash as the ship came to ground. All *they* witnessed was the rapidly disappearing cover devoured by fire and the vast skeleton exposed in blinding light. Blistering hot walls turned their cocoon into an oven. Flames licked their feet and legs through holes in the floor.

"Safety first. What a *bloody* joke!" Bell shouted.

"Sweet Mother of Jesus, save us," Binks cried.

"We've got to get out. This petrol tank's gonna blow any second."

Binks suddenly remembered the old gypsy.

"Hey, hold on a sec, Ginger. Trust me on this," Binks shouted, putting both his hands on Bell's chest. Bell frowned at Binks, but didn't move. A few moments later and without warning, one of the ballast tanks above ruptured, sending a torrent of water cascading over them and the car. The flames were doused and the car cooled momentarily. The two men picked up their wet coats and threw them over their heads.

"Come on Joe, let's get out of here."

"Thank you, dear merciful Lord God in Heaven!" Binks exclaimed. "Through fire, rain and fog she said! Yes! Yes! That old witch was right."

They climbed out onto the car's entry platform into the intense heat and blinding fire and jumped. They fell down on their hands and knees into the mud, then dashed, slipping and sliding through smoke and steam to a safe distance. They collapsed on the ground, burned, but alive.

"I owe you one, Joe. Thank you for being late, mate!" Bell croaked. "But how did you know water would come down on us like that, eh?"

Binks smiled. " 'Ee who 'esitates ain't always lost, is 'ee!"

Lou's worst claustrophobic nightmares had materialized. In this tomb, at the center of hell, in total darkness, they'd surely be cooked alive. His fear was increased when the rumbling floor above collapsed. They were knocked down as the ceiling fell, leaving them four feet of headroom. Aside from his phobias, Lou was in a bad state.

Burns to his body and face stung with salty sweat. What was left of his hair smelled singed.

"This ain't no way to die, is it, sir?" Leech said.

"We've got to get out," Lou yelled.

"I'll try the door." Leech crawled to the first door. The frame and structure of the opening were askew. The door wouldn't budge. He found the drinks trolley, ripped off the cigar lighter and lit the space with the flame.

"Cigar, anyone?" Leech said, holding up the cigar box.

"Nice, Harry," Lou croaked.

Leech stuffed two cigars in his inside pocket.

"We've got to break through this wall," he said.

In insufferable heat, they crawled on their hands and knees through broken glass around the sheet metal-lined walls. Lou heard Leech pulling on a settee screwed to the wall on the starboard side. He scrambled across the floor to help him and they yanked it free.

"I need a knife," Leech said.

Lou reached gingerly inside his pocket and pulled out his old *R38* switchblade. He opened it and passed it to Leech. Lou held up the flaming lighter while Leech went to work on the hot wall. He was able to pry away the sheeting at one of the seams, exposing asbestos boards behind it. He frantically beat the asbestos with his fists and stomped it with his heels until it cracked and fell to pieces. After more furious moments of clawing and pulling, he'd made a hole big enough for them to pull themselves through. Leech went first. As Lou struggled out, he ripped a deep gash in his left arm on the jagged metal sheeting.

Outside, the cover had disappeared entirely, but the fire was still raging. Making their way through the flames to the perimeter of the structure, they stepped on red-hot girders, burning the soles of their feet. Once there, they had no choice but to jump for it. Lou guessed the ground was thirty or forty feet down, although he couldn't see for smoke. Again, Leech went first. Lou heard crackling sounds, and then Leech shouting up to him.

"It's okay, sir. There's a tree there. Jump for it."

Lou leapt out as far as his strength would allow. He could just make out branches and leaves that shook cold water over him as he jumped. He caught hold of one branch, but it snapped. He grabbed wildly at others, but they slipped through his grasp, tearing his face. He fell to the ground head-first, strangely evoking a vision of Irwin reading the lesson in church. He hit the ground with a snap, as his right arm was broken. He rolled across the grass and lay there feeling like Jonah spat from the whale onto the dripping shore. Irwin's gentle Irish voice filled his head. *"...And the Lord spake unto the fish, and it vomited out Jonah onto the land ..."*

Water continued to shower upon him.

Ah, blessed cool water!

Leech knelt down beside him. "Are you okay, sir?"

"You know what? I reckon we're gonna get to smoke those cigars you stole from His Majesty's airship, Harry."

"Damned right we are! Powerful stuff, this heather, sir."

Leech helped Lou to his feet and they limped away from the smoke and flames. From out of the haze, they heard a shout.

"Anybody out there?"

"Me, Leech!"

Two men, their heads covered, emerged like desert tribesmen in a war, their faces black and blistered, clothes burned. But Lou recognized the voices. "Thank God, you're all right, sir," Binks said. "And you, too, Mr. Leech."

"Anyone seen Potter or the captain or Pierre?" Lou asked.

They shook their heads.   Three additional men approached out of the smoke: more engineers who'd escaped from their aft port and starboard engine cars. Two of them were supporting their companion, who looked close to death.

"Who are you?" Lou asked.

"I'm Cook, sir, and these are Savoury and Radcliffe." Cook nodded to Radcliffe. "This man's hurt pretty bad."

"You two lay him down over here and stay with him. We'll go and see if we can find anyone else," Lou said.

Radcliffe was burned all over his body, face and hands. He cried out in agony as they laid him down. Both Lou's arms throbbed and blood ran from the cut he now realized was deep. He held on to his broken arm as they moved along the wreck, feeling dizzy and nauseous.

"Hey look, there's another one," Binks said.

"Who are you?" Leech shouted.

"It's me, Disley."

Disley, his hands badly burned, was in terrible pain. He, like the others, was hardly recognizable, being black with soot and oil. He grimaced and moaned. They came to the position where the control car should've been. Not much was left. It was flattened into the ground.

"If the captain was in there, he had no chance," Leech said.

"Thomson stayed with him 'til the end," Lou said.

"I guess you gotta hand it to the man for that," Leech said.

Lou had been in that control car only minutes ago. All this was *déjà vu*—he'd survived again. He felt wretched. They moved on toward the ship's bow in the woods. Someone was on all fours, trying to crawl away from the intense heat.

"Sammy, is that you? Yes, it's Sammy!" Binks cried, sinking to his knees beside Church.

"Oh, Sammy, thank God you're alive. Are you all right?"

Church was far from all right. He, too, was barely recognizable— his hair completely gone, face and hands horribly burned, his jacket smoldering.

"Get me jacket off ..." Church mumbled, fighting to breathe.

Church cried out in pain as Binks and Bell gently turned him and sat him up to remove his jacket. They lifted him carefully and moved him further from the burning wreck.

"Oh, Sammy," Binks sobbed.

"Get me cigs," Church whispered, his eyes beseeching.

"He wants a cigarette," Lou said.

"In me jacket," Church said.

Binks fished through Church's jacket pockets and found a tin of Players. He lit one from a piece of burning wreckage on the ground. He stuck the cigarette in Church's mouth and took hold of his injured hand, but had to let it go. Church winced and took a long drag and blew the smoke out. He looked thankful for a moment, nodding to indicate they should help themselves. They each took a cigarette. He looked up at Lou.

"I'm sorry sir, I tried to release that ballast, but I got there too late," Church whispered.

"Don't worry about that, Sam. It wouldn't have made much difference," Lou told him.

"I was so looking forward to a life with Irene," Church said, looking up at the swirling clouds.

"You'll have that life, Sammy," Lou assured him, knowing it was a lie.

"Not now. They don't call me 'Bad-Luck Sam' for nothing." He closed his eyes. "I shoulda stayed home. Joe, me cards. You take 'em."

Binks fished out the playing cards loose in Church's coat pocket. "Don't worry, mate. I'll look after 'em for yer."

Lou hobbled away coughing and holding his broken arm. He beckoned to Disley with his head to follow him.

"Dizzy, can you make it to that town over there?"

"Yeah, I reckon."

"Call the Air Ministry. Tell them what's happened."

"The police station's the best bet, sir," Disley said. Despite the pain, he stumbled off across the field toward the lights of Allonne.

Lou sank to the ground as an army of villagers approached—there must have been a hundred of them. They moved slowly up the hill in the darkness, carrying lanterns and rescue equipment. At last, they arrived. Nuns, nurses, doctors, firemen, policemen and farm workers made up the procession. They carried stretchers, first aid supplies, picks, shovels and digging bars. The fire had died down some and Leech implored them to help him try to find his shipmates inside the wreck. Lou didn't have the strength to assist them. He lay on his side watching, until he faded into blackness.

PART THREE

Crowds throng the wreck of *Cardington R101* on Beauvais Ridge, France.

AFTERMATH

24

MOGOSOËR

Sunday October 5 & Monday October 6, 1930.

While Thomson had been enjoying a cigar in the smoking room and scribbling a message, Marthe was kneeling beside her sumptuous bed praying to God for Him to watch over Thomson and his airship and for his voyage to India to be a resounding success. She shuddered with cold as she climbed into bed and burrowed under the bedclothes. As she drifted off, she considered Thomson's marriage proposal. Had she, deep in the furrows of her subconscious, already made up her mind? She prayed again in a whisper for an answer. Guilt and depression hung over her like a guillotine.

Please God help me, please help us all.

Marthe woke in the darkness Sunday morning and let out a piercing scream. Isadora burst in from the adjoining room.

"My dear baby, what's the matter?"

Marthe sat up clutching her chest, her face screwed up in agony.

"I'm dying. I'm dying. Fetch the doctor! The pain is terrible!"

Isadora rushed off and telephoned Marthe's doctor, asking him to come at once. She also called Marthe's husband, who was in bed fast asleep with this mistress. George arrived before the doctor.

Isadora sat with Marthe on the bed, her arm around her. Other servants came and joined the vigil. Gradually, the searing pain subsided, only to be replaced by despair. Just before dawn, the French windows to Marthe's bedroom burst open and the sheer curtains flew out from the wall. To the women gathered around Marthe's bed, this was a dreadful, supernatural sign.

"Oh, my God! Oh, my God!" Marthe moaned.

"It's only the storm," Isadora assured her.

"No, no, it's not."

"What is it, my darling?"

"It's Kit."

"What about him?"

"It's him—he's dead," she whispered.

"Oh, Marthe. Don't be so dramatic."

"He's dead! Isadora, I know he's dead ..."

The next day, the pain had subsided and despite her anguish, Marthe wrote in her journal.

Sunday October 5th, 1930.

Last night, I was awoken by Kit's voice calling to me in a dream. So loud, it woke me. I managed to get back to sleep, but was awoken again by a dreadful pain in my chest. It felt so bad, I thought I would surely die. I called for Isadora, and she sent for George, who came immediately. He is very good these days. The doctor came at last, but found nothing. A heart attack, perhaps. He gave me pills to sleep, but they did no good. I could only think of Kit. I long for him to be back from his voyage and for us to meet again in Paris. Oh Kit, my dear friend, Kit. May God preserve you.

The following morning, Isadora came to Marthe's bedroom with two telegrams—both from Thomson. One was from the post office in Westminster on the evening of departure and the other from the airship itself, during the early hours of Sunday morning. Marthe derived no comfort from them.

Half an hour later, Marthe was informed Prime Minister MacDonald was on the telephone. She knew the reason for his call. Her heart sank.

"Good morning, Prime Minister."

"Marthe, I'm calling with news which breaks my heart ..." He sounded shaken.

"Yes, Ramsay?"

"His airship has crashed in France."

"He's dead?"

"I'm afraid he is. All but nine perished."

"It happened at just after 4 o'clock Sunday morning?" Marthe said, managing to stay composed.

"Yes, my dear. Today they'll lie in state in Beauvais. They'll be brought home tomorrow from Boulogne and thence by train to Victoria. I shall be there to meet him ..." his voice faltered.

"He'll be glad of that."

"I've arranged for them to lie in state in Westminster Hall."

She pictured Thomson's handsome face as he stood in the center of Westminster Hall, staring up at the structure before they parted, as he always did.

"When?" she asked.

"Friday ...The damned blabbermouths have already started with their mischief."

"What do you mean?"

"Some newspapers are asking questions. They're blaming him. He hasn't even been identified and buried ..."

She heard him draw in his breath as he choked up.

"You think they'd leave a man *something* ..." he whispered.

"Sickening!" she said.

He rallied suddenly.

"I shan't allow his name to be tarnished. I'll not *stand* for it!"

"Has the funeral been arranged?"

"Saturday. Will you come?" MacDonald asked.

"I wish that were possible, but I'm feeling quite ill."

"I understand. Please take good care of yourself, Marthe."

"Will you do something for me?" she asked.

"Anything."

"Place a single red rose on his coffin from me."

"I shall make a point of obtaining one of his special roses—*Variété Général Jacqueminot*, I believe."

"Bless you, dear Ramsay."

They said their goodbyes and MacDonald promised to keep her informed. Marthe retired to her bedroom, where she remained for the next three days.

25

THE NUNS OF BEAUVAIS

Monday October 6, 1930.

Lou found himself riding into the Cardington Fairground on the *Brough Superior*. The colors were vivid, unnaturally so, the cloudless sky a deep sapphire, the sandy ground, violent ginger. Above, he heard unnerving screams of girls on the Ferris wheel, not of joy, but of horror and behind him, more screams…those of crewmen trapped inside *Cardington R101*. He looked back over his shoulder at the tower. The ship, shining like polished silver, was enveloped in orange flame from end to end. He turned the bike and stopped. He saw no one, but could hear their cries inside. Turning away from that miserable sight, he coasted on through the fairground toward the carousel, its music gently playing. Sound came intermittently, as though from a speaker with a bad connection.

He passed the crimson tent where Madam Harandah stood with her hands on her hips. She gave him an off-hand look as he neared the gilded, red and gold carousel of bobbing horses. He stopped to watch it. Charlotte was the first person he spotted, with her parents standing beside her. She rode a white horse, her eyes vacant. She took no notice of him. Others were seated behind her on multi-colored horses: his own father and mother, Tom and Anna, Julia, old Jeb, his hair dazzling white, and wife, Alice, and their children dressed in fluorescent colors. Following them, from *R38* was Josh, Capt. Wann soaked in blood, Capt. Maxfield and Commodore Maitland horribly burnt. They were in uniform. The commodore looked ridiculous, wearing a black Napoleonic bicorn hat. Lou's dead German boy, with the broken neck, sat beside New York Johnny, Bobby and Gladstone the cabin boy—all dripping wet. Three satanic Ku Klux Klansmen followed in flowing, white robes. The leader, on a black and white appaloosa, held a blazing cross. Lou sat motionless, realizing why no one would acknowledge his presence—they all hated his guts. He couldn't contain himself any longer.

"Dad!" he screamed in desperation, but not one head turned in his direction. They remained like tailors' dummies, riding up and down and round and round, in a slow motion parade.

Then, off to one side, he saw two women. They were both gorgeous and beautifully dressed and made up, unreal, like shop-window mannequins. One was Helen Smothers (in her magnificent hat), and the other, Mrs. Hinchliffe. "Hey, Commander Remington, come ride with us," Helen Smothers called.

"Yeah, come on, Remy," Mrs. Hinchliffe said.

But he knew they didn't mean it. They were taunting him.

"Come on Lou, I was hoping we'd meet again," Helen Smothers said, her voice silky and inviting.

"Don't forget to call me Millie when we meet again, Lou …" Mrs. Hinchliffe shouted.

Lou rode away from them, over to the coconut shy, where he found Potter at the entrance, playing his accordion. He smiled as he squeezed the bellows, playing a polka. On the ground in front of him was his airshipman's cap full of coins. Lou tossed in a silver half crown. Potter smiled and nodded his thanks. At the rail, Church stood holding Jessup's grimacing head high in the air like a trophy. Disley, Binks, Cameron, Freddie and Billy fell about with laughter while the fairground attendant angrily shook his fist. Behind him, the heads of Jessup's friends cried out from their coconut cups, tears streaming down their cheeks.

"See, I told you those 'eads were glued in, didn't I, boys!" Church was yelling.

Beside Lou, there was more laughter. The clown's head in its glass box stopped its cackle and glared, and as Lou rode away, it threw its head back and roared.

The carousel music and Potter's accordion were drowned out by sounds of sita, flute and beating percussion. A group of Indian musicians in national garb sat playing their captivating music. In front of them, a huge silver cobra reared up and swayed from side to side, its evil eyes on Lou, ready to strike.

Lou drove away through the chestnut fencing and was overpowered by the smell of fish and seaweed-filled air. Finding himself on top of a sand dune, he left the bike and began to walk, hoping to find relief from all this weirdness and misery. Directly ahead, in the distance, he saw an airship. It was black. He knew it was *Howden R100* by its rippling cover. The gentle surf monotonously sucked the seashore, while gulls sounded their warnings overhead. Lou's eye traced the curved, sandy beach stretching to a low-lying headland, where the great Egyptian Pyramids stood silhouetted against a rising sun. In the opposite direction was another headland where the dome and minarets of the Taj Mahal stood in shining orange against another, dying sun. The airship passed directly over his head and disappeared behind him.

From the direction of the pyramids, a tiny, open-topped vehicle approached. As it drew nearer, he saw four figures inside, woodenly upright, rocking to and fro. The vehicle sped up the sand dune and came to an abrupt halt in front of him, the figures' heads bobbing and jerking comically. The car and its occupants were made of molded red and blue plastic. Lou recognized Scott as the driver. He wore a tall pointed hat with the letters R101 embossed across the front. Next to him, was Irwin. Thomson sat in the back, complete with overcoat and trilby, Brancker beside him, wearing his pith helmet. Each of them appeared weary and forlorn.

"I say old man, could you tell us, which way to India?" Scott called.

Lou pointed along the beach toward the Taj Mahal on the other headland. With a wave of Scott's hand, they sped off in their strange contraption, doomed to an eternity of searching—melded together for all time. Lou felt abject pity for them.

The sound of Potter's accordion in an overlapping dream woke Lou from his morphine nightmare. He was glad to be released from that, but overwhelmed by loneliness. Voices of dead crewmen screamed in his head. The sickening horror of the ship's last moments flooded back to him—the massive boom and blinding light, not being able to breathe or hear. Then, more detonations as the rest of the gas bags ignited in succession. He couldn't get Potter out of his mind—in plain sight one moment, gone the next. Again, there was the accordion.

Damn it, Walt—why didn't you stick close to me?

Lou wished he'd waited for him, perhaps even shared his fate. He wondered where Leech was—he owed that man his life.

There'll be so many devastated families in Bedford.

He thought about Church and Irene and hoped Church was going to make it. Was he still alive? Then Captain Irwin ...

Poor Olivia.

Did Charlotte know yet? She'd been right all along. Who could blame her for getting out?

I should have listened. She knew something others didn't know— except for that damned gypsy ...and Mrs. Hinchliffe ...Millie!

Lou couldn't see—his eyes and ears had been covered, further impairing his hearing. He hoped he wasn't blind and dreaded the thought of the nuns removing the bandages. When the French villagers had come to their aid in Therain Wood, he'd felt as if he was coming around from a deep sleep. His eyes hurt from being blinded by the hydrogen fire, and he was still half deaf—he supposed his eardrums had been damaged. He wondered if this would be permanent. Would his hair grow back?

I'm a wreck—but most of the others are dead. Oh God, why do you do this to me?

The nuns and nurses had been caring and gentle on the field—so reassuring, although he couldn't understand a word they said. They'd lifted his arm carefully and tied it in a sling and bound up and bandaged the cut on the other arm. They applied cool lotion to his burning face and head. He was in and out after that.

The journey in the field ambulance had been agony. It bounced and squeaked across the field, jarring his injured body. A couple of others were with him—probably Radcliffe and Church. He heard their cries and whimpers.

The next thing he remembered was the removal of the bandages; the brightness was blinding—overhead lights above the table, glistening white walls, smocks, headscarves. They washed his wounds and burns. That hurt like hell. They also stitched the cut on his arm. Other victims had been in the room. He could tell by the chatter of nurses and doctors close by, and from groans on their creaking gurneys.

The nuns have been kind and soothing—with voices of angels.

Lou slept for what seemed like ages, in and out of consciousness, depending on the morphine doses they gave him. It caused him to seriously lose track of time; he drifted off to sleep for a minute and think he'd slept for an hour or two. During one of his conscious moments, he heard the voices of his men—those not too badly hurt—probably Binks talking to Bell. They must have thought he was asleep. One of them was mumbling close by his bed.

"…Jessup …'is 'ead exploded, you should 'ave seen it …it was 'orrible! …Damn! …I couldn't …" Then more muttering—most likely Bell. Lou drifted off to sleep, those phrases repeating themselves over and over, like an infuriating recording that just wouldn't stop. Sometimes, he sensed the guys hovering by his bedside only to be shooed away by nuns.

Allez-vous en! Go away!

He thought about Disley. He hadn't heard his voice. He wondered if he'd managed to call London. The smells of the hospital got to him, particularly the disinfectant. Once, he smelled the perfume of one of the nurses. Though not the same as Charlotte's, it made him think of her. She'd always worn the same perfume, which he loved. He'd first noticed it in the hospital in Hull when she leaned over him and stitched his face. He'd concentrated on her perfume to block out the pain as she stuck in her needle and pulled the thread.

What seemed like a week later (he had no way of knowing), he thought he smelled the scent Charlotte used. It came to him so strongly, it was jarring.

Must be another crazy dream.

He faded back to sleep again, sensing the aroma of Balkan Sobrani and he thought of Norway. It was all a confusing muddle. Then, that same damned recording began playing over and over again in his brain, " …Jessup …'is 'ead exploded, you should 'ave seen it …it was 'orrible …Damn! …I couldn't …"

He came to, smelling the same perfume and shook his head, trying to snap out of it. He felt delusional, saddened and comforted at the same time. There was more mumbling and he strained to listen; first a woman's voice then and a man's, possibly two. Then nothing. Now, a soft woman's voice which he figured had to be a nun. He drifted back to sleep. When he awoke, the muttering continued and he caught the smell of that magnificent perfume once more. What was it called? Who could it be?

If only she were here—if only it were she!

He breathed in the scent and wept and lay there listening to those incoherent voices. Someone wiped the tears from his cheeks and gently took his hand.

Must be a nun—thank God for her.

"Can you hear me, my love?" a voice said.

But the voice was *English*—perhaps even *Yorkshire!*

"It's me," the voice whispered close to his ear. A soft loving kiss covered his mouth—the lips moist and luscious. There could be no mistaking those lips, or that perfume.

Damn these dreams! Damn the morphine!

One of the nuns spoke and his bandages were gently unwrapped. Though hazy, Charlotte's face came into focus, appearing more beautiful than he'd ever seen her—her lips full and red and her eyes so huge and clear and sparkling and blue. Short hair accentuated her elegant neck and high cheekbones.

Thank God, I can see, but is any of this real?

And she looked so well—she had an aura about her—not the same Charlotte he'd last seen. Behind her, he made out Norway and John Bull standing against the wall. He was overwhelmed.

"*Je Reviens,*" he said softly.

"*Je Reviens,*" she repeated.

Lou didn't speak again for some moments. A cloud descended over him. He stared blankly at Charlotte in a daze, remembering. He wrapped his bandaged arm around his head. His shoulders shook and he fought for breath. Charlotte embraced him, believing he was overcome with joy at the sight of her. But it wasn't that emotion which had enveloped him. He'd finally collapsed under his burden and his demons. Her appearance fuelled the agony caused by burgeoning guilt, smothering him with feelings of self-loathing and unworthiness. Again, why hadn't he been allowed to die in peace with the others? He gasped for breath.

"I threw myself down, you know," he said at last.

She leaned over him. He was obviously delirious.

"I didn't black out. That was a lie."

"What, my darling? What do you mean?"

"The machine guns cut my buddies down. I didn't black out."

She understood perfectly. In that moment, she knew all there was to know about Lou Remington. He wasn't worthy to live, or to have her return to him. It was all too much.

"I cheated God. He'd sent me to that front line that last day as punishment for killing the German boy. I really didn't have to kill him. I should've died that morning with the rest."

"No, Lou. You did what any man would've done."

"They said I was a hero. I was a cheat and a liar who deserved to die—and now my punishment is to live."

"Oh, Lou, please don't say that, my darling."

"Julia's prayers saved me …She made a pact."

"*Julia* …a pact?"

"With God," he said.

She waited.

"And look at her—she has *nothing!*"

Charlotte was thrown even more off balance. "Who is *Julia*?"

The nun came to Lou's bedside and glared at Charlotte and then at Norway and John, who was himself, choking up.

"*Ça suffit! Vous le contrariez. Il est temps de partir.* That's enough! You're upsetting him. It's time for you to leave."

And then something happened that astonished Lou and Norway, but not John Bull. Charlotte smiled and turned to the nun and spoke perfect French.

"*Je vous supplie de me laisser rester. Je suis une infirmière. Je connais bien cet endroit. S'il vous plâit, laissez-moi rester un peu plus longtemps, j'ai des choses importantes à dire à mon mari.* I beg you to let me stay. I'm a nurse. I'm familiar with this place," she said, lifting her hands and gesturing to their surroundings. "Please allow me to stay a little longer. I have important things to say to my husband."

The nun's manner changed as she looked into Charlotte's face. She showed a hint of recognition and relented. Norway pulled a chair up to the bed for Charlotte to sit close. He and John went into the corridor. Charlotte took Lou's hand again.

"Julia—she was waiting for you back home, wasn't she? I always had the feeling there must be *someone*."

"Charlotte, she's a wonderful person. She asks for nothing."

"I'm sure she is. She deserves you more than I, especially—"

"My darling, don't …I missed you so much," he said.

"Lou, I'm so sorry I didn't let you in that day—"

"I came to tell you I was ready to give it all up."

Charlotte felt sick.

"Kiss me again," he said.

She leaned over, kissed him and then took out a folded, white handkerchief from her handbag. She opened it, revealing his gleaming gold wedding ring. She gently slipped it back on his finger and kissed him again. He became calm.

"I figured Robert had shown up again and you'd run off with him."

She was shocked at the suggestion. She held up her ring finger.

"I never took mine off," she said. "Poor Robert is dead—long dead, poor boy."

For the first time, Charlotte pronounced 'Robert' the French way (Ro-bare), which strangely, she'd never done, even in her own mind.

"I love you, Charlie," Lou said.

"Now, there's something I must tell *you*, Lou," Charlotte said, pausing to recall dreadful memories, her voice a whisper. "I was at the Western Front, too."

It took a few moments for it to sink in. He was speechless.

"What …!" he stammered. "Where? …When?"

"I was at different field hospitals …the last one was at Saint-Mihiel …near you."

"Oh, my God …" Stunned, Lou put his hand to his head, it explained a lot of things.

"I decided you should know."

Tears welled up in Lou's eyes.

"Many of *them* were American," Charlotte told him. "So many died. I'll never forget their pleading eyes …they were so far from home. I couldn't talk about it. I'm sorry. I've never spoken of the horror of that place to anyone." She wiped her eyes with a handkerchief smudging her eye makeup and then blew her nose.

"Baby, I'm so sorry. I wish I'd known. A fine pair, huh. So that's where you learned to stitch—and speak French!" He closed his eyes and smiled as he remembered.

She had things she could not share …Another victim of war …She was a brave girl that one …And the Red Cross pin!

Charlotte smiled now, too. They consoled each other until the nun returned and told them visiting would be suspended for a couple of hours. Lou's dressings had to be changed and he needed rest. Before leaving, John came in and patted Lou's shoulder, overjoyed Lou had survived and that he and Charlotte were reunited.

26

BLACKOUT IN BEDFORD

Sunday October 5, 1930.

Around 6.00 a.m. on that chilly Sunday morning of the crash, Charlotte and her parents were roused by pounding on the front door that shook the whole house. When Charlotte heard it, a feeling of doom overcame her and her heart began to race. Instinctively, she knew. She *had* listened to the 9 o'clock news the night before. Her heart had skipped a beat when she heard it mentioned that a representative from the United States was on board. She put on her dressing gown and went down to the living room where her father was already on his way to the front door. Charlotte's mother followed her. Mr. Hamilton nervously switched on the vestibule light and opened the front door. Two familiar figures stood on the step: Norway and John Bull. Their faces said it all.

"W-we're s-sorry to d-disturb y-y-"

"Lou's ship went down," John said.

Charlotte felt as though she'd been stabbed in the chest. She let out a gasp and her mother caught her and led her back into the living room. They followed. Mother eased Charlotte down into an easy chair.

"What happened?" Charlotte's father asked.

"I got a c-call from George Hunter of the *D-Daily Express*, he's a r-reporter," Norway said.

"What did he say?" Charlotte asked.

"He said the airship had crashed in France."

"Where?"

"B-Beauvais," Norway answered.

"Beauvais!"

"There are survivors. I'd been following it all night on my short wave radio. I don't speak French, but I was able to pick up parts of it," John said.

"What about Lou?" Charlotte asked.

"We d-don't know."

"All we know is that nine survived and they're in hospital," John said.

Charlotte's father went to the radio and switched it on. There was nothing but church music on and a program about birds in Newfoundland on the other station. He looked at the clock.

"We must listen to the seven o'clock news," he said. It was twenty minutes to seven.

"When did you last see Lou?" Charlotte asked.

"I saw him off last night," John replied.

"From Cardington?" Charlotte's mother asked.

"Yes. I was worried when I left. The weather was shocking. I got home and sat by the radio all night. It came on in France at four o'clock this morning."

"And they said there were survivors?"

"Yes, they said *neuf survivants*—that's nine," John said.

Charlotte nodded.

"George Hunter confirmed nine," Norway said.

"And all the rest are dead?" Charlotte asked.

"Yes, but we've got to keep our hopes up for Lou," John said.

"His luck may've run out," Charlotte said. She remembered the nine lives he joked about.

"We're going to f-f-fly down to Cardington and then F-France. Depending on what we f-find out," Norway said.

"Depending on if he's dead, you mean?" Charlotte said, her eyes flashing at Norway, who looked away, badly stung.

"There were a l-lot of good people on that flight. P-people I liked," Norway said.

"It's all *your* bloody fault!" Charlotte snapped.

"Char-Char-Char ..."

"I'm coming with you," Charlotte said.

"I'd hoped you'd say that. Bring your passport," John said, "and don't forget your door key."

"We're going over to Sh-Sherburn to pick up a plane," Norway said.

"Okay, I'll make you breakfast before you go," Charlotte's mother said, rushing off to the kitchen. There was now a great sense of urgency. Charlotte dashed up stairs to get dressed. Mr. Hamilton put the radio on just before 7 o'clock.

"They'll make an announcement, I'm sure," he said.

They listened closely to the news while they ate breakfast, but the BBC didn't mention a word about *Cardington R101*. It made them wonder if it'd all been a cruel hoax. There'd been false stories put out when *Howden R100* flew to Canada—rumors it'd gone down in the Atlantic. Within half an hour, they were on their way to Norway's flying club in John's car. Once there, they found that the plane they needed was already rented, but the club-member allowed them to take it when he heard the news. Everyone at the club was deeply shocked.

Two hours later, they landed on Cardington Field, parked the aeroplane close to St Mary's Church and tied it down. That morning, the weather was perfect for flying; the wind had dropped and the sky was clear. Charlotte stared at the leaves stuck to the damp, autumn-smelling ground. Their colors reminded her of khaki blankets and dried blood. Across Church Lane, they heard the congregation singing. There wasn't much gusto in the voices; it was supposed to be Harvest Festival with worshipers there to give thanks. Charlotte remembered being in church with Lou last year, this very day. She looked across at the Ferris wheel. It was still. The fairground, like the aerodrome, was empty and quiet except, for the sound of birds in the hedgerows and men dismantling the rides. Perhaps the gypsies knew there'd be no business here now—maybe never.

They walked across the field, past the sheds and up to Cardington House. The doors were locked. Booth's Sunbeam Talbot was parked outside next to Scott's Morris Oxford and two other cars. Norway pounded on the door. Eventually, they saw Booth through the glass, walking toward them. His face was grave. He reluctantly let them in.

"Look Nevil. I can't tell you anything and you're the last person they want to see around here right now!" Booth whispered.

"What are *you* d-doing here, then?" Norway asked.

"They called me at four-thirty this morning."

"I got a c-call from a reporter at the *D-Daily Express* at four o'clock," Norway said. He pointed at John, "And he heard it on shortwave radio."

"Most people round here don't have radios," Booth said.

"So people in Bedford don't know?" John said.

"They didn't, but a rumor has spread like wildfire," Booth said.

"Are you sure it's actually *true*?" Charlotte said.

Booth nodded. "Disley, the electrician called from the police station in Allonne."

"But there *were* survivors?" Charlotte asked.

Booth wouldn't say, but he did nod his head slightly.

"What about Lou?"

Charlotte could see, Booth was in a terrible position. He kept looking nervously toward the corridor behind him. "I'm so sorry I can't …Orders have come from the highest levels," he said. "The *very* highest!"

"I need to know if my husband's alive!" Charlotte whispered, her eyes like daggers. Booth nodded his head silently so that others listening couldn't tell he was communicating. Charlotte closed her eyes in relief.

"Is he going to live?"

Please God.

"*That,* I can't say. I don't know. Honestly, I'd tell you if I knew," Booth murmured. And then, in a loud voice, "Nevil, you must leave! You really shouldn't have landed here, you know."

"I'm s-sorry if I hurt anyone's f-feelings, but this was important to Mrs. Remington. We're going on to F-France tomorrow morning," Norway said.

"So am I. I'm leaving this morning," Booth whispered and then in a loud voice, "I'm sorry I can't tell you anything. They'll put out a statement later, when in possession of the facts." Booth opened the front door. "That's all I can tell you. Goodbye."

Booth's face was more kindly than his words sounded down the corridor.

"We'll see you over there," Norway muttered.

Booth shut and locked the doors behind them.

They left Cardington House and walked the half mile down to the gate, where a crowd had gathered. Norway went to the gatekeeper.

"Jim, what's going on?"

"Mr. Norway, they've 'eard something about the airship. They keep asking me. I can't tell 'em anything. No one's told me a damned thing and they won't come down 'ere and talk to these people. It ain't right, keepin' people in the dark like this!"

The gatekeeper unlocked the small side gate and Charlotte and her companions stepped outside. The desperate crowd surged forward. Charlotte found it heartbreaking to see people in such a state. They rushed at Norway.

"Is it true, sir?"

"What can you tell us?"

The crowd surrounded them.

"You've h-heard something about the air-sh-ship?"

"You heard it went down?" Charlotte said.

All eyes centered on Charlotte.

"Yes, we 'eard a rumor, m'am, my boy's on that ship," one desperate man said.

"Look, I'm going to be honest with you. My husband's on that ship, too. We heard it went down and there are a few survivors. That's all we know. I'm so sorry. We must go."

A bus drew up nearby.

"Oh, yes. You're the American's wife."

"God Bless you, miss. I hope your 'usband's all right," someone said.

The crowd parted for them as they went for the bus. They climbed aboard and looked back at the unhappy faces. Charlotte wondered when they'd be told the facts.

They got off at the top of Kelsey Street and walked to No. 58. It felt strange seeing her old house again. Charlotte was desolate—she'd betrayed Lou. She found herself staring at the oil patch where he always parked his motorbike. She wondered where it was now. She'd heard about Lou and Billy's accident from Fanny, who'd been to see her the previous evening. After receiving Lou's phone call at Goole Hospital, Fanny had been shocked to learn from other sources that

Charlotte had walked out on Lou weeks earlier. She dashed over to Charlotte's parents' place to find Charlotte. After catching up, Fanny told her about their collision with the painter's van. Charlotte had been relieved the boy was safe and *not* aboard that damned airship.

As she walked across the concrete parking area in front of the house, she looked at Mrs. Jones's window. Fluffy was sitting on the windowsill, inside. She'd seen Charlotte and was making a fuss. Soon, Mrs. Jones appeared at the window. Her face lit up.

Charlotte stood at the foot of the steps and looked up, noticing the stains. She had no idea what it was. It looked like dried blood. It made her shudder. She unlocked the door and they went in. There was a white envelope bearing her name lying on the hall table. She slipped into the living room and opened it. The card simply said,

> *My Darling Charlotte,*
>
> *I'll take you to see the full-size statue one day soon.*
>
> *God, I've missed you!*
>
> *All my Love*
>
> *Lou XXXX*
>
> *Many more kisses to come!*

She wasn't sure what it meant until the clock chimed on the mantelpiece. Next to it, was the Sitting Lincoln statue he'd bought for her. She felt empty inside. They trooped down to the kitchen where Charlotte opened the window to let in some fresh air. Everything was tidy. Mrs. Jones knocked on the front door and came down stairs with Fluffy, who was making a hell of row—admonishing Charlotte.

"What's happening, Charlotte? Are you back?" Mrs. Jones said.

There was an awkward silence. Mrs. Jones looked from one to the other. Then she realized something was up.

"What is it, dear?"

"There's been an accident," John said.

"The airship?"

"It crashed," Charlotte said.

"What about Lou?"

"We think he may have s-survived," Norway said. "But we d-don't know for sure."

"What about the rest of 'em"

"Nobody knows, or at least they ain't telling anybody," John said.

"Well, there's been nothing in the paper about it," Mrs. Jones said.

"It happened in the night, so there won't be," Charlotte said.

"George Hunter said the *Express* stopped the presses early this morning and was doing a special late edition. Maybe we can get one," Norway said.

Charlotte said, "Look, if you don't mind, I'm going to walk round to Olivia Irwin's house. I must see her."

Before leaving, Charlotte went upstairs to their bedroom. It was tidy, but not as tidy as she'd left it. Their portraits were still on the wall. She spent a moment studying them. Lou looked handsome. Happier days. Then she noticed his guitar was missing from its hook on the wall on his side of the bed—then the gaping hole in the wardrobe door. She pictured the scene, feeling regret she'd caused Lou so much pain.

Oh, God, that must have hurt. My poor dear Lou.

She opened the wardrobe door and peered inside. Her heart sank. In the bottom was the guitar, or what was left of it, in a thousand pieces. It broke her heart. She realized just how much she'd hurt him. She sat on the edge of the bed and wept. She got up and went to the sink in the bathroom, washed her face and re-did her makeup. He was all that mattered.

Please God, let him live.

Twenty minutes later Charlotte was on Olivia's doorstep ringing the bell. It was some minutes before Olivia appeared in her dressing gown, her eyes cast down. There was both rage and sorrow in her lovely, ashen face. She held the door open in silence for Charlotte to enter. As soon as the door was closed, Charlotte put her arms around her and they both cried bitterly. They went into the living room.

The house felt dead. Only the ticking clock on the mantelpiece made any sound.

"How did you find out?" Charlotte whispered.

"We both knew he wasn't coming back ..." Olivia dropped her head. "...Booth was here early this morning."

"You both sensed all this coming?" Charlotte asked.

"Yes. I went back to the ship last night. I begged and pleaded with him."

"But he *still* went?"

"Yes. How could he not? They made him go. They damn-well forced him!"

Charlotte didn't want to talk about survivors. It'd seem cold. But Olivia brought it up. "Booth said Lou's alive," she said suddenly. "He's injured. He said some won't live."

Charlotte let out a sob. "Oh God!"

He could still die.

She was brought back by Olivia's weary voice.

"I went and saw that damned gypsy last week." She sounded bitter.

"Oh, Olivia!"

"I just couldn't resist. Fat lot of good it did. She said, 'the bells will toll for them'."

"She was right."

"And then, that pilot's wife came to see me."

"Mrs. Hinchliffe?"

"Yes. She came knocking on the door just before they left. She told me they had no chance of survival. She said her dead husband had told her this."

"I wish I'd known."

"What could you have done? You were gone. Anyway, it wouldn't have made a difference. That bloody Thomson had his own agenda. It was all *his* damned fault!"

"I suppose he's dead, too," Charlotte said.

Charlotte left Olivia and walked back toward Kelsey Street. On her way, she went past the corner store to see if she could get the *Sunday Express*. Inside, there was a crowd of nervous people with the same idea. News of the crash was out. People in the corner store were desperate and very angry.

"We need news," somebody said, as if Alan, the store owner, had influence with the press. He held up both his hands, trying to quell the storm.

"I made a phone call. The *Sunday Express* has printed a late edition, but we've not been able to get any yet. The *Bedford Circular* is printing a late paper right now. It should be getting here any time," he told them.

Somebody saw a *Daily Express* van slowing down outside. A bundle of newspapers tied up with string was thrown out on the ground from the tail gate and it tore off up the street. Everybody stampeded from the shop and grabbed at the newspapers like crazy people. In seconds, they were all gone. The lucky ones stood reading the front page with people gathered around them. Charlotte read the headlines of the *Sunday Express* over someone's shoulder.

CARDINGTON R101 CRASHES ON FRENCH HILLSIDE

Air Minister Lord Thomson and Director of Civil Aviation Among the Dead Nine Survivors: Some Severely Injured In Beauvais Hospital

Charlotte's heart sank. She kept thinking of how she'd refused to let him in her parents' house. She'd deserve it if he died now. She couldn't help thinking of old Mrs. Tilly's last words.

You'll find someone special. I just know you will. And when you do, you grab 'im and 'old on to 'im and never let 'im go.

In despair, Charlotte headed for the *Bedford and District Circular's* office on the High Street in town. As she approached the square, she heard a brass band playing Chopin's "Funeral March."

Damn! As if people aren't depressed enough.

She walked round the square to the newspaper office where a crowd had gathered. This'd become a command post for news and exchange of information. She spotted John on the other side and went over to him. He'd come here, leaving Norway at home in case the phone rang.

Bundles of newspapers were being unloaded from a van and put into a stack for people to take free of charge. A blackboard had been chalked up with survivor's names. Charlotte read them, knowing most of these men. Their faces came to mind. The reality of seeing Lou's name made her stomach turn over.

Dear God, please let him live. ...They all die someday, Charlotte.

<u>Survivors as of 10 a.m. this morning – Unconfirmed.</u>

L. Remington	3rd Officer USN
A. Disley	Electrician
H. Leech	Foreman Engineer
J. Binks	Engineer
A. Bell	Engineer
W. Radcliffe	Engineer
V. Savoury	Engineer
A. Cook	Engineer
S. Church	Rigger

While everyone gathered around the blackboard in hushed silence, the Salvation Army band marched up the road spreading the gloom. There was little or no traffic and people spoke reverently in whispers, as if in church. People sobbed into their handkerchiefs. A bell tolled close by. As soon as one stopped, another started elsewhere. And so it went. It was unnerving to hear the howling of someone's dog.

There was one girl Charlotte recognized after a few moments. It was the pregnant Rosie Cameron. Well, that was no surprise. She wondered whose child it was.

"I'm walking with the Lord," Jessup had told her.

What a laugh!

Charlotte wondered what had happened to him.

They're probably both dead. ...Poor Doug.

She watched Rosie trudge off up the road in tears and felt enormous sympathy for her.

Silly little fool! Where's the justice?

A man came out of the newspaper offices and whispered behind his hand into the ear of the man at the blackboard. He picked up a damp cloth and rubbed out Radcliffe's name. A great moan went up in the crowd. One woman let out a terrible scream.

John put his hand on Charlotte's shoulder. "Come on, let's go home," he said.

"I must go and see Sam Church's girl, Irene, on the way. She's probably at his parents'."

"Okay, I'll come with you," John said.

They talked as they left the square. It was good to see John again. Charlotte realized how much she'd missed him.

"I must say, Charlotte, you're looking well."

"Yes, I'm getting better and I feel stronger."

"And you still love him?"

"Yes, of course I do."

John appeared relieved. "You can tell him when we get to Beauvais."

John was easy to talk to, caring, as always. It was then, that it all came spilling out, like a dam bursting, surprising her and shocking John.

"Beauvais …I know it …only too well," Charlotte said dreamily.

"What d'you mean?"

"I was *there*."

Now she screwed up her face as though in terrible pain. John put his arm around her shoulder, totally confused.

"You mean you were at Cardington Tower when they left last night?"

"No. I was a nurse in *France* during the war."

Her voice was a whisper, her eyes fixed on his. This came as a hammer blow to John. His face expressed horror as he remembered his son.

"Dear God! When?"

"I got there in 1917, before the Americans arrived."

Charlotte described how, at the age of seventeen, after working at Pontefract Hospital for two years, and after being inspired by Red Cross recruitment posters, she'd joined to do her bit for King and Country, to care for her sick and dying countrymen. No one in her village, except for her parents and an aunt, knew where she'd gone. They thought she was working in Guy's Hospital in London. After additional training, she'd been sent to various front-line field hospitals, the first near Arras.

Morale was in decline; it looked as though the war was lost. The Germans were pounding on the gates of Paris. For French soldiers, Aisne was the last straw—tens of thousands of them were slaughtered

—their lives counted for nothing. One regiment mutinied and it spread like wildfire throughout the French Army.

Nothing could have prepared Charlotte for what she encountered in the squalor of those khaki tents. Hundreds of seriously wounded men lying on cots in states of agony and distress, lingering for days; arms and legs blown off, faces and jaws gone, gaping bleeding wounds —all made worse by plagues of rats and lice. It was their cries that got to her the most: cries for their mothers, cries to be put out of their misery. She'd been proposed to by many soldiers. She'd usually accepted. They always died within a day or two.

As soon as she arrived at the Front, she assisted a weary, irritable surgeon with amputations and stitching wounds, things she'd never done before. It was a horrific baptism, but she carried on while enemy guns roared close by. She spent eleven months in the field with little or no rest, except for short breaks in Paris, when all she could think of was getting back to care for those poor wretches.

Charlotte didn't tell John everything. During one of her Paris breaks she'd met a young French soldier. He'd sat next to her on a bus. His face was beautiful, but full of despair. It broke her heart to look into his mournful, grey eyes. His name was Robert. They'd struck up a conversation. Her French was improving, and he was able to muster a few words in English. He looked at her nurse's uniform with admiration, as if she were holy.

"Ange de la miséricorde. Angel of mercy," he said. "Vous êtes magnifique!"

They spent the day trudging the streets amongst weary Parisians whose faces registered the same despair, while German guns boomed only forty miles away. They sat in a café drinking coffee where Robert told her sadly that the war was lost. Many in his regiment had torn off their uniforms and thrown down their rifles. Dozens had been shot for desertion.

"Lâches! Cowards!" he called them. *He* wouldn't do that. He'd rather die in the mud of no man's land than leave France to the barbaric Boche. He was due back at the Front the next morning and reconciled to his fate. After a light meal, they walked in the park, chatting. His mood was elevated. At the end of the day, just before dark, he bade her farewell and kissed her tenderly on the lips.

"Thank you for everything, angel," he said. "You have lifted me up. I now go goodly."

"You mean, gladly."

"Yes, *gladly*," he said with a slight bow and a smile.

He saw her onto a bus to her pension. She watched him as it pulled away. She never saw him again, although she looked for him in every crowd and at the café when she returned to Paris. She knew he was dead.

When the Americans entered the war, Charlotte was sent down from the north to the Château-Thierry/Saint-Mihiel arena with British Forces. A new American offensive had been opened led by General Pershing, along with the revitalized French Army.

When the war ended, she was sent to Beauvais Hospital to care for those too ill to be moved, or who were chronically sick from the influenza pandemic nicknamed the 'Spanish flu'. She remained there for six months. When she got back to Ackworth, she never spoke of her experiences, and people, including her parents, knew well enough not to broach the subject. On her arrival, they tried, but she lifted a finger to her lips, and they understood. Soon after that, one of Charlotte's aunts brought up the war and Charlotte flew into a rage— out of character for her. The war became like the mad relative in the attic—ignored and never to be mentioned. Charlotte erased the horror from her mind. Or so she thought.

John was deeply touched. "Does Lou know you were there?"

"No."

"My Goodness! You must tell him."

"Perhaps you're right."

"What about Fanny, did she know?"

"No. The only person that knew was the matron at Bedford Hospital. I forget how it came up, but it turned out that she'd been at the Front herself—and somehow she just knew. I confided in her and she completely understood. She was very kind to me."

They walked in silence for a few moments and then Charlotte spoke again. "Do you know why I really hate airships, John?"

She went on to relate how during her first week of training at Guys Hospital, she'd taken a bus ride to Westminster. Suddenly, the bus in front exploded—bombed from the air. Charlotte jumped from her bus and looked up in time to spot the guilty culprit: a tiny, silver Zeppelin lurking high in the sky. She watched it disappear behind a cloud. Seven died that sunny afternoon and eight were severely injured. Setting up a triage station had been her introduction to the war and she knew she'd made the right decision to go to France to help beat this evil enemy.

After baring her soul, Charlotte felt indescribable relief. She was now, more than ever, desperate for Lou's survival. A massive load had been lifted. Yes, she'd tell him everything. He'd understand why she'd held it back.

Please God let him live.

They were interrupted by a great rumbling. They looked round. Coming toward them on the London Road was a gaggle of motorcycle dispatch riders dressed in Air Force blue, helmets and goggles. When they reached the main square they split off and went their separate ways. Charlotte looked startled.

Angels of Death!

After a fifteen minute walk, Charlotte and John reached Church's parents' house on Doctor Street. It was on a run-down, working-class row of terraced houses on a narrow, cobblestone street. Charlotte lifted the old black knocker and rapped gently on the door. Church's father answered, and by the look of his haggard face, he obviously knew. Irene stood behind him.

"Mr. Church?"

"Yes, that's me."

"I'm Charlotte—"

"It's Charlotte, Dad—Sam's commander's wife," Irene said.

"Come in, love," Mr. Church said.

They followed Irene down the narrow, dark passageway into a small back room with brown lino and a small piece of faded carpet in front of the fireplace. On the way, Charlotte caught the smell of a dog, and a roast cooking in the oven. In the tiny living room, a coal fire burned in the black iron grate. On one wall was a small crucifix and on another, a painting of The Holy Virgin with Child. The dining table under the window was set with a white table cloth for Sunday dinner. Church's mother came out of the kitchen in her apron. All eyes in the Church family were red and swollen.

"We've got to keep our strength up, 'aven't we?" Church's mother said, apologizing for cooking dinner in these circumstances. Charlotte put her arms around Irene and Irene's tears started again. An old, black mongrel in its basket in the corner, trembled uncontrollably, watching them with sad, knowing eyes.

"That's Sam's dog. He won't come out of 'is basket. *He* knows," Mr. Church said.

"I was down at the newspaper office earlier," Mr. Church said. "They've got Sam's name up on the board as a survivor—I hope it's still up." He almost broke down again.

"Yes, it is, Mr. Church," Charlotte said.

Irene looked down and shook her head. "God, I'm so thankful," she said, "If anything happens to him, I don't know what I'll do."

"There's nothing on the bloody wireless. It's disgusting," Mr. Church said.

"What about your 'usband, Miss?" Mrs. Church said.

"They've got his name up, too. We hope he's going to be all right," John said, although he hadn't been introduced.

"This is Mr. Bull—he's a close friend of ours," Charlotte said. Everyone nodded. "We're flying over there tomorrow. Another friend has a plane—"

They were interrupted by the sound of a motorbike outside in the street and then a loud bang on the front door. Mr. Church disappeared. They heard muttering. Irene ran up the passage and Charlotte heard them talking. They came back a few moments later. Mr. Church was holding a letter.

"It's from the Air Ministry. It says the airship crashed and Sam's been severely injured and he's in Beauvais Hospital…" He broke down and couldn't speak for a few moments. "…It says his condition is …'grave'."

Irene began sobbing. "We've got to get to him," she cried.

Mr. Church stopped crying. He was suddenly calm. He had a plan.

"We'll go to Henlow in the morning. I'll borrow the money and charter a plane. We've got to be with the boy."

Charlotte and John headed back to Kelsey Street. After they'd mounted the front steps, a dispatch rider drew up on the road outside and parked his motorbike. He shuffled through some envelopes in his shoulder bag and pulled one out. He came up the steps to Charlotte.

"Excuse me, m'am, I'm looking for a Mrs. Remington."

"I'm Mrs. Remington."

"This is for you. Please sign for it."

He held out a clip board and Charlotte signed her name.

"I'm so sorry, m'am," he said.

Charlotte's heart missed a beat. He turned away and went back to the curb. His words worried Charlotte, had something happened to Lou? Was he dead? She opened the front door and they went into the living room. John stood by while Charlotte ripped open the envelope. Her eyes quickly scanned the letter. John waited.

Air Ministry,

Gwydyr House,

Whitehall, London,

5th October, 1930.

REF. HMA CARDINGTON R101 G-FAAW.

Voyage to India. Departure 4th October 1930.

Dear Mrs. Remington,

Regretfully, I must tell you that at nine minutes past two this morning, His Majesty's Airship Cardington R101 crashed into a hillside in Beauvais, France. Your husband, Lt. Cmdr. Louis Remington U.S.N. survived the crash and is in hospital in Beauvais. Your husband's injuries are extensive. His chances of recovery are favorable.

Yours truly,

Hugh Dowding,

Air Member for Supply & Research. (AMSR)

"Thank God. He's still alive," Charlotte said.

They went down to the kitchen, where Charlotte showed Norway the letter. John switched on the wireless.

Beep Beep Beep Beep Beep Beeeep.

This is the BBC Home Service. We interrupt this program to bring you a special news bulletin ...'

"Here it comes. It's about bloody time an' all!" John growled.

...It has just been confirmed by the Air Ministry in Whitehall, that His Majesty's Airship Cardington R One hundred and One crashed on a hillside in Beauvais, France at nine minutes past two last night. The airship had been in the air since leaving Cardington at seven thirty-six on Saturday evening in weather conditions not thought, at the time, to be severe enough to delay the flight. However, weather conditions grew steadily worse over Northern France. There are nine survivors. Among the dead are, Brigadier General, Lord Thomson of Cardington, Secretary of State for Air, Air Vice Marshall, Sir Sefton Brancker, Director of Civil Aviation, Wing Commander Reginald Colmore, Director of Airship Development ...'

The following morning, Charlotte, flew with Norway and John to Beauvais. Weather conditions were extremely unpleasant. Charlotte was badly shaken and wondered how Irene and Mr. Church were faring with their charter flight. When they got to Allonne, Norway took the plane over the crash site before landing.

The wreck looked like the skeletal remains of a massive, prehistoric sea creature. The front section had ploughed into the woods and crumpled up. The rear portion appeared intact. They could see the ensign fluttering in the breeze on the tail—the only fabric left on the entire craft. Hundreds of people stood around the edge of the site, with police keeping them as far away as possible—a virtually insurmountable task. Charlotte hoped all the bodies had been removed. Norway put the plane down at Beauvais Airport and they took a taxi to the hospital.

27

THERAIN WOOD

Monday October 6, 1930.

After she'd decided to unburden herself with Lou, Charlotte had been transformed. Her crushing depression was gone. Liberation had made her radiant. Lou had survived, knocked about, but he was going to be okay. In all this devastation, there were positive signs which she couldn't dwell on due to the terrible price others had paid—people she'd come to love. She left the ward and went into the corridor where she found Norway and John chatting with Booth and McWade.

"Fred and I walked the wreck site yesterday afternoon and this morning," Booth said. "We came here to speak to survivors and take statements."

"We can't go back in the ward for a couple of hours," Charlotte said.

"I'd like to take a look at the ship," Norway said.

"The bodies have been removed," Booth told them. "When we arrived yesterday they were pulling them out and laying them under sheets along the edge of the wood. It was bloody gruesome."

"Horrible!" McWade said, shuddering.

Booth glanced at Charlotte. "He had a lucky escape, this one," he said, pointing at McWade.

Charlotte remembered first meeting him on Victoria Pier nine years ago. She went to him and put her arms around him. "Fred, Fred, Fred," she said, burying her head in his shoulder.

"All those men. I warned them," McWade said, his eyes welling up.

"If you're going, I'm coming with you," Charlotte said.

"Are you *sure* you want to do that?" John asked.

"Yes, it's important we bear witness. We'll need to tell people what we've seen," Charlotte replied.

"I should warn you. Four more Air Ministry officials flew in today. They're probably over there right now," Booth said .

They took a taxi to the wreck site and asked the driver to wait. They trooped across the field toward the blackened and twisted structure. It stood higher than the tallest trees of Therain Wood, alien and tragic. The odor of diesel and other burnt substances hung in the air. For Charlotte and Fred McWade, the scent of death brought back awful memories of a sunny evening on the waterfront in Hull.

Gendarmes stopped them and asked for ID. Booth was in uniform and Norway held up his Cardington pass. They were waved on without argument. Charlotte walked between Booth and Norway to the stern. She stared up at the Air Force ensign attached to the crow's nest, still fluttering nobly in the breeze. The rudder above them swung from side to side, squeaking. One of the workmen came to them, appearing friendly and wanting to talk.

"Messieurs et Madame, were any of zeese people your friends or family?" he said in passable English.

"Friends," Charlotte said.

"*Ah, vos amis*. What a conflagration! They were so burned they were small like children, their 'eads shrunken like zis," he held his hands together indicating the size of an orange. "There wasn't much left of zem, Madame. They were light as a fever when we put zem in zee coffins."

"Have all the remains been removed now?" Booth asked.

"*Oui, oui*—to zee town 'all. Possessions we found—we found all sorts of fings er—watches—all stopped at ten minutes past two, er fountain pens, cuff links. We put everyfing in boxes and give zem a number—zee same as on zee coffin."

The Frenchman stooped down and picked something up and held it out to Charlotte.

"Look at zis," he said.

She stared at the blackened, rubbery object, puzzled. He was holding the remains of an old-fashioned, black and dark green, steel beaded, kid pump with a Louis heel. The workman threw the shoe down in disgust.

"Pah!" he muttered.

My God, was there a woman on board?

The man drew her attention away from the shoe, pointing up at the ensign.

"Do you want it? I can get it for you."

While they were gazing up at the ensign, Norway hurriedly picked up the shoe and stuffed it in his pocket.

"Yes, please. We'll take it home," Charlotte said.

"I will have it for you before you leave," the man said, going off to find a big ladder.

They moved on to look around the wreck. Charlotte stuck close to Norway the boffin, intensely interested from a technical standpoint. McWade stayed with them. John followed on behind, silent and forlorn, hands behind his back. No one from the Air Ministry appeared to be around. They went to the bow, where the remains of a bundle of fabric was still smoldering. McWade poked at it with a steel bar he'd picked up.

"Look—a carpet," he said.

"It's a Persian," Charlotte said.

"What's left of it," Norway said.

"Probably worth a few bob—or was," McWade said.

"I wonder what it was doing there," Charlotte said.

"Strange place to s-stow it," Norway said.

Charlotte glanced at the ground nearby. Something red caught her eye. She picked it up. It was half of a playing card, burned and blackened at the edges; the Jack of Hearts. She slipped it into her handbag.

They proceeded through the wreck with plumes of smoke rising from the ground around them. They gazed at the remains of the fluted columns, some still bravely standing, their little gold-leaf heads mostly gone. Charlotte felt sad; those false columns represented false hopes and misguided dreams. The group stopped and stared at the starboard engine car—now a melted, tangled piece of wreckage driven up into what used to be the envelope.

"The poor devil in this thing didn't have a chance," Booth said.

"Must've been blown to kingdom come," McWade said.

They went next to the location of the control car, its structure crushed, the silver coxswain's wheels bent and twisted, along with the instrument panels and telegraph board. The water ballast main piping above the car and leading down to the valves in the car was mangled and broken. The floor was covered in a layer of black ash and soil washed in from the field by rain and ballast.

Something caught Charlotte's eye. "Nevil, what's that?"

Norway pulled out his knife and opened the blade. He poked around to expose the object—a ring with a red metal plate attached. Norway wiped the dirt off. "It's a key ring with *Cardington R101* on it. Look."

"I wonder who it belonged to," Charlotte said.

Norway slipped the keyring into his pocket. They left the control car and arrived next at a tree standing mysteriously in the middle of the wreck, undamaged, save for burn marks.

"This tree is clear evidence of how gently this ship settled down," McWade said.

"They must've b-been head to w-wind, t-traveling at virtually z-zero," Norway said.

They stood looking at the tree as if it were sacred. They were joined by two more Englishmen, dressed in raincoats and trilby hats. Charlotte presumed them to be from the Air Ministry. They appeared officious, but not overly so. McWade seemed familiar with them. Charlotte and Norway wandered away into what Norway explained was the passenger cabin area. Charlotte spotted a glint in the dirt. She pointed it out to Norway who took his knife out again. He carefully unearthed a chain with a silver medallion attached. He cleaned it off, squinting closely.

"Look, it's a St. Christopher," Charlotte said.

Norway got down on his haunches once more and poked around.

"There's something else here," he said. Pretty soon he had another object in his hands—a monocle. "Oh my goodness. Brancker must have died on this very spot. Oh, dear," he said, painfully closing his eyes. He didn't know Brancker personally, but the man was legendary and so was his monocle. He gave both objects to Charlotte. "Put them in your handbag." They moved on and joined the others, where

McWade showed them a broken cable on the ground. "Look at that, s-snapped clean in two," Norway said.

"We saw this earlier. That's the elevator cable," McWade said.

"I expect the heat of the fire and the explosion caused that," an Air Ministry man said.

"Maybe and m-maybe n-not," Norway said.

"What do you mean?" the man said.

"C-could have been caused by t-too much strain on the elevators, if they were t-trying to get out of a steep d-dive," Norway replied.

The Air Ministry man said nothing. They moved and stood between frames 8 and 9, where the extra bay had been inserted.

"And that c-could've been what broke her b-back," Norway went on.

"Broke her back! I don't see any evidence of structural damage," the second Air Ministry man said.

"She's *hogged*. Look here," Norway said, pointing at the keel structure. "She's compressed at the keel, but the top members are stressed and broken apart, look. See that!"

Two more Air Ministry officials joined them, obviously desperate to know what assumptions were being made. Both were dressed in black overcoats and bowler hats. The tall one had a beaky nose and the short one, a limp. "May I ask if you're authorized to be in this location? Who *are* you, exactly," the short one said curtly.

Booth stepped forward. "I'm an officer with the Royal Airship Works. I was sent here yesterday to carry out an inspection and make a report after interviewing the survivors."

"And what about *these* people?" said the tall one with a smell under his beak. Charlotte stepped forward, ready to let him have it, her eyes blazing.

"My husband was an officer aboard this airship. He's severely injured, lying in Beauvais Hospital. I came here to visit him and to see this bloody wreck—and, I might add, he was a representative of the United States government!"

The tall man's face showed little emotion, but she perceived a trace of caution in his manner. He turned to Norway and McWade. "I just heard you making statements about structural damage. Be *very careful* what you imply."

"We're n-not *implying* anything. The f-facts speak for themselves," Norway said.

"And who are *you?*" the short one said, glaring at Norway.

"My name is N-Nevil N-Norway."

"With whom?"

"V-Vickers Aircraft Company."

The man's eyes bulged in horror. "What the dickens are *you* doing here? You're *certainly* not authorized!"

"He brought me here. He's my pilot," Charlotte said.

The man turned his gaze on John. "And *you*, sir? Who are you, may I ask?"

"I'm taking care of Commander Remington's wife. They're my family," John said.

"He came and got me in Yorkshire and informed me about the crash—unlike you people at the Air Ministry, who failed to tell anybody what was going on for more than *twelve hours!*" Charlotte snapped.

The short one glared at Norway. "You have no business being on this crash site. Are you here to gloat?"

"H-how d-dare you, sir! M-many of the men on this ship were good f-f-friends of mine."

"Well, you need to leave. Immediately."

"You d-don't have any j-jurisdiction. This is F-France, not W-Whitehall. And I should have thought you'd have been p-pleased I am here. I'm one of the last remaining airship engineers in England. Anyhow, we've seen enough," Norway said.

"Remember what I said—do *not* talk to the press," the tall one said.

The French workman came to Charlotte holding out the folded ensign. "Madame, pour vous," he said.

"I'll take that," the short one said, putting out his hand. "Give it to me at once."

The Frenchman sneered in disgust. "Non, non, non. First, I give it to zee lady. I got it for 'er. She can give it to you, *if* she pleases." He handed the ensign graciously to Charlotte, as though it were a ceremonial relic, bowing his head. Charlotte received it solemnly, hugging it to her breast.

"Merci, monsieur. C'est très gentil de votre part. Vous êtes un gentilhomme." Then, turning to the Englishman, she said, "You shan't have it! My husband will take the flag home."

Norway took out the red keyring and placed it in the man's upturned palm. "Here, you c-c-can have this s-souvenir instead," he said. "And by the way, w-were there any w-women on board?"

"Of course not," the tall one grunted.

Norway fished out the woman's shoe and thrust it at him.

"I s-suggest you do m-more investigation," he said.

28

CHURCH

Monday & Tuesday October 5 & 6, 1930.

After Charlotte's party had arranged for somewhere to stay, Charlotte spent the afternoon visiting hours with Lou. He told her about his trip to Canada—not so much about the trip as the plans he'd been making. He'd had a lot of time to think, he said. He mentioned his encounter with Bobby's parents at Union Station. He was surprised when Charlotte told him she'd tracked Elsie down and given her Bobby's message, still in its cardboard tube attached to its parachute, just as the girl on the waterfront had found it. Charlotte said Elsie had never married and had 'matured into a fine-looking woman' and her daughter 'was a sweet lass'. When Charlotte showed up at her door, Elsie had been touched and thankful. Charlotte was happy to find out that Bobby's parents had already made contact and were making plans to visit England to see their granddaughter. Elsie was looking forward to seeing them. Bobby's note in the tube, she said, had seemed like a miracle from heaven, coming when it did.

While Lou and Charlotte caught up on events, the others sat and talked with Leech, Binks, Bell and Disley. They were all able to sit up in bed, despite dressings on their burns, mostly to their hands, arms and faces. They were delighted to see Charlotte. Church lay in an adjacent room at death's door, swathed in bandages. Charlotte was granted permission to go in and see him.

"He's very ill, madame," the nun whispered.

"Can I speak to him?" Charlotte asked.

"He *may* hear you. You can try."

Charlotte leaned over Church. Only his eyes and blistered lips were visible. His eyelids fluttered.

"Sam, this is Charlotte. Irene and your Dad are on their way. Please wait."

Church made a little noise in acknowledgment and blinked his eyes. He moved his head slightly from side to side.

"Dear Sam, try to get better," Charlotte whispered.

The nun shook her head. "He may last until tomorrow," she whispered.

Charlotte wondered what had happened to Irene and Church's father.

They should've been here by now.

She returned to the main ward where Norway and John were chatting with Lou, who seemed much brighter. Lou's face dropped when he saw in her eyes that Church was not long for this world.

Church hung on bravely through the night. Irene still hadn't arrived by morning and Charlotte was worried. Later in the day, after spending a couple of hours with Lou and visiting with survivors, Charlotte, Norway and John went to the town hall, where the dead lay in state in pine wood coffins, each draped with a small Union Jack.

Charlotte counted five as having been identified, their names on the coffins. Walter Potter was the only name she knew. It made her cry. The rest had a number written on the end in large numerals. A small, wooden box rested on each coffin with its number. The back wall had been draped with black fabric.

Four solemn French guards stood to attention with two Red Cross nurses. A line of people carrying flowers filed past, their heads bowed. A huge crowd had gathered around the square. It was time to load the coffins onto carriages, drawn up at the bottom of the steps. Charlotte and her companions left the town hall and stood at the curb in the crowd. Soldiers brought the coffins down and laid them in pairs in the backs of the twenty-three open carriages, each drawn by four magnificent horses. By 11 o'clock, forty-six coffins had been loaded.

John tapped Charlotte's shoulder. "Look—the survivors, who are well enough."

Binks, Bell and Leech were led to a place of honor in the procession. Charlotte pitied them. *Those poor devils didn't ask for this.*

As a band played *God Save the King* and the *Marseillaise,* a hundred and one gun salute was fired.

"Lord Thomson is getting the full treatment today," Charlotte muttered.

"While the w-world watches," Norway replied.

The procession of firemen, policemen and all branches of the military moved off around Beauvais Square toward the railway station. A formation of aeroplanes flew overhead.

They returned to the hospital in the middle of the afternoon. Lou was making progress, but Church was slowly slipping away. Charlotte couldn't believe Irene still hadn't arrived. The funeral procession to the station ended and Binks, Bell and Leech returned to the ward to rest.

Later, a priest carrying a small case was led into Church's room by the Mother Superior. Charlotte, Norway and John went in, too. Binks, Bell, and Leech stood along the wall beside Church's bed. The priest put on a sash and took out bottles of holy water and oil and put them on the side table and administered last rites.

Church opened his eyes, appearing fearful at first, then at peace. Charlotte took Church's bandaged hand. She felt him squeeze hers weakly. Ten minutes later, Church breathed his last. The priest put his bottles away, took off his sash and put it in his case. He nodded his head and left. A nun pulled the sheet over Church's head. Binks sobbed.

Not an hour later, Charlotte heard hurried footsteps in the corridor. She jumped up and went to the door, stopping Irene and Mr. Church in their tracks.

"We couldn't get a plane. They said the weather was too bad."

"Irene."

"We took the boat train to Calais ..."

"*Irene!*"

"...and we've been travelin' by car ..."

Irene's voice trailed off as she stared into Charlotte's face—the truth dawning on her.

"Oh, no, no! Please, no!"

Irene and Mr. Church wept as they were gently led away by the Mother Superior.

MacDonald called Marthe on Wednesday, as promised.

"Dearest Marthe."

"Ramsay."

"He came home last night. I was at Victoria at midnight to meet their train."

"So many times, he met me there."

"They crossed the Channel aboard *Tempest* yesterday afternoon," he said. "The strange thing is—there's one man they cannot account for."

"How odd. Perhaps the fire ..."

"They're in the Westminster morgue trying to identify them."

"What about *him*?" she asked.

"No."

She heard him choke up. "I shall miss his friendship and his counsel ..." he said.

"Yes, he always said he protected you."

"Aye, he did that."

"You know you can count on me, Ramsay."

"Thank you, lassie."

"He'd want that."

29

ANOTHER FUNERAL

Friday & Saturday October 10 & 11, 1930.

The airshipmen lay in state in Westminster Hall the following Friday, their coffins draped in Union Jacks smothered with flowers. Thousands filed past in silence, paying their respects, including Lou, Charlotte and John. Lou had barely recovered, his head and arm in bandages, his other arm in a sling, but he insisted on being there. Lou was in awe of the place. The room was so massive. He stood at center looking up at the enormous roof beams. The scale reminded him of one of the sheds. He read a plaque on the wall. It said this was where King Charles I had been tried before being executed. Lou was enthralled. Now, he supposed they'd install another plaque dedicated to the victims of the *Cardington R101* disaster.

Later that day, memorial services were held in both St. Paul's Cathedral and the Catholic Westminster Cathedral. Lou and Charlotte sat with the heartbroken Olivia Irwin. Before the service began, Lou gave Mrs. Richmond the ensign. "I know you'll remember his last words to you from the elevator," he said. She received it gratefully and asked the chaplain to lay it on the altar.

Lou and Charlotte took part in the funeral procession the following day, riding in a car with Binks, Bell and Leech behind the twenty-four gun carriages. Each was drawn by four black geldings, their coats groomed to a sheen that glistened in the autumn sun. The number of coffins had risen to forty-eight, now including Radcliffe and Church. Disley was not up to taking part and Lou couldn't help marveling that he'd managed to get to a phone in Allonne that night, despite his injuries.

The two-mile procession wended its way from Westminster Hall, past Gwydyr House, to Whitehall, around Trafalgar Square and on to Euston, passing hundreds of thousands of grieving people. All flags were flying at half-mast. At Euston, the coffins were loaded onto a train, itself covered in wreaths. The mourners made the slow journey to Bedford, passing thousands standing silently beside the tracks, at railway crossings, on railway stations, on their allotments and in their back gardens.

On reaching Bedford, the coffins were placed on trucks and taken to St. Mary's Church, where a single grave had been dug in the tiny cemetery within sight of Shed No.1, where the hated *Howden R100* remained in her prison, awaiting sentence. As the procession passed by, the bells of Bedford's churches tolled. Hundreds of thousands of mourners stood in stunned silence.

While prayers were being said by the RAF chaplain, coffins were walked slowly down a ramp into the grave and laid side by side. Lou thought it ironic that Thomson's coffin wasn't marked. He hadn't been identified. He was just one of the unknown airshipmen.

Lou and Charlotte stood at the grave's edge with Olivia, Rosie, Irene and Sam Church's family. Charlotte made a point of holding her hand out to Rosie and giving her a hug. She invited her to stand with them. Binks, Bell and Leech stood behind them with the legend of the airship world, friend of Brancker, Scott and Richmond—Hugo Eckener, the great German Zeppelin designer.

Lou spotted Norway standing in the crowd with Barnes Wallis and John Bull. What must they be feeling right now? No one in the crowd recognized Wallis, who was wearing a flat cap. Where was Burney?—probably in America. Lou wondered about his own family in Great Falls. He'd write to them this week. He'd already sent them a wire to let them know he was okay. He and Charlotte needed to arrange a visit as soon as possible.

Across the mass grave, he saw Prime Minister MacDonald in a black overcoat, hat in hand—with his mane of white hair and magnificent mustache—but, like everyone else, he looked desolate. When the last hymn ended, MacDonald walked slowly down the ramp to the coffins. He seemed lost, not knowing where to place two vivid, red roses he was clutching. Finally, he laid them down on the nearest unmarked coffin, where he stood, head bowed.

After a few moments, he turned and walked up the ramp, glancing at Charlotte as he passed. Charlotte began to shake, as if he were an apparition. She'd seen MacDonald's picture in the newspapers over the years, but it wasn't until this moment that she recognized him. It was the same face she'd seen years ago, eyes full of bewilderment and sorrow as he'd approached her dressed in black, carrying his hat, then as now, in a casualty clearing station in Arras in 1918. She heard the voices of those two officers escorting him as plain as if it were yesterday.

Our future Prime Minister!

Preposterous!

She was jarred back to the present by a covey of crows breaking from a tree. They swarmed across the cemetery above the mourners' heads, a swirling black cloud, twisting and turning, over the gravesite and away across the vacant fairground. But for the sound of their wings, they were completely silent. Their disturbance had been caused by an approaching squadron of aeroplanes.

As the service ended and the shadows grew long, the crowd stood in the chilly wind and watched MacDonald climb wearily into the blue Rolls. Everyone had a sense, not only of profound loss, but of uncertainty, which added to their misery. They knew this was the end of 'Airship City'. They'd been cut adrift.

Before leaving, Lou and Charlotte placed flowers on Freddie's grave. They were driven home by Booth and his wife and, after an early dinner, went to bed. It was the first time they'd been in their own bed together since Lou had left for Canada aboard *Howden R100*. In spite of the dreadful events of the day, Lou's injuries and weariness, it was a joyful occasion for both. Never before had Charlotte been so gloriously satisfied as she was that night—with all her mind, with all her heart and with all her soul. The airship was out of her life; so was Jessup; she knew she was going home; the unspoken had been spoken. At last, she was free.

On Sunday, there was a knock on the door. The person standing on the step was someone Charlotte had never seen before. She introduced herself as 'Mrs. Beasley'. She said she was William Jessup's landlady. In her hand, she had a large, white paper bag, which she handed to Charlotte.

"These belong to you," she said. "I laundered them myself. I know the whole story. I wanted to make sure you got 'em back."

Charlotte was mystified. She opened the bag and peeked inside. She gasped.

"Now, don't you worry, Mrs. Remington. You take 'em. No telling when you might be needing 'em."

"Let me give you something," Charlotte said.

"Don't you dare think about that, my girl," the woman said, turning away.

When she reached the bottom step she stopped and shook her head. "That Jessup was a bad lot. Got what he deserved I reckon—the only one that did."

She left with a nod. Charlotte closed the door. Lou was standing behind her. "What you got there, Charlie?" he asked.

She opened the bag for him to look. He was puzzled.

"The baby clothes! I thought you'd taken them with you," he said.

"It's a long story, Remy," Charlotte said.

Lou smiled, "I've got plenty of time, honey."

Later that day, Lou wrote to his mother.

58 Kelsey Street,
Bedford.
12th October, 1930.

My Dearest Mother,

I hope you and Dad are holding up. Tell Dad I think of him always and that I am praying for him. I want you to know I am doing okay. I will make a full recovery. I am so sorry if I caused you and Dad and everyone a lot of worry. Charlotte is with me! She came to Beauvais in France immediately after the accident.

Please write to me often and tell me how Dad is doing. Not quite sure what the future will bring, but I guess I will leave the Navy soon. We plan to visit you and Dad as soon as possible via New York.

Fondest Love,

Your loving son, Lou.

During the following week, his arm in a sling, Lou went to Cardington on the bus and wandered around. He looked inside the customs shed. Potter's accordion was still on the back table where he'd last seen it. He picked it up. It made a few wheezing sounds. Terrible sadness washed over him.

With the accordion slung over his good shoulder, Lou went to Shed No. 1 where he met Booth and Meager. They preferred to sit around next to *Howden R100* than in Cardington House. They'd had no direction and went through the motions of going in each day and filling out pointless daily reports. He asked Booth if he wouldn't mind dropping the accordion off at Kelsey Street. He'd take it to over Potter's wife later.

Lou went next door to Shed No.2 and looked inside. It was empty but for two men sweeping the floor. Lou stood quietly for a few moments remembering the noise, echoes, shouts, singing and laughing ... The silence was now absolute. He stood at the shed doors staring at the tower, remembering his morphine dreams. He turned away. It was all over. This was a milestone in his life, one also marking the end of an era in British aviation.

He walked to Cardington House between the autumnal trees. Everything had a depressing air about it. His first visit, when Thomson had made his grand announcement had been enveloped in optimism. When he got to the great house, he saw two grey Air Ministry vans parked outside. A gang in grey boiler suits were busy loading them with file cabinets and office furniture. He went to Colmore's office. It was bare: furniture gone; lockable filing cabinet gone; wall pictures gone. There were only clear patches where things had been and impressions in the green carpet where his desk had stood.

Lou went to his own office. His files and logs were being removed, the operation supervised by two men in bowler hats—a tall one with a beaky nose and a short one with a limp.

"And who are you, sir?" the short, officious one said.

"Commander Remington, U.S.N., Special Assistant to Wing Commander. Colmore, Third Officer, Royal Airship Works, Cardington."

"Hmm, I see. Got any documents in your drawers or at home—any records pertaining to airships *R100* and *R101*, including any memos, instructions, letters, logbooks, photographs, reports, progress records, drawings, calculations ...?"

"No, I don't."

"Are you quite sure?"

"Yes, I'm quite sure. What's happening to all the files?"

"Going up to Central Filing. They'll be available on an 'as needed' basis by request after special approval."

"Right."

"There is one other thing. There was a lady. I presume she'd be your wife, who brought back the Royal Air Force flag. Do you know where it is?"

"Yes, it was on the altar in St. Paul's. Now it's on the altar of St. Mary's," Lou said.

"I see," the man said. He seemed resigned and turned briskly away.

Lou went home.

PART FOUR

Cardington R101 Court of Inquiry.

EPILOGUE

30

ANOTHER COURT OF INQUIRY

November 1930.

Tthe Court of Inquiry began a month after the crash. It was held
in the auditorium of the Institution of Civil Engineers on
George Street, close to Westminster Hall. Lou sat with
Charlotte and Olivia Irwin. The hushed room was full of Air Ministry
officials, government bureaucrats, world press reporters, French
witnesses and survivors, Binks, Bell, Disley, Leech, Savoury and
Cook.

Some aspects of the proceedings bothered Lou. He often saw small
groups gathered around the entrance lobby or about the corridors
engaged in deep conversation. The feeling of conspiracy was
heightened when he saw the two bowler-hatted Air Ministry men
jawing with Thomson's secretary, Knoxwood, on various occasions.
One time, he saw the same men in a deep conversation with Leech.
They appeared to be bullying him, laying down the law, pointing
fingers in his face. It all seemed irregular. These people seemed intent
on keeping control of the evidence, lines of questioning and testimony.

Furthermore, Lou heard the president of the court complaining on
more than one occasion that the Air Ministry hadn't provided
requested documents. They were usually 'about' to send them, or
'trying' to locate them, or declared the said documents had been
'mislaid' or simply 'gone missing'. It was unfortunate, they said. The
court would just have to glean information through witnesses. But, of
course, most of the people who knew the answers were dead.

No meaningful discussion was had about the 'grand competition'
set up by Thomson, pitting the teams against each other. The two most
qualified and experienced airship designers in the country, Wallis and

Norway, weren't consulted, invited to testify or offer an opinion. They may have shown government as incompetent, or Thomson in a bad light. Instead, they preferred to interrogate people like their German airship competitor, Hugo Eckener or Monsieur Rabouille from Allonne, button maker by day, rabbit poacher by night. Wallis and Norway and the Vickers team were excluded, just as they'd been from the great funeral.

Lou and Charlotte listened patiently while forty-two witnesses were cross-examined, charts explained, and models displayed. It was all terribly well-managed, but devoid of any real research. The ground rules were set early in the proceedings by the president of the court, who praised the design team and all those in government having anything to do with the structural integrity and vetting of the airship— clearly the structure wasn't in question and therefore, not worthy of any discussion at all. The notion that the airship could have broken or deformed in the air, besides being painfully embarrassing, would have been intolerable to the public, especially after all the hoopla. The court and the public were skillfully directed by the President away from the subject and any notion that the crash may have been caused by or contributed to a massive structural failure. The press eagerly took this and disseminated it as truth. At least, they said, we can rest assured the ship didn't break apart like *R38/ZR-2* or *Shenandoah*.

Lou believed, however, as did Capt. Irwin and McWade, that with the additional bay, her resilience had to have been diminished to some degree. Under 'full elevators' she'd broken her back—just as ZR-2/*R38* had done under 'full rudders'. The one thing Richmond had striven to avoid at all costs had occurred. But still, none of that would be examined—it'd all been under the government's care and control and, therefore, off limits. Lou knew that if her back hadn't broken, she might have made it out of Therain Wood, but only just; all that was moot. With the cover damaged beyond repair and the catastrophic loss of gas, both gradual and sudden, there was no hope for this ship's survival and the officers knew it. The crash was inevitable. McWade had sounded the warning, but no one would listen.

No questions were asked regarding the airworthiness of the ship or its fitness to make this journey. No mention was made of the fact that the ship had never flown in adverse weather conditions, nor been properly tested at full speed. No one questioned the qualifications of the main players, including the Minister of State for Air himself. No one asked what all these civilians (including Thomson) were doing on board this untested, unproven, experimental aircraft, making a ten thousand mile return trip to India. Neither was there any discussion concerning the fitness of Scott, Colmore, Richmond, or Rope to oversee this project or supervise or schedule such a voyage.

Of course, despite the move afoot to create a whitewash, someone would have to take the fall. Lou sat fascinated when he realized just who'd been selected for that honor. It was a logical choice—one that the public would buy into. He remembered Commodore Maitland and he smiled to himself.

Not on my watch, good buddies!

The president of the court reminded Lou of the president of the court in Hull—another Oxford man, or was it Cambridge? Beautifully spoken, beautifully dressed. Lou watched as he addressed his own questions to one of the faceless senior Air Ministry bureaucrats.

"What we need to know is: Who made the final decision to fly? Who was the man in charge of this airship?"

"Captain Irwin, sir."

"He was the pilot in command. Is that correct?"

"Yes."

"But Major Scott was on board, also. Is that correct?"

"Yes, he was, but—"

"In what capacity was he on board?"

"As Rear Admiral or Commodore—a ceremonial position."

"He was a uniformed officer?"

"He was wearing his uniform on the night in question, yes."

"He outranked the pilot in command, did he not?"

"Yes, technically, but he was wearing his uniform more as a ceremonial thing."

"So, if he was the most senior uniformed officer ...I'm confused."

"It sounds confusing, sir, but really, it's not."

"All right. Let's look at the flight to America in 1919. Who was the pilot in command of that ship?"

"Major Scott."

"He was the captain?"

"Yes."

"Was there a commodore or rear admiral on board that voyage?"

"Yes, Commodore Maitland, sir."

"But Scott, as the captain, had full control?"

"Absolutely, sir."

"Then it follows that this logic applies to this voyage to India. Captain Irwin was in full control. If he thought it imprudent to attempt to fly this ship to India then he should have—"

A terrible shriek erupted in the courtroom. Olivia Irwin jumped up beside Lou. "*How dare you! How dare you!*" she screamed.

Lou and Charlotte stood up and helped Olivia, now in a state of total collapse, out of the courtroom. Officials directed them to the library where she fell into a leather armchair, sobbing hysterically. A doctor was sent for and Olivia was given a sedative. Lou and Charlotte sat beside her and she took Lou's hand. "Please, Lou, don't let them destroy my husband. They forced him to do what he knew was suicide. It was insane and he knew it. Now, they intend to destroy his memory." She buried her face in her hands. "Oh my poor Blackbird, what are they trying to do to you," she whispered.

The following day, it was Lou's turn to take the stand. He was examined by the same solicitor general who'd cross-questioned him in Hull in 1922. They exchanged pleasantries, the solicitor general showing much respect for Lou. He questioned Lou about his role at the Royal Airship Works and his experience aboard *R38*. Then Lou's perspective on the voyage to India was discussed in detail. Finally, Capt. Irwin's role was called into question. It was what Lou had been waiting for. He was quick jump to Irwin's defense.

"You are *not* here, Commander, to give Captain Irwin a character reference!" the solicitor general snapped.

"That may be the case. *Nevertheless,* sir, I shall give one to this court, just the same." The court was stunned into silence. The solicitor general fumed. "Captain Irwin was one of the most skilled officers it has been my honor and pleasure to serve—and he was one of the finest human beings I've ever known. I would not be standing here today, if it were not for him. No blame should be cast on him, *none* whatsoever! The world must know that."

"So are you trying to say the captain was *coerced?*"

"Yes, *absolutely* he was coerced!"

The court went silent. No one asked by whom. No one needed to. That ploy turned out to be a miserable failure and abandoned immediately. Capt. Irwin's name would be preserved for all time.

When the court adjourned the next day, Lou caught up with Binks and took him in the library, having asked Charlotte to wait for him in the reception hall. They went in and stood by the window.

"Tell me what happened on the ship that night, Joe."

"What d'you mean, sir? *When*?" Binks replied, his eye and cheek twitching furiously. This almost made Lou break into grin, but he managed to remain stern.

"What did you do to Jessup?"

"I don't follow you, sir."

"Joe, you had blood on your jacket, Cameron had an envelope in his back pocket smeared with blood and Disley had blood on his right shoe. And if I'd seen Church, he probably had blood on him, too."

"Not much gets past you, does it, sir?"

Lou held both his hands out, curling his fingers to his palms.

"Come on, Joe, let's have it!"

"Well, before we left, we got together and decided we'd put Jessup out of action—just hurt him a bit."

"On my account?"

"Yes, but Doug got a bit carried away and bashed 'is 'ead in and killed 'im."

"His head exploded, did it?"

"Well, yeah."

"Just like the gypsy said it would?"

"That's right."

"What did you do with his body? It wasn't found in the wreck."

"We cast him into the sea—just like *Jonah*, sir."

Lou screwed up his face. This was a conundrum, or was it? Maybe not.

"I s'pose you're gonna have to tell 'em, sir, aren't you?"

"I have no idea what you're talking about, Joe. I thought Jessup had been incinerated."

Binks sighed in relief then smiled fondly at Lou.

"Oh, Joe, I want you to do something for me. You're a good artist. Do some sketches for me of the goings on over these past years: the *R100* the *R101* and all the characters involved."

"Sure I can sir, I've done loads already. What do you want 'em for?"

"I thought maybe we'd put them in a book someday," Lou said.

Lou and Binks came out of the library as Big Ben was striking four. Lou stood a moment, as he'd done many times in the past, admiring Charlotte from a distance. She was looking out of the window at the traffic, unaware of him. She looked so beautiful. He shook his head in wonder of her. Even though he'd used up all nine lives, he was still the luckiest man in the world! As he was thinking this, he put his hand in his pocket and pulled out the burnt remnants of Church's Jack of Hearts. He'd brought it for Binks to put with the rest. But then, he decided to keep it. He put it in his wallet, where it would remain always. Church wouldn't mind.

The day after the Court of Inquiry ended, Lou received a telegram from Great Falls.

Dearest Brother STOP Regret to inform you Father died last night at 3 am STOP Letter to follow STOP Love Anna

A letter arrived three weeks later.

Remington's Farm,
Virginia U.S.A.

Dearest Brother,

I am sorry to tell you that on December 5th, at 3 a.m., our beloved father died at home on Remington's Farm. During that last day, he asked Mother and me to tell you he loved you. He asked that you forgive him. He said he is thankful you are safe and that Charlotte is with you. A funeral service will take place at St. Peter's this Saturday. We know you will be there in spirit. I will place a wreath on his coffin from you and Charlotte.

You'll be happy to know Jeb's house is finished and they are pleased with it. Dad saw it when it was nearly complete and he liked it very much. Jeb is a lot better now, but his hair is snow white. Julia came and sat with Dad every day and during many nights over the last month. We all long to see you and Charlotte soon.

Your ever-loving sister,

Anna.

P.S. In all this sadness and grief, there is some good news. Julia is to become our sister-in-law. (Father knew about it and it made him a very happy man.)

P.P.S. What was it you whispered in Tom's ear at Union Station?

Lou smiled. He remembered word for word what he'd whispered:

'Put your arms around Julia and never let her go. Thank you for everything you've done. I am very proud of you. I love you, my dear Brother.'

When he'd got home to find Charlotte gone, he'd had a few moments of regret for uttering those words, but he knew he'd never have gone back on them. Would he answer Anna's question? He would need to think about that.

31

CHRISTMAS EVE IN PARIS

December 24, 1930.

On Christmas Eve, Marthe was joined by Abbé Mugnier, her Catholic priest, spiritual adviser and friend, in her Paris apartment on the Left Bank. It was a frigid day. They sat drinking coffee at the window overlooking the stone terrace, bright in the morning sunshine. They reflected on their trip to the wreck site on Beauvais Ridge earlier that month.

Marthe had dressed in black from head to toe and worn a veil. What a miserable day it'd been—cold and blustery—not unlike the conditions *he* must have faced that terrible night. It took them a long time to find the wreck, but in the end, after making enquiries, they discovered it some distance from the Meru road. Half of it was in a field, the rest in the woods—woods infested with rooks, their ghostly calls rasping and mocking. The birds were irritated still by the great incursion of the flaming beast and all the activity ever since.

Marthe had taken a dozen red roses with her and laid them on the ground. A workman had shown them the exact spot in the mass of tangled steel where Thomson had died. Of course, Marthe knew this was impossible, but gave him a franc anyway. The man was helpful, but much too descriptive about the scene the morning of the crash. Marthe got down on her knees on a blanket while the Abbé conducted a short Requiem Mass for Thomson and all those who'd perished. After that, they visited Beauvais Cathedral where Marthe lit a candle for Thomson and said more prayers.

"I shall miss him so much. No one could ask for a better friend," Marthe had said, sadly.

"Indeed. He was a very fine fellow, and now he is with God," said the Abbé.

Their reverie was interrupted by the sight of a boy entering the courtyard and climbing the steps. He carried a basket of flowers. He crossed the terrace with its stone balustrade and knocked on the door. Isadora ushered him in and told him to place the basket on the table in the circular entrance hall. Marthe was disturbed. They were *Général Jacqueminot* roses—only *he* sent her those... She jumped up and pulled out the card. Her eyes became wide with astonishment as she read the words.

If I cannot be at your side on this joyous Christmas Eve, then my love comes to you with fifteen of our special roses, one for each of the splendid years I have known you since the banks of the Cotroceni— years which have given me exquisite pleasure and exquisite pain; pain which I have endured happily. Until we meet again, your eternally devoted love and friend.

Now and forever,

Kit.

32

A NEW DAY

July 1931.

It was a magnificent new day—a beautiful morning in July. Marthe delighted in the song of the larks drifting through the open windows. Ah, how she loved that sound.

Yes, yes, so unmistakably English!

She reflected on how beastly the last year had been.

Thank God this year is showing signs of improvement.

Luxuriating in the enormous bed, she stretched her limbs and let out a sigh of pleasure. The fine silk sheets felt good against her naked body.

This bed is the very center of power. The most powerful place on earth! Kit was right. I am Cinderella! And who knows—perhaps the wife of a British Prime Minister one day…

MacDonald, dressed in his black and burgundy silk dressing gown, awkwardly pushed the door open with his elbow. He entered slowly, concentrating on the tray of tea and buttered toast he held out before him.

"What a darling man you are!" Marthe exclaimed.

"Made it all ma self, in the scullery."

"Even the toast?"

"Aye and I buttered it, too," he said. "There's marmalade and honey if you want some." They sat in silence for a few minutes, enjoying their breakfast.

"We owe everything to *him*, you know," she said suddenly.

"Aye, we do. It was he that brought us together."

"Dear Kit, I do miss him," she said.

MacDonald looked genuinely pained. "No one misses him more than I. He was the only person I ever confided in."

She gave him her most endearing look of compassion. "Then, from now on, you must confide in *me*, mon chéri."

"I shall. And I will confide this to you: When I first saw you with him at the House of Lords that day, I fell hopelessly and passionately in love with you. I felt so desperately guilty. I was beside ma self," he said, shaking his head, re-experiencing his pain.

"And I felt exactly the same about *you*," she said.

"And when we all played croquet together, I'm ashamed to say, my longing was unbearable. It was pure *agony!*"

"And me," she said, clapping her hand to her breast.

"But I have to tell you, in all seriousness, if he were still with us, none of this would be happening," MacDonald said.

"Of course not! ...He was such a dear, dear man. Now, *I* have two confessions of my own to make to *you*."

"Oh, how I love these love-bed confessions!" MacDonald said, chuckling.

"When Kit came to Paris that Christmas, we went into Notre Dame and I lit four candles. One was for my beloved father, one was for Isadora, one was for Abbé Mugnier and the other was for someone else. Kit was dying to know who, and I wouldn't tell him."

"Who was it for?"

"It was for *you*."

MacDonald blinked in disbelief. "Good grief!"

"I felt so bad about it afterwards."

"And what else are you going to tell me?"

"Kit always had a recurring dream about this ..."

"Girl in the carriage! Oh yes, he was mesmerized by it," MacDonald said, his face lighting up.

"He dreamed of it time and time again and told me about it over and over—it was an obsession!" she exclaimed.

"Aye, it was that."

"He swore it was me, but in the dream the coachman always drove off before he could get a closer look."

MacDonald pursed his lips and dropped his head. "Poor Kit," he said sadly.

"I told him it couldn't possibly have been me."

"No, of course not, my love."

"But Ramsay ..." She faltered, her beautiful bosom heaving, about to burst into tears. She pressed the heels of her palms into her eyes. "...it *was* me!"

"Oh, my goodness gracious!"

"I never owned up to it. It would've been too painful for him. I was there in Paris with Isadora to pick up my wedding gown. I was to be married in Bucharest the following month, on my fifteenth birthday."

"Well, I never did!" MacDonald exclaimed.

"The sad thing is: I never remembered seeing a young officer on Rue de Rivoli that day."

"Poor CB. He loved you so much, sweet lassie." She watched him reminisce. He looked away into the garden and his face clouded over.

"I blame myself. I wondered if he was driving them all to their deaths, including his own. It was foolhardy and somehow I *knew* it. I should've put my foot down and stopped him. Now, I doubt my own motives. I canna help myself! It's something I'll have to live with. Did I feel about him, the way he'd felt about your husband—hoping for the worst? Nay, I had my doubts and I stood idly by and let it happen. It makes all this bitter sweet." He put his hands to his head.

"Oh come, my precious. You tried to stop him—you know you did! Don't blame yourself. He did what he did of his own free will. He truly believed it would all turn out well. But it just wasn't to be."

Bolstering a man's spirits was one of her most unique skills. His face brightened; his depressing thoughts banished, for now.

"What happened to his precious painting?" Marthe asked, changing the subject.

"It's hanging in Mother's room up in Lossie. He loved that room."

"Good," she said.

"Do you want it in your flat? I'll send it over to Paris, if you like?"

"Dieu non! God no! It would remind me of that detestable, bloody airship."

"Mr. Churchill came back and painted some clouds over the damned thing before we took the painting down."

"Dear old Winston …" she said.

"So you *wouldn't* see it," he reassured her.

"No. *I'd* know the beastly thing was lurking behind those clouds. I don't want it! There's just one thing, Ramsay …" Her voice tapered off.

"I was just thinking the same thing, my darling. When you come up to Lossie, I'll have to find a new home for it."

"Would you dearest? I'd appreciate that."

"Perhaps we can stick it out in the shed," he said.

Having unburdened themselves, they sat in silence for a few moments. Marthe lay back down on the pillows with a sigh of contentment—and now, exquisite longing.

"You know, my darling Marthe, from the moment we met, I knew you were a passionate woman—*and very highly sexed*—if I may say so!"

To her, when he said this, his Highland accent, sounded like beautiful music, pleasing and seductive—as sweet as Eros' lyre.

"You're such a perceptive man. I always *knew* you understood me perfectly."

"And now, I do believe our wee friend is beginning to raise his head yet again," MacDonald said, leaning over and gently kissing her hardening nipples. She sighed with pleasure.

"He is *relentless*, and we shall not disappoint him. Come back to bed, Ramsay."

"Oh, my dear Lassie. Love is all …"

"Come to me, you sweet, gorgeous man," she purred.

33

THE TOMB

July 1931.

Lou and Charlotte stood in silence, reading the names on the tomb. They hadn't wanted to visit previously; they'd put off coming to pay their respects until it was finished. The dedication ceremony had taken place the day before, but Lou could not bring himself to attend. Red wreaths from that ceremony lay under the carved spread eagle. Lou placed a bouquet of white roses at the foot of the monument, beneath Captain Irwin's name.

Each name on the seven-foot-high edifice brought a face vividly to Lou's mind. At some, he smiled wistfully, at others, he felt intense sadness. Potter was such a name …and Capt. Carmichael Irwin …and Peter 'Pierre' Higginbottom. Lou was pleased they'd had the decency to put up the name he preferred. He was unable to suppress a smile when he remembered Pierre telling him his last name was Higginbottom. "No saucy remarks from you, sir, if you don't mind," he'd warned with one of his cheeky looks.

Lou forgave those whom he knew had made wrong decisions. They were all human—*only* human. It was pride that killed them, ultimately. He realized why Scott drank too much; who could blame him? Deep down he must have been a worried man—perhaps scared—caught in a trap not entirely of his own making, like everyone else. There was also the possibility that he was actually a sick man—something Lou had never considered until this moment. Perhaps he should've been knighted back in 1919 when he'd astonished the world with his two-way Atlantic flight. Who knows? Perhaps they wouldn't be standing here now if he *had* been.

He thought about his own role in this saga. Had he done enough to try to prevent it? He remembered his own irrational guilt over *R38*—which obviously he knew he couldn't have prevented. He considered all this and finally felt guilt-free. He'd tried his damnedest. It must've been Fate. He was satisfied about that. One of life's big learning experiences!

Lou was brought back from his thoughts by the sound of footsteps on the gravel. Turning, he was surprised to see the Prime Minister with a beautiful lady on his arm—and by the way they looked into one another's eyes, they were pretty darned close. MacDonald's blue Rolls was parked outside the iron gate in front of John Bull's van. Two men in dark suits hovered nearby. The woman carried a bunch of exquisite red roses.

"Good morning, laddie. I hope we're not disturbing you," MacDonald said, while Marthe placed their flowers in one of the tomb's stone flower pots.

"Not at all, sir."

"How old is your baby?" Marthe said, coming close to Charlotte and peering at the newborn in Charlotte's arms.

"He's two weeks," Charlotte answered.

"Oh, how *adorable!* Such thick, black hair. May I hold him?"

"Yes," Charlotte said.

She carefully transferred the infant into Marthe's arms.

"Just look at those *blue, blue* eyes. He's so sweet. What's his name?" Marthe asked.

"Christian—Christian Carmichael."

"How lovely. Did you have friends aboard the airship?"

"Yes," Lou said, "...*many* good friends."

"He was on board *this* ship and *R38,*" Charlotte said.

MacDonald and Marthe were taken aback. MacDonald studied Lou thoughtfully for a moment. "You must be the *American* I've heard about."

"Yes, Prime Minister. Formerly, Lieutenant Commander Louis Remington, U.S. Navy."

MacDonald put out his hand. "I'm *very* honored, sir," he said. "This is Princess Marthe Bibesco."

"I heard Lord Thomson speak of you once, ma'am," Lou said. "This is my wife, Charlotte."

Charlotte smiled.

"He spoke to you of *me?*" Marthe asked her eyes full of curiosity.

"No, ma'am, I *overheard* him speaking to Captain Irwin, by accident really."

"How nice."

"He spoke very highly of you."

Marthe seemed delighted. Even in death, Thomson complimented her.

"Tell me, laddie, with all your experience: What do you think of airships now?" MacDonald asked.

"Sir, if you want to know the truth—I'd have to say: The concept is flawed—at least for the present."

MacDonald was thoughtful.

"Fate has had a hand in me running into you like this. There is much you have simplified for me today with just those few words. I must say, I had reservations myself and I was told I was worrying unduly. What are you going to do now, son?"

"I'm going back to fixing cars and pumping gas in Yorkshire, sir, and living a comfortable, quiet life in a lovely cottage with Charlotte and Christian."

"That's a noble thing to do."

"And maybe I'll write a book—a novel—about these airshipmen with some sketches—like a tribute," Lou said, nodding toward the monument. "I asked a writer-friend of mine to write it once, but he wouldn't. Perhaps I'll do it myself."

"Wonderful idea," Marthe said. "Let me know if I can be of any help to you.'"

"The Princess is an acclaimed writer," MacDonald said.

"And what will you call this book of yours?" Marthe asked.

"*The Next Big Thing*," Lou said, without hesitation.

"Yes, wonderful!" MacDonald said. "I look forward to reading it."

After a few more pleasantries, Marthe eased the baby back into Charlotte's arms and Lou and Charlotte turned to leave. As they did so, Charlotte whispered to Lou.

"Charlotte has just reminded me of something, Princess. I understand you are you a friend of Lady Cathcart."

"Yes, indeed I am."

Lou put his hand in his pocket and pulled out the silver St. Christopher on its chain.

"Charlotte found this at the wreck site in Beauvais. I've had it in my pocket ever since. Sir Sefton Brancker proudly showed it to me on the ship. He said he'd promised to return it to Lady Cathcart on his return from India. I wonder if you'd be kind enough to give it to her—I know he'd appreciate that."

"I shall make a point of it."

"Thank you, m'am."

"It will be my pleasure, Commander Remington."

Lou and Charlotte made their way out of the cemetery to their restored motorcycle, now with a shiny, new sidecar attached. Lou held Christian while Charlotte tied her white headscarf under her chin over her now almost shoulder-length hair. She put on her sunglasses and climbed in. Lou kissed Christian's forehead and carefully slipped him into her arms. He covered them both with a blanket, tucking them in snugly before leaning over and kissing Charlotte's lips. He waved to John and Billy sitting in the van with Fluffy in her cage on the seat between them. Potter's accordion was in the back of the van with the furniture. He'd taken it to Potter's wife, but she'd refused to take it.

"You keep it safe for Walt—he thought the world of you—and the kids ain't musical," she'd said.

He vowed to himself that he'd learn to play it—if he could bring himself to try. Perhaps Walt would look over his shoulder and show him how—he had *promised*, after all.

Lou kicked over the engine, put on his gloves and goggles and climbed aboard. They drove away slowly up Church Lane in convoy, careful not to dislodge the small, black and white Jack Russell sitting in the dicky seat behind Charlotte. With his chest out and his nose in the air, Spot sniffed the chilly breeze like some little, but very noble, lord.

Later that year, MacDonald went on the floor of the House of Commons and announced that the British Airship Program had come to an end. A small amount of money was budgeted merely to keep an eye on what other countries were doing. The Germans and Americans continued with their programs until *they* too, reached the same conclusions as the British after their own similar, painful experiences.

Soon after that, the government decided *Howden R100* had to be destroyed. Lou, Charlotte and Norway made a point of going down to Shed No.1 in October to witness her execution. Norway paced around as though in pain, gnashing his teeth while Wallis's sacred creature was roughly dismantled and put to death under a great steamroller.

"If they couldn't b-bloody-well succeed, then n-nobody else would be allowed to either—despite Thomson's promise," Norway seethed.

"Calm down, Nev, maybe it was all a bad idea. Let it go," Lou said.

Charlotte remained silent, but she couldn't help smiling radiantly.

"I should remind you that on two occasions we almost lost *your* precious airship over the St. Lawrence—*we* very nearly became part of the Canadian landscape—or had you forgotten about that?"

Norway thought for a moment. "I wonder what in the world would have happened then."

"I reckon *we'd* have been the ones having a lovely funeral in Montreal and Thomson's trip to India would have been delayed for a year or two. It would've turned out to be a fabulous success and *he'd* have gotten the girl—*maybe*."

Norway calmed down, as though he'd had an epiphany. "Okay, I suppose you could be right," he said finally. "We took a huge bloody risk and we got away with it."

Lou looked across to where the fair usually stood at that time of the year. It never returned to Cardington and he never saw Madam Harandah again.

Around this time, Lou received a brown envelope from Certified Accountants, Bennett, Wicklow & Brown from an address on K Street in Washington, D.C. It contained a full report on the Holdings of Tyson's Lumber and Hardware and a number of other related companies, including real estate holdings. Julia's name appeared throughout as a fifty-one percent shareholder. The accompanying letter described Lou as an interested party representing the interests of one Mrs. Julia Remington, Joint Chairman of the Board. Lou was fairly satisfied, at least for the time being. The fifty-one percent was intriguing; maybe Julia's father had owned more than that before his death. He'd look into that when he and Charlotte paid their next visit to the U.S.A. Now that Tom and Julia were married, maybe it was time for Tom to become a member of the board. Lou was sure Uncle Rory would be agreeable to this, after they'd had one of their 'little chats'.

The Report of the Cardington R101 Court of Inquiry was issued. Though beautifully written, it did little to determine the real cause of the disaster. It was found that the crash involving His Majesty's Airship *Cardington R101* was due to a loss of gas in bumpy weather conditions. No one was to blame. It would have made any fiction writer proud.

During these months, while he sat in the garden at Candlestick Cottage with Christian asleep on his chest, Lou often wondered what became of Jessup's body. Had he washed up on a beach or floated into the marshes of some French backwater? Or was he somewhere out in the endless sea, destined to float around in the Atlantic Drift until he disintegrated and sank to the black depths of the ocean floor? He'd never know.

THE END

Cardington Prepares for R101's Voyage to India

A Certificate of Airworthiness is hurriedly issued for *Cardington R101*.

246

Life aboard a British airship.

Crowds gaze at *Cardington R101* at the tower.

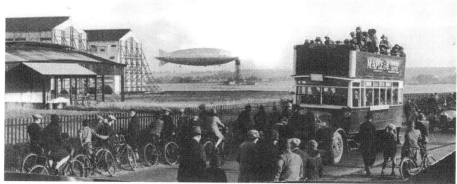

Crowds gather at the fence to catch a glimpse of *Cardington R101*.

Cardington R101 Officers, Crew & Passengers

Lord Thomson poses with his airshipmen before boarding *Cardington R101*.

Cardington R101 officers: Johnston, Irwin, Scott, Atherstone and Steff.

Sir Sefton Brancker poses for a photograph with *Cardington R101* crewmen before boarding for India.

Officers and crewmen of the *Cardington R101*.

Flt. Lt. H. Carmichael Irwin, Captain of *Cardington R101*.

Lt. Cmdr. N.G. Atherstone 2nd officer of *Cardington R101*.

Sqdn. Ldr. Ernest 'Johnny' Johnston, Navigator for both *Howden R100* and *Cardington R101*.

George W. 'Sky' Hunt, *Cardington R101* Chief Coxswain.

Mr. Maurice Giblett, Cardington Meteorologist.

A *Cardington R101* crewman's cap badge.

A *Cardington R101* officer's cap badge.

Cardington Airship R101 Sets Off for India

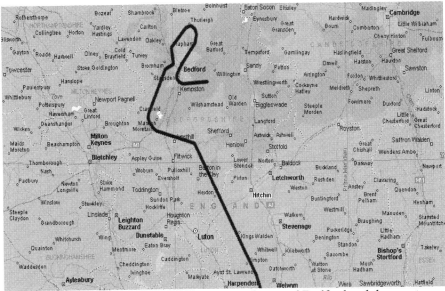

October 4th, 1930: *Cardington R101's* track around Bedford and then on to London and the English coast.

Cardington R101 passes over The Old Inn at the English coastline and disappears over the English Channel. Painting by Ken Marschall.

Cardington R101's track across the English Channel and France toward India, October 4, 1930.

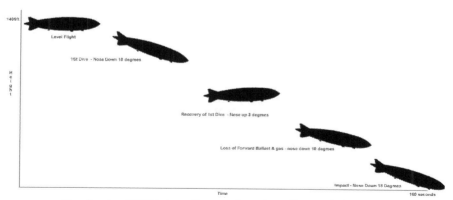

Cardington R101's two dives and crash on Beauvais hillside.

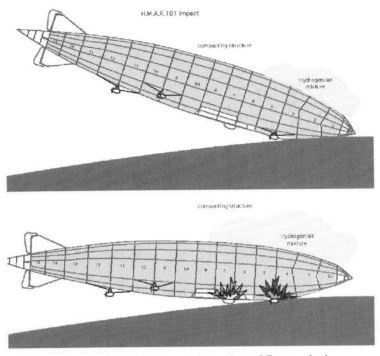

Cardington R101's impact and location of first explosions.

Witness to the crash, Monsieur Albert-Eugène Rabouille, the rabbit poacher.

The Crash Site on Beauvais Ridge.

Cardington R101 came to rest in a field on Beauvais Ridge, her bow in Therain Wood.

Cardington R101 tail section of the wreck, her ensign still flying.

Daily Express reports the crash of *Cardington R101*.

French firemen search the wreck.

The Great R101 Funeral

Funeral procession in Beauvais, France.

Binks, Leech and Bell follow the funeral procession in Beauvais, France.

Coffins are loaded aboard British warship *Tempest* at Boulogne.

Forty-six coffins lie in state at Westminster Hall.

Honor guard at the lying-in-state at Westminster Hall.

The funeral procession passes the Cenotaph on Whitehall.

The King's wreath leads the procession past Aldwych.

The procession moves along Kingsway toward Euston Station.

RAF trucks carry the coffins from Bedford Station to St. Mary's, Cardington.

Coffins are carried to the mass grave, St. Mary's Churchyard, Cardington.

Buglers sound the Last Post.

The Tomb in St. Mary's Churchyard, Cardington.

Survivors of the *Cardington R101* disaster: Bell, engine car No 5; Disley, electrician; Cook, engine car No 4; Binks, engine car No 5; Savory, engine car No 3; and Leech, foreman engineer.

The scorched ensign on the wall inside St. Mary's Church, Cardington.

Sam Church died of his burn injuries in Beauvais Hospital.

AUTHOR'S NOTES

This is a work of fiction—pure fantasy, if you like—based on actual events. It is not a historical nonfiction documentary written to 'set the record straight'. It is my hope that this novel piques the reader's interest in this dramatic era of aviation history. Some characters are based on real people, others are fictional. Some events in the novel took place, others did not. After some years of research, I took what I thought was the essence of the characters involved and built on those qualities for dramatic effect, with fictional characters woven into the story to take part and to witness events. In the end, Lou Remington and Charlotte Hamilton became as real to me as Brigadier General Christopher Birdwood Thomson and Princess Marthe Bibesco.

I did not see any real villains in this story and did not set out to portray anyone as such. But I did see all the characters as suffering with that one trying malady—being human. The myriad symptoms of this disorder include: unconditional love, passion, ruthless ambition, pride, megalomania, greed, spinelessness, jealousy, deviousness, murderous intent, loyalty, duty, trust, obedience, honor, patriotism and selflessness.

I took liberties for dramatic effect: Scott and McWade were *not* on Victoria Dock in Hull when the *R38* went down, as far as I know. Hull Infirmary is not on the waterfront. The scenes aboard *R38/ZR-2, Howden R100* and *Cardington R101* during their flights and crashes are painted mostly from my imagination with information drawn from many books (see bibliography). Actual events on board those ships, as well as the dialogue throughout the novel is, of course, conjecture. And no, as far as I know, Cardington R101 did not deviate from her route to India in order to show herself over London on that fateful night.

There is a great deal of truth in what I have written as a fictional account, but like the extraordinary Princess Marthe, the truth is elusive. Much I have taken from reading between the lines, exaggerating or emphasizing for dramatic effect. Some is pure speculation. The grand events are true, save for those actions carried out by fictional characters.

Lord Scunthorpe, the Tyson family and Tyson's Lumber & General Hardware Co. are fictitious entities, not based on any persons living or dead, any organization or corporation.

In order to help differentiate between airships *R100* and *R101*, I took the liberty of adding the prefix of the place of their birth, calling them *Howden R100* and *Cardington R101*.

ACKNOWLEDGMENTS

I have been blessed with a tremendous amount of help from many amazing people while researching and writing this book. Very special thanks are due to my consulting editor at LCD Editing (lcdediting.com) who has put many years into this project and kept me focused and on the straight and narrow. Thanks also to Steven Bauer at Hollow Tree Literary Services for his expert guidance and editing. Grateful thanks must go to Edith Schorah for additional editing and proofreading. My appreciation also goes to Kathryn Johnston and Jon Eig at the Writer's Center, Bethesda, Maryland for their patient and professional coaching during workshop sessions.

I am indebted to John Taylor, lighter-than-air flight test engineer and consultant and writer of *Principles of Aerostatics: The Theory of LTA Flight,* who conducted a technical review and spent many hours reading and critiquing this manuscript and offering a wealth of advice, not only regarding airships, but also on formatting and preparing these books for publication.

Special thanks to Eddie Ankers who worked tirelessly on book design and artwork, producing the cover for Volume One - *From Ashes.* Thanks also to Bari Parrott who created cover art for *The Airshipmen* and *Volumes 2 & 3.*

Deep gratitude is due to Katie Dennington who did a wonderful job of designing and setting up the website http://www.daviddennington.com (although she is not accountable for its content). Katie was also responsible for helping me get started in the realm of novel writing. Throughout this five year process, she gave me the spiritual fortitude and encouragement to see it through.

I am also very grateful to Frank Dene at Act of Light Photography who produced the website video and assisted Katie.

I owe a debt of thanks to the people at Cardington Heritage Trust Foundation for their kind help over the years, especially Dene Burchmore and Sky Hunt's son, Albert, who showed me around Shed No. 1. Special thanks to Alastair Lawson, Chairman of the Airship Heritage Trust for providing extra images for the trilogy. Thanks also to Alastair Reid, C.P. Hall and to Dr. Giles Camplin, editor of *Dirigible Magazine, Journal of the Airship Heritage Trust,* who kindly assisted with contacts in the airship community and photographs for these books and for my website. Many thanks to Paul Adams of the British Airship Museum and Jane Harvey of Shortstown Heritage Trust, Christine Conboy of Bedfordshire Libraries, Paul Gazis of The Flying Cloud, Trevor Monk creator of Facebook pages relative to the sheds and airships, and John Anderson of the Nevil Shute Foundation, all of whom advised on or shared photographic information.

I would like to thank the following for their help and encouragement: my dear wife, Jenny (my own special Yorkshire lass), Lauren Dennington and Lee Knowles, Richard and Katie Dennington, Dawn and Nick Steele, Alan and Violet Rowe, John and Sandy Ball, Katya and Michael Reynier, Edith and

Michael Schorah, Cliff and Pat Dean, Ray Luby, Chris and Jan Burgess, John and Sally Slee, Richard Lovell, Julie and Marty Boyd, Karel Visscher, Aaron Kreinbrook, Derek Rowe, David and Susan Adams, Commander Jason Wood, Graham Watt, brothers Karl and Charles Ebert, Ruta Sevo, Harry Johnson, Alan Wesencraft of the Harry Price Library at the University of London, and Mitchell Yockelson at the U.S. National Archives. I am grateful to Isabelle Jelinski for consultation regarding French translation (any errors are mine).

And lastly, my sincere appreciation goes to the marine who helped distill into words what I thought it must be like to search for a reason to go on after surviving horrific events and having experienced your friends and brothers-in-arms dying all around you. He confirmed that 'survivor's guilt' is all too real. He told me how once home from the war in Vietnam, he was unable to speak of it to anyone, even to the woman he married after coming out of the VA hospital. He allowed his wife to believe for years that his wounds were the result of a traffic accident. This veteran's experiences and his reactions to them are, seemingly, not uncommon.

BIBLIOGRAPHY AND SOURCES

Inspiration, information and facts were drawn from an array of wonderful books, as well as newspapers, magazines and documents of the period, including:

Report of the R101 Inquiry. Presented by the Secretary of State for Air to Parliament, March 1931.

Eleventh Month Eleventh Day Eleventh Hour. Joseph E. Persico. Random House, New York.

American Heritage History of WW1. Narrated by S.L.A. Marshall, Brig. Gen. USAR (ret). Dist. Simon & Schuster.

Icarus Over the Humber. T.W. Jamison. Lampada Press.

To Ride the Storm. Sir Peter Masefield. William Kimber, London.

Lord Thomson of Cardington: A Memoir and Some Letters. Princess Marthe Bibesco. Jonathan Cape Ltd., London.

Enchantress. Christine Sutherland. Farrar, Straus & Giroux. Harper Collins Canada Ltd.

Barnes Wallis. J. Morpurgo. Penguin Books, England. Richard Clay (The Chaucer Press) Ltd., England.

Howden Airship Station. Tom Asquith & Kenneth Deacon. Langrick Publications, Howden UK.

The Men & Women Who Built and Flew R100. Kenneth Deacon. Langrick Publications, Howden UK.

Millionth Chance. James Lessor. House of Stratus, Stratus Books Ltd., England.

Sefton Brancker. Norman Macmillan. William Heinemann Ltd., London.

The Tragedy of R101. E. F. Spanner. The Crypt House Press Ltd., London.

Hindenburg: An Illustrated History. Rich Archbold & Ken Marschall. Warner Bros. Books Inc.

My Airship Flights. Capt. George Meager. William Kimber & Co. Ltd., London.

Slide Rule. Nevil Shute. Vintage Books/Random House. William Heinemann, GB.

Chequers. Norma Major. Cross River Press. Abberville Publishing Group.

The Airmen Who Would Not Die. John Fuller. G.P. Putnam's Sons, New York.

R101 - A Pictorial History. Nick Le Neve Walmsley. Sutton Publishing, UK. History Press, UK.

Airship on a Shoestring: The Story of R100 John Anderson. A Bright Pen Book. Authors OnLine Ltd.

Airships Cardington. Geoffrey Chamberlain. Terence Dalton.

Dirigible Magazine: Journal of the Airship Heritage Trust, Cardington UK.

Aeroplane Magazine.

Daily Express, October 4, 1930 newspaper articles.

Daily Mirror, October 4, 1930 newspaper articles.

Daily Mail, October 4, 1930 newspaper articles.

Journal of Aeronautical History.

IMAGE SOURCES AND CREDITS

Cover Art: 'Taj Mahal' by Bari Parrott.

Front Material

Girls & R101 at tower: Courtesy of Martin Edwards, Roll of Honour and Bedford Borough Council website: Photographer unknown.

Part One: R100 at Cardington Tower: Photographer unknown, public domain.

Part Two: Boarding R101: Photographer unknown.

Part Three: Wreck of R101: Australian Airforce website, public domain.

Part Four: R101 Court of Inquiry: Nevil Shute Foundation, public domain.

Epilogue: Tomb at St. Mary's Church, Cardington: courtesy of Jane Harvey.

Back Material Images in order:

CARDINGTON PREPARES FOR R101's VOYAGE TO INDIA

Certificate of Airworthiness for R101: Courtesy of Airship Heritable Trust.

Artist's impressions: Life aboard a British airship: Courtesy of Roll of Honour.

Crowds gaze at Cardington R101 at the tower: Courtesy of the British Airship Museum.

Crowds gather at the fence to catch a glimpse of Cardington R101: Courtesy of the British Airship Museum.

CARDINGTON R101 OFFICERS, CREW & PASSENGERS

Lord Thomson poses with his airshipmen before boarding R101 for India: Courtesy of the Airship Heritable Trust.

Cardington R101 officers: Johnston, Irwin, Scott, Atherstone and Steff: Courtesy of the Airship Heritable Trust.

Sir Sefton Brancker poses for a photograph with Cardington R101 crewmen: Courtesy of the Airship Heritable Trust.

Officers and crewmen of the Cardington R101: Courtesy of the Airship Heritable Trust.

272

Flt. Lt. H. Carmichael Irwin, Captain of Cardington R101: Courtesy of the Airship Heritable Trust.

Lt. Cmdr. N.G. Atherstone, 2nd Officer of Cardington R101: Courtesy of the Airship Heritable Trust.

Sqdn. Ldr. Ernest 'Johnny' Johnston, Navigator for both R100 and R101. Courtesy of the Airship Heritable Trust.

George W. 'Sky' Hunt, Chief Coxswain for Cardington R101: Diss Mercury.

Mr. Maurice Giblett, Cardington Meteorologist for Howden R100 and Cardington R101:Jane Harvey: britishairshippeople.org, uk.

A Cardington R101 crewman's cap badge: Courtesy of the Airship Heritable Trust.

A Cardington R101 officer's cap badge: Courtesy of the Airship Heritable Trust.

CARDINGTON AIRSHIP R101 SETS OFF FOR INDIA

First part of R101's journey around Bedford and on towards London. Courtesy of Airship Heritable Trust.

Cardington R101 passes over The Old Inn at the English coastline: Painting by Ken Marschall. From Airship Heritable Trust website.

Cardington R101's track toward India. Courtesy Airship Heritable Trust.

Cardington R101's two dives and crash on Beauvais hillside: Courtesy Airship Heritable Trust.

Cardington R101's impact and location of first explosions: Courtesy Airship Heritable Trust.

Monsieur Eugene Rabouille, rabbit poacher by night, button maker by day: Photographer unknown.

THE CRASH SITE ON BEAUVAIS RIDGE

Cardington R101 came to rest in a field on Beauvais Ridge, her bow in Therain Wood: Journal of Aeronautical History/ABC Aus. (Also appears in Chapter 23 text.)

Cardington R101 tail section of the wreck: Australian Airforce website. Public domain.(Also appears in Chapter27 text.)

Daily Express reports the crash of R101. Daily Express.

French Firemen search the wreck: Courtesy Airship Heritable Trust.

THE GREAT R101 FUNERAL

Funeral procession in Beauvais, France: from Funimag/Twitter.

Binks, Leech and Bell follow funeral procession in Beauvais, France: Courtesy Airship Heritable Trust.

Coffins are loaded aboard British warship, Tempest: Courtesy Airship Heritable Trust.

Forty-six coffins lie in state at Westminster Hall: Courtesy Airship Heritable Trust.

Honor guard at the lying in state, Westminster Hall: Courtesy Airship Heritable Trust.

The Funeral procession passes the Cenotaph on Whitehall. Courtesy Airship Heritable Trust.

The King's wreath leads the procession and borne past Aldwych. Courtesy Airship Heritable Trust.

The procession moves along Kingsway towards Euston Station. Courtesy Airship Heritable Trust.

RAF trucks carry the coffins from Bedford Station to St. Mary's, Cardington: Courtesy Airship Heritable Trust.

Coffins are carried into the mass grave, St. Mary's Churchyard, Cardington: Courtesy Airship Heritable Trust.

Buglers sound the last post: Courtesy Airship Heritable Trust.

The Tomb in St. Mary's Churchyard, Cardington: Photograph courtesy of Jane Harvey.

Survivors of the R101 Disaster: Courtesy Airship Heritable Trust.

The scorched ensign on the wall inside St. Mary's Church, Cardington: photograph by author.

Sam Church died of his burn injuries in Beauvais Hospital: Courtesy Airship Heritable Trust.

Every effort has been made to properly attribute images reproduced in these pages. If errors have occurred, we sincerely apologize. Corrections will be made in future issues.

ABOUT THE AUTHOR

As a teenager, I read all Nevil Shute's books, including *Slide Rule,* which tells of his days as an aeronautical engineer on the great behemoth *R100* at Howden and of his nights as an aspiring novelist. I was fascinated by both these aspects of his life. He inspired me to write and to fly (ignorance is bliss!). The writing was put on hold while I went off around the world assisting in the management of various construction projects and raising a family. I picked up flying in the Bahamas, scaring myself silly, and sailing in Bermuda. This was all good experience for writing about battling the elements, navigation and building large structures.

Many years later, I read John G. Fuller's *The Airmen Who Would Not Die* and my interest in airships was rekindled. It was time to pursue my dream— writing. My daughter was in Los Angeles, trying to get into films. I thought, stupidly, I could help her by writing a screenplay.

I had done extensive research on the Imperial British Airship Program and attended many screenplay writing workshops at Bethesda Writer's Center. I wound up writing two screenplays which had a modicum of success. The experts in the business told me the stories were good and that I just *had* to write them as novels. So, back to the Writer's Center I went to learn the craft of novel writing. Five years later, with my daughter working as my editor and muse, *The Airshipmen* was finished and later turned into this trilogy.

CAST OF CHARACTERS FOR THE TRILOGY
(*Fictional)

A

*Alice—Jeb's Wife.

Atherstone, Lt. Cmdr. Noël G.—1st. Officer, *Cardington R101*.

B

Bateman, Henry—British Design Monitor, *R38/ZR-2*, National Physics Laboratory.

Bell, Arthur, ('Ginger')—Engineer, *Cardington R101*.

Bibesco, Marthe, ('Smaranda')—Romanian Princess.

Bibesco, Prince George Valentine—Princess Marthe's Husband.

Binks, Joe —Engineer, *Cardington R101*.

Booth, Lt. Cmdr. Ralph—Captain of *Howden R100*.

Brancker, Air Vice Marshall, Sir Sefton, ('Branks')—Director of Civil Aviation.

*Brewer, Tom—*Daily Telegraph* Reporter.

Buck, Joe —Thomson's Valet.

*Bull, John—Lou's Employer and Close Friend.

*Bull, Mary—John Bull's Wife.

*Bunyan, Fanny—Nurse at Hull Royal Infirmary and Charlotte's Best Friend.

*Bunyan, Lenny—Fanny's Husband.

*Bunyan, Billy—Fanny and Lenny's Son.

Burney, Dennistoun—Managing Director, Airship Guarantee (*Howden R100*).

*Brown, Minnie—Nurse at Hull Royal Infirmary.

C

*Cameron, Doug—Height Coxswain, *Howden R100* & *Cardington R101*.

*Cameron, Rosie—Doug Cameron's Wife.

*Cathcart, Lady—A Friend of Brancker.

Church, Sam, ('Sammy')—Rigger, *Cardington R101*.

Churchill, Winston—Member of Parliament.

Colmore, Wing Cmdr. Reginald—Director of Airship Development (R.A.W.).

Colmore, Mrs.—Wing Cmdr. Reginald Colmore's Wife.

D

*Daisy—Thomson's Parlor Maid.

Disley, Arthur, ('Dizzy')—Electrician/Wireless, *Howden R100 & Cardington R101*.

Dowding, Hugh—Air Member of Supply & Research (AMSR), Air Ministry.

F

*Faulkner, Henry—WWI Veteran—Lou's Wartime Friend.

G

Giblett, M.A.—Chief Meteorologist at Royal Airship Works Met. Office.

*Gwen—Thomson's Housekeeper.

H

*Hagan, Bill—*Daily Mail* Reporter.

*Hamilton, Charlotte, ('Charlie')—Nurse at Hull Royal Infirmary.

*Hamilton, Geoff—Charlotte's Cousin.

*Hamilton, Harry—Charlotte's Father.

*Hamilton, Lena—Charlotte's Mother.

*Harandah, Madam—Gypsy Fortune Teller at Cardington Fair.

Heaton, Francis—Norway's Girl.

*Higginbottom, Peter, 'Pierre', Chief Steward, *Cardington R100 & Howden R101*.

*Hilda—Forewoman at the Gas Factory, Royal Airship Works, Cardington.

Hinchliffe, Emily—Wife of Captain Hinchliffe, MacDonald and Thomson's Pilot.

*Honeysuckle, Miss—Brancker's Pilot.

Hunt, George W. ('Sky Hunt')—Chief Coxswain, *Cardington R101*.

*Hunter, George—*Daily Express* Reporter.

I

Irene—Sam Church's Girl.

Irwin, Flt. Lt. H. Carmichael, ('Blackbird')—Captain of *Cardington R101*.

Irwin, Olivia—Captain Irwin's Wife.

Isadora—Princess Marthe's Maidservant

J

*Jacobs, John—*Aeroplane Magazine* Reporter.

*Jeb—Tenant and Friend Living at Remington's Farm.

*Jenco, Bobby—American Trainee Rigger, *R38/ZR-2*, Elsie's Boyfriend.

*Jessup, William, ('Jessie')—Charlotte's Ex-boyfriend.

*Jessup, Angela—William Jessup's Sister.

Johnston, Sqdn. Ldr. E.L. ('Johnny')—Navigator for *Howden R100 & Cardington R101*.

*Jones, Edmund—*Daily Mirror* Reporter.

K

*Knoxwood, Rupert—Thomson's Personal Secretary, Air Ministry.

L

Landsdowne, Lt. Cmdr. Zachary USN—Commander of *Shenandoah*.

Leech, Harry—Foreman Engineer (R.A.W.), *Cardington R101*.

*Luby, Gen. Raymond—U.S. Army Chief of Staff, Fort Myer, Arlington.

M

MacDonald, Ishbel—Daughter of Ramsay MacDonald.

MacDonald, Ramsay—British Prime Minister.

Mann, Herbert—Cardington Tower Elevator Operator.

*Marsh, Freddie—Cardington Groundcrewman, Joe Binks' Second Cousin.

McWade, Frederick—Resident R.A.W. Inspector, Airship Inspection Dept. (A.I.D.).

Maitland, Air Commodore Edward—British Commodore, *R38/ZR-2*.

*Matron No. 1—Matron at Hull Royal Infirmary.

*Matron No. 2—Matron at Bedford Hospital.

Maxfield, Cmdr. Louis H. USN—American Captain of *R38/ZR-2*.

Meager, Capt. George—1st Officer, *Howden R100*.

Mugnier, Abbé—Princess Marthe's Priest and Spiritual Advisor.

N

*Nellie—Worker at the Gasbag Factory, Royal Airship Works, Cardington.

*'New York Johnny'—American Trainee Engineer, *R38/ZR-2*.

Norway, Nevil Shute, ('Nev')—Chief Calculator.

O

O'Neill, Sqdn. Ldr. William H.L. Deputy Director of Civil Aviation, Delhi.

P

Palstra, Sqdn. Ldr. MC, William, Royal Australian Airforce, Liaison Officer to the Air Ministry—representing the Australian Government.

*Tyson, Rory—Julia's Uncle, Proprietor, Tyson's Lumber and General Hardware Co.

*Tyson, Israel—Rory Tyson's Son.

W

Wallis, Barnes—Designer-in-Chief, *Howden R100*.

Wallis, Molly—Barnes Wallis' Wife.

Wann, Flt. Lt. Archibald —British Captain of *R38/ZR-2*.

*Washington, Ezekiah, II—Train Steward aboard *The Washingtonian*.

*Wigglesbottom, 'Moggy'—Owner of a 15th Century Cottage, Bendish Hamlet.

Y

*Yates, Capt. USN—Washington Navy Yard, Washington, D.C.

THE GHOST OF CAPTAIN HINCHLIFFE

Some characters in *The Airshipmen* also appear in *The Ghost of Captain Hinchliffe*. Available online at Amazon worldwide and at retail booksellers.

Millie Hinchliffe lives a near perfect existence, tucked away with her loving fighter-pilot husband in their picture-postcard cottage in the glorious English countryside. As a mother, artist, classical pianist and avid gardener, Millie has it all. But when 'Hinch' goes missing with a beautiful heiress over the Atlantic in a bid to set a flying record, her world is shaken to the core. Heartbroken and facing ruin, she questions the validity of messages she receives from 'the other side'—messages that her husband is desperate to help her. In this suspenseful tale of unconditional love, desperate loss and wild adventure, Hinch charges Millie with an extraordinary mission: *Put a stop to the British Airship Program and prevent another national tragedy.*

PRAISE FOR *THE GHOST OF CAPTAIN HINCHLIFFE*

Another riveting tale from David Dennington, author of The Airshipmen. This time, he cleverly weaves together a couple's amazing love and the temptation it faces with the drama of a transatlantic flying record attempt and spine-tingling psychic connection from beyond the grave that becomes the only hope of preventing a horrific aviation disaster. It's an intriguing recipe that makes it hard to put down *The Ghost of Captain Hinchliffe*.

David Wright, Daily Mirror Journalist, London.

YouTube promo: The Ghost of Captain Hinchliffe

Available worldwide in paperback or Kindle from Amazon

Author's website: http://www.daviddennington.com

Printed in Great Britain
by Amazon

60388123R00175